A new shipment arrived today. Dry goods, clearly marked, along with a small package. This shipment needs special handling, and I fear I am not up to the task.

I can't help but remember my own days of torment, ripped away from my parents, sent to a strange place, and subjected to sights no child should see. At times like this, my commitment to the Cause is reaffirmed.

One thing I know for certain: there is no curse on God's earth equal to slavery.

Prudence Willard
Marietta, Ohio
October 6, 1857

Secrets of Wayfarers Inn

SECRETS OF
WAYFARERS INN

A Flame in the Night

VIRGINIA SMITH

Guideposts

New York

Secrets of Wayfarers Inn is a trademark of Guideposts.

Published by Guideposts Books & Inspirational Media
110 William Street
New York, NY 10038
Guideposts.org

Cover and interior design by Müllerhaus
Cover illustration by Bob Kayganich, represented by Deborah Wolfe, LTD.
Typeset by Aptara, Inc.

Printed and bound in the United States of America
10 9 8 7 6 5 4 3 2 1

Editor's Note

William Still's legacy as an abolitionist and a leading figure of the Underground R ailroad still echoes through history. In *A Flame in the Night*, we meet a fictional descendent of Still's named Marla, and discover a tangible memento of Still's legacy in an old Bible that belonged to him. While both the character of Marla and the heirloom keepsake of William Still's Bible in this story are fictional creations of our author, Virginia Smith, you can learn much more about the real William Still, his family, and his legacy starting on page 285 of this book.

CHAPTER ONE

The aroma of cumin from the day's butternut squash soup lingered in the kitchen at Wayfarers Inn, though the café had closed several hours ago. The mood of those gathered around the table was at complete odds with the room's cheerful atmosphere. Janice Eastman slumped in her high-backed chair, her mind reeling with the news Tess Wallace had just delivered.

"I don't understand." Janice shook her head. "How can we be broke?"

"We're not broke." Tess tapped the document resting on the surface of the table between them. "We even showed a profit last month, which Jeff says is terrific for a start-up business. It usually takes years to start making money."

Jeff, Tess's son, served as advisor to the three owners of Wayfarers Inn on financial matters, since he was a CPA.

LuAnn Sherrill, the third member of the Inn Crowd, as they called themselves, stirred her tea with slow circles. "That's because most businesses have to take out huge loans to get enough operating capital to open. Thanks to my inheritance from my father, we didn't have to borrow that much."

Janice shifted in her seat. Terms like *operating capital* made her uncomfortable. In fact, discussions of finances in general left her feeling uneducated and dull, which was ridiculous since she'd earned her living as a teacher for several decades. But Lawrence, her late husband, had always handled the money. When he passed away, almost two years ago now, she'd had a terrible time trying to gather all the information she needed to pay the bills, much less keep track of their modest investments. When she and her two best friends opened Wayfarers Inn, she'd been happy to leave the day-to-day financial matters in Tess's capable hands.

"So we're not broke," she said to Tess, "but we're losing money?"

"Given the number of reservations we have—or don't have—we'll be operating at a loss for the next month or two."

"But the café is full to bursting almost every day." Her glance slid from Tess to LuAnn. "Aren't we making money there?"

LuAnn's features scrunched. "A little, but we didn't open the café to make money. There was never any expectation that we'd support the inn by selling soup and bread."

"I know," Janice said. "But it has become far more popular than we imagined. That's got to help."

"The café pays for itself." Tess tapped on the document again. "The income from there pays Taylor's hourly wage and buys all the supplies. It even covers part of the utilities but not nearly enough to keep the whole inn running."

"We've had a lot of business in the couple of months since we opened." LuAnn made the statement sound like a question. "We were even booked to capacity during the Sternwheel Festival."

Tess nodded. "The revenue from that week helped out a lot. But the projections for the next couple of months, as we head into winter, might be bleak. Nobody's visiting Marietta. Or if they are, they've not made reservations to stay here."

"If only people knew how beautiful the area is this time of year," LuAnn said. "The leaves are at their peak all up and down the Ohio River. It's a wonderful time to visit Marietta."

"We do have a lady arriving soon and staying for two weeks." Janice had taken the reservation on the phone herself. "That ought to help, right?"

"Definitely. And we have two more at the end of the month. But we need a steady occupancy rate of at least"—Tess glanced at the columns of numbers on the paper—"forty-four percent. That means we need to have four rooms rented at all times. And that's just to break even."

Silence fell around the table while thoughts whirled through Janice's mind. She and Lawrence had faced some lean times back when the kids were young. "We need to close off the vents in the rooms we aren't using. That'll save on the heating bill. And we've got to turn off lights. I can't tell you the number of times I've come into an empty room and found the light left on." She purposefully didn't look at Tess, whom she suspected was the light-leaver-on-er.

Both her friends nodded, and then an uncomfortable expression stole over Tess's face. "I hate to even mention it, but should we consider a layoff?"

Janice jerked upright. Fire one of their friends? Taylor Smith needed the money from his part-time job waiting tables in the café. College students were notoriously short on cash. And Winnie…she banished the thought of letting Winnie go.

"No." LuAnn's tone left no room for arguments. "I've still got money from my inheritance."

Tess leaned toward LuAnn, frown lines on her forehead. "We're not taking more of your money for the inn. We agreed on that. You've already paid for far more than you should have."

"Pshaw." LuAnn flipped a dismissive hand in the air. "That's what money is for. Besides, it all belongs to the Lord. We opened this inn and the café as a ministry, remember?"

Her words served to loosen a couple of knots in Janice's stomach. "You're right. We did. So let's leave it up to God to work out."

Tess gave Janice a grateful smile. "Good idea. Would you lead us in prayer?"

Not long ago that request would have sent Janice into a quiet panic, but she'd warmed up to praying in public. Now she even welcomed the task. The three grasped hands and bowed their heads.

"Lord, we're sitting here worrying over money, which is exactly what Jesus told us not to do. You know what we need, and You are more than capable of providing for us and for this inn. Please send guests so we can pay the bills and continue to welcome people in Your name. Help us not to worry or be anxious over anything but instead to trust You even more than we ever have before. In Jesus's name we pray."

"Amen," the three chorused together.

Tess squeezed her hand before releasing it. "Thank you. I feel better."

"Me too." LuAnn picked up the financial document and flipped it face down on the table. "Not only that, but I have an idea. Why don't we host a big celebration feast? You know, to celebrate the harvest like the farmers did in the old days."

"A harvest celebration." Tess said the words slowly, as if testing them out on her tongue. "Isn't that what Thanksgiving is?"

"Yes, but I don't want to wait until November. Besides, everyone is too busy with their own family plans then. Let's do it in October. Say, the last Saturday of the month." LuAnn's voice grew animated. "We'll decorate the inn with fall colors and have a huge meal where we thank God for blessing our harvest."

"And not just the harvest of our garden." Janice gazed around the kitchen. "We'll thank Him for the harvest of our ministry here at Wayfarers Inn."

"Exactly." LuAnn beamed at her.

Janice clapped her hands. "I love the idea. We'll invite all our families. I'm sure Stacy will help with cooking and decorating."

At least, she hoped Stacy would help and not put up a fuss. A tiny frown tugged at Janice's lips. Her relationship with her daughter had definitely improved since she'd moved from the apartment over Stacy's garage and into her cozy quarters on the fourth floor of the inn, but Stacy still tended to be a bit, well, prickly. Though she loved the idea of Wayfarers Inn, she'd never fully accepted Janice's involvement. Stacy insisted that launching a business this late in life would be a drain on all three women at a time when they should be slowing down and enjoying their retirement. Though Janice's son, Stuart, shared his sister's concern, he was far more easygoing and made a point to support the three friends in their venture. "And Stuart will come wherever there's food."

"Jeff too. I'm sure Lizzie and Michael will come and bring the kids." Tess glanced toward the giant vintage stove that resembled a fire engine in both color and size. "One thing's for certain. We could cook the entire meal at once in Big Red. No trying to juggle casseroles so they all stay hot."

Big Red was the highlight of the inn's industrial kitchen—an authentic 1954 O'Keefe & Merritt Aristocrat stove that had been fully restored and boasted a bright coat of fire engine red paint. The vintage appliance was as good as, if not better, than any modern commercial range, with two baking ovens, two broiling ovens, six cooktop burners and many other features that only Winnie had figured out.

Just then, an idea occurred to Janice. "Perhaps we could invite our friends as well. Like Thorn and Winnie and maybe Robin." As the last name left her lips, an excited tickle fluttered in her stomach. She'd grown fond of Robin in recent weeks and had developed a growing respect for her dedication and work ethic. Though Janice knew better than to meddle in the romantic lives of her children, she couldn't help but think Robin and Stuart would be good for each other. If only they would exchange more than a few words. Maybe Janice could finagle things so Stuart and Robin were seated next to each other.

An artful smile curved Tess's lips. "And Brad, of course."

Janice glanced at LuAnn in time to see a spot of color appear on each cheek. Bradley Grimes had become a fixture in their lives since he sold them the building that now housed Wayfarers Inn. In particular, he and LuAnn had become close friends.

LuAnn ignored Tess's suggestive tone. "We must absolutely invite our friends. But I was thinking of something on a larger scale. What if we opened the inn's doors to anyone who wants to come?"

"We could charge a fee," Tess said slowly. "That might help generate some income, but I don't—"

LuAnn held up a hand. "Actually, I was thinking of doing it for free. Kind of the inn's way of saying thanks to the community."

Tess's jaw dropped while Janice sat slowly back in her chair. A free Harvest Celebration dinner for everyone in Marietta? Of course, not everyone would come, but if they opened the doors to anyone and everyone, they might have hundreds of guests.

"But it wouldn't be free, would it?" Janice searched LuAnn's face. "Think of all the food we'd have to buy. How can we afford that?"

"Janice is right." Tess gave a firm nod. "We're sitting here talking about how tight our finances are, so we decide to spend a bunch of money throwing a party?" Her mouth twisted. "'Cause that makes sense."

LuAnn acknowledged the sarcasm with a dip of her head. "I know it sounds crazy, but what better way to show God how grateful we are for this inn than to welcome people to a celebration dinner?"

Tess appeared ready to argue, but a Bible verse crept to the front of Janice's mind. "'Give, and it will be given to you,'" she quoted.

A smile crept onto LuAnn's face, and she continued the quote. "'A good measure, pressed down, shaken together and running over, will be poured into your lap.'"

They both peered at Tess, who continued to look stubborn. Then her expression softened and she completed the verse. "'For with the measure you use, it will be measured to you.'" She heaved a sigh. "Okay, I get it."

Janice rested her hands on the table. "Finances aren't my strong point, but I'm perfectly happy trusting in God's economy. If He wants to bless hundreds of people with mashed potatoes and gravy, I'm happy to dish them out."

A pained look creased Tess's forehead. "Could we at least make it a potluck? For those who can afford it, anyway. That'll spread the cost around a bit."

LuAnn tilted her head to consider the suggestion. "I don't see why not."

Janice clapped her hands, delighted. "I love potlucks! At Christ Fellowship we used to have a potluck once a month on communion Sunday." She grinned. "Lawrence said it boosted attendance. Some people used to stay home on communion Sunday because the service tended to run long." Her grin faded. "I wish Pastor Ben hadn't stopped the potlucks."

The young pastor who'd taken over Lawrence's pulpit had introduced many changes to Christ Fellowship, and not all of them were well received by longtime members of the congregation. A touch of irritation niggled the back of Janice's mind. Things had run smoothly at the church for more than a decade before Lawrence's death. The two of them had operated as a team in ministry. They'd worked hard at maintaining the relationships within the church family and had learned to introduce changes slowly in order to keep people happy and in agreement with the direction in which the church was headed. Ben and his wife, Paige, didn't seem to understand the importance of gradual change.

She forced the disloyal thought from her mind. The young couple had treated her well, and she had grown quite fond of them both. And, after all, their attention had been focused elsewhere. They'd certainly done a good job of attracting younger people to the church. Nearly every week new faces appeared in the padded pews, and the Sunday school classes were full of children. Those were good changes.

Chair legs scraped across the gleaming tiles as LuAnn left the table to retrieve a notepad from one of the drawers.

"All right," she said when she'd resettled. "Let's plan the menu."

The three exchanged smiles. Planning was one of the things they loved to do.

"Let's stay away from turkey since next month is Thanksgiving. We don't want people to be all turkeyed out," Tess said. "Ham. I like honey-baked ham."

"I'll make my butternut squash casserole." The list of ingredients formed in Janice's mind as LuAnn wrote. "And corn bread. That will keep in the freezer, so I can start making it now."

"Scalloped potatoes with lots of onions and cheese." LuAnn recorded the items in her neat script. "Anybody have a good baked apple recipe?"

Tess raised a hand. "My mother-in-law made the best cinnamon apples you've ever tasted. It's a favorite dish in our family. I'll make that."

The ding of a bell reached them through the open doorway. The front door.

Janice scooted her chair back. "I'll get it. Maybe it's a walk-in guest."

"Where is everybody?" A familiar voice called from the café.

"We're in here, Marla," LuAnn shouted back.

A moment later, Marla Still charged into the kitchen. That was the only way to describe the near-run that catapulted the well-padded woman through the doorway. She marched to the center of the room, whirled to face the table, and planted her feet shoulder-length apart.

"Y'all will never guess what's happened."

Janice eyed the woman. Clearly, something had excited her, something good, judging by the toothy grin that carved dimples into her nut-brown cheeks and awarded them a clear view of her molars. Her eyes practically sparkled as she paced across the room with a lilting step and turned with something just short of a hop. Coarse dark hair with a liberal smattering of gray danced around her head, escapees from the tight braids gathered together at the base of her hairline.

"It must be something good," LuAnn said.

"Good? It's downright fabulous." Marla's deep laugh filled the room. "It's finally happenin'. I cain't hardly believe it. I keep pinchin' myself. Go ahead. Guess. You'll never guess."

Janice couldn't hold back a chuckle. How could she not laugh in the face of such exuberance? "Why don't you sit down and have a cup of tea?"

Tess cocked her head, her gaze fixed on Marla, who cavorted from the counter to Big Red as though unable to stand still. "Better make it herbal. Caffeine might send her blasting into orbit."

"Tea?" The woman pirouetted and bounded across the room again. "Who's got time for tea? I want you to guess my big news before I bust." She grabbed the back of Janice's chair with one hand and LuAnn's with the other. "Here's a hint. The Sternwheel Festival."

Janice exchanged a blank glance with Tess. Marietta's annual festival had been held over a month ago.

LuAnn ventured a guess. "You're entering next year's boat race?"

Marla threw back her head and released a peal of laughter. "Not even close. Guess again."

"Does it have something to do with fireworks?" Tess asked.

Another loud laugh and Marla bounced on her toes. "Sort of, but not the kind you think. C'mon. Keep trying."

The guessing game, and particularly the high-schoolish shenanigans coming from a woman in late middle age, was quickly growing old. Janice pasted on a smile. "I'm completely stumped."

"Me too," LuAnn said. "Don't keep us in suspense."

"All right." Marla released the chair backs and gathered herself to her full height. "I'm getting married!" She let out a startling shout that made Janice jump. "Yippee-skippy, I'm getting hitched!"

Janice's jaw went slack. She couldn't have been more stunned if Marla had announced that she was planning to dye herself purple and parade down Front Street in a polka-dot bikini. As far as she knew, Marla hadn't been on a date in more than ten years. And Marla being Marla, she wouldn't have kept the existence of a boyfriend secret. Judging by the stunned expressions worn by Tess and LuAnn, they were as shocked as she was.

"Well, that's..." Tess appeared to grope for a word. "Surprising."

"Yes, it certainly is," LuAnn agreed. "Who's the lucky man?"

"Byron Wickham." Marla breathed the name on a sigh.

The name sounded vaguely familiar. "Is he from around here?" Janice asked.

"He's from Canada, but after we're married he's going to work remotely down here. Y'all met him, though." The wide grin returned. "Guess where."

Janice took a stab at the obvious. "At the Sternwheel Festival?"

Marla pointed at her. "Bingo. He stayed over at the Lafayette, on account of he didn't know any better." She cast an apologetic glance toward the ceiling, beyond which lay the inn's beautiful guest rooms. "He came here for lunch one day and hasn't stopped talking about Winnie's gumbo since. Told me he can hardly wait to come back and order a big bowl of it."

Though the weekend of the festival had been hectic, an image rose from Janice's memory. A tall, nice-looking black man, midfifties maybe, who asked a ton of questions about the inn's history. After lunch, he'd requested to meet Winnie to compliment her gumbo and then had succeeded in charming the recipe from her.

Tess found her voice. "Did you know him before the festival?"

Marla shook her head. "He came into the store looking for earplugs on account of the noise, and it was love at first sight."

LuAnn's eyebrows arched. She stood up and gestured toward her chair. "Sit down, dear. We want to hear all about it. I'll get you some tea." She glanced at Tess. "Chamomile."

Marla hesitated, her knees bent as though poised for take-off. But then she relaxed and sank into the chair. "Well, okay. Truth be told, I could talk about Byron all day long."

Since Janice had never known Marla to be at a loss for words on any subject, she settled back and prepared to listen.

"I was working the photo counter at Walgreens, and the store was packed. Always is during the festival." Marla's eyes grew dreamy and distant. "I was printing a one-hour order and I saw him wandering through the cough-and-cold aisle, looking kind of lost. I've got to tell you girls, he is one good-looking man. About took my breath away. Tall, shoulders wide like a football player, and skin the color of Hershey's best. No." She closed her eyes and continued in a dreamy tone. "Not Hershey's. Ghiradelli. Rich and dark and delicious."

The description conjured a clearer image in Janice's mind. Yes, that was the man she remembered.

LuAnn returned with a clean mug, the tag of a tea bag dangling over the rim. "Love at first sight, huh?"

"It was for me. Took Byron a week or so to come around. He went back to Toronto, where he lives. He's an accountant in a big firm there, Godfrey and Associates." With a grin the size of Texas, she watched steam rise from her mug as LuAnn poured water from the kettle. "But he couldn't forget about me. And then, bam!" The grin doubled in size, though Janice wouldn't have thought it possible. "Our wedding's going to be October 20th."

Tess's eyes widened. "But Marla, that's in eight days."

"Don't I know it? Fast, but neither of us are getting any younger."

Janice forced her face to remain impassive. In her years as a pastor's wife, she'd cultivated a calm demeanor that masked any amount of concern, worry, or even shock. "But Marla, you barely know him. Marriage is a lifelong commitment. How can you be sure he's the right man for you after such a short time?"

"I know him better than if we'd been sweethearts for years," Marla assured her. "Not a single day has gone by when we didn't talk on the phone. Last month I got me a tablet with Facetime so we could see each other every day."

"Phone calls and video chats are hardly sufficient to get to know a potential spouse," Tess said.

"Nonsense." Marla picked up the tag and swirled her teabag in the mug with the force of a whirlwind. "We aren't teenagers, you know. We didn't spend all that time mooning at each other. We talked about serious stuff. Our goals and our childhoods and our beliefs." She dropped the tag and picked up the mug, then caught Janice's eye over the rim. "He's a good Christian man, my Byron is."

"Well at least you discussed the important things," LuAnn said.

"Of course we did. We can't afford to waste time. And we both want a big wedding. A big church wedding." The wide grin returned, and Marla directed it toward Janice. "And I want you to help me with it."

Surprised, Janice slapped her hand to her chest. "Me?"

"Yes, you. You've planned some of the most beautiful weddings I've ever seen at Christ Fellowship. You know exactly what to do in that church, how to have it decorated, and where all the flowers should go."

It was true that Janice had helped many a bride enjoy her dream wedding in that church over the years she and Lawrence ministered there. But that was her former life.

She spoke slowly, allowing hesitation to creep into her voice. "Maybe it would be better if you asked Paige to help you."

"Psht!" Marla flipped a hand in the air. "That young thing? She's still wet behind the ears, she and Pastor Ben both. I like them, don't get me wrong. But this is my wedding. And I want everything perfect. Not only perfect but big. Flowers everywhere.

The organ turned up full volume. And bells." Once again her eyes sparkled. "I want those church bells tolling, telling everybody all over town that Marla Still's done got herself a husband."

Despite her misgivings, Janice completely understood why a woman in her fifties, who never expected to get married, would want to celebrate her big day in a big way. But this whole thing just felt wrong. To marry a man she'd known only a month and met only once in person? Janice needed to think about this, to pray about this.

To cover her conflicted thoughts, she voiced the first thing that came into her mind. "Those bells haven't rung in years."

"I know it. But for my wedding I want those bells ringing." Marla set her mug down on the table with a thud and shot out of the chair. "I've got to go. I have news to spread, and I'm spreading it all over town." She headed toward the doorway and then stopped. "One more thing I nearly forgot. Byron and his friend are coming to Marietta tomorrow, and they're planning to stay until the wedding. I told him they just have to stay here because y'all run the best inn in the whole state." An anxious expression crept over her features. "You do have openings for them, don't you? Oh, and for Byron's family a few days before the wedding? There's a whole bunch of them."

Janice exchanged a glance with her friends. Was this God's answer to their prayer?

"Of course we will make room for them," LuAnn assured Marla.

"I knew I could count on you." Marla looked down at Janice. "This wedding's going to be one to put at the top of the best weddings you ever arranged. And besides, after you get that belfry cleaned out, the church bells can ring again."

Then she was gone, leaving the three in the kitchen in a stunned silence.

"My goodness," LuAnn said. "That was certainly a shocker."

Tess picked up a napkin and wiped up the tea that had splashed out of Marla's mug. "At least this man is a Christian."

"He says he is." Normally Janice took people at face value. After all, she was in no position to judge someone's heart. But Marla had been a friend for a long time. She was one of the flock Janice and Lawrence pastored together. She was a dear woman, but she did tend to be a bit gullible and had been known to rush into situations without thinking them through. "A lot of people claim to be Christians. I've seen enough fakes in my years of ministry alongside Lawrence to know just because you park yourself in a garage and call yourself a car doesn't mean you are one."

LuAnn picked up the deserted mug. "Aren't you a sourpuss?"

Yes, Janice supposed she was being pessimistic. But she couldn't shake the feeling that Marla Still was making a mistake of epic proportions.

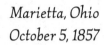

Marietta, Ohio
October 5, 1857

Prudence held her apron in a makeshift pouch with one hand and scooped out a portion of feed with the other. Her hens raced toward her as she slung the grain across the ground in front of the coop.

"Enjoy thy breakfast and show thy gratitude with more eggs tomorrow." She glanced at the basket resting in the grass nearby. Her pet goose, Patience, had struck a regal pose standing guard over the morning's scant offering of only three eggs. A fox may have frightened the brainless birds in the night. Either that or the October wind had picked up a chill as it blew across the Muskingum River. Some of her hens laid poorly in the cooler weather.

When her apron was nearly empty, she released the fabric and brushed the last of the feed from its white starched surface. Though she carefully kept her gaze from straying toward the oak tree near the river, the sides of her eyes strained in that direction. Was there a message among the golden autumn leaves? She would not, *could* not glance fully in that direction. Not yet.

Instead, she dusted her hands and left the hens pecking the last of the grain.

"I thank thee for thy service." Though she awarded Patience a bow, the goose did not deign to reply. Instead, the creature, who knew the morning routine well, strode regally toward the house. Prudence fell in behind her, noting that the twelve-pane windows could do with a scrubbing. Though the trees surrounding her home tried bravely to hang on to their leaves, the wind that blew through them picked up a generous amount of dust from the drying underbrush.

Inside the house, she found Jason still seated at the breakfast table, sipping the last of the coffee. His injured leg rested on a pillow-covered chair. Pain had disturbed his sleep most of the night, which meant sleep had eluded Prudence as well.

After placing the eggs in the crock, she crossed the room to press a tender kiss against his forehead. When she started to move away, he grabbed for her hand. "Is there a message?"

"I am about to look."

She squeezed his hand and left the kitchen. When she had let herself out the front door, she made a show of rubbing her fingers across the dirty windowpane. She dusted her hand against her apron while scanning the tree line. The hair on the back of her neck prickled. Among the autumn leaves fluttered a tattered scrap of brown fabric.

Back in the kitchen, she retrieved her gathering basket, aware of Jason's gaze fixed on her. With the calmest smile she could manage, she faced him. "I am going to the woods to gather walnuts."

Concern carved deep crevices between his eyebrows. "Shall I join thee?"

With an effort, Prudence averted her eyes from his leg. Jason's deepest desire was to protect her, and since the accident that had injured him, he felt he failed in that endeavor. Though the pain periodically receded enough that he could join her in the work the Lord had called them to, today was not one of those days.

"I will not be long. When I return will thee inspect the walnuts for worms?"

He nodded, though the worry did not leave his face. Prudence tucked the handle of the basket in the crook of her elbow and left the house. Overhead, a bright sun attempted to warm the morning's chill. She lifted her face toward it as she walked, her basket swinging casually at her side. She prayed that, to anyone who may be watching, she appeared to be nothing more than a farmer's wife going for a morning stroll in the woods, though inside her muscles were tight with tension.

Lord, keep me safe as I do Thy work.

A frantic honking filled the air as Patience, who had just realized she was about to be left behind, rushed toward her with her wings flapping.

Prudence laughed at the bird's antics. "Thee knows I wouldst not leave thee behind, silly one. Come along then."

Her back burned as though hostile eyes bored into her. *No one is watching,* she told herself. Still, she slipped past the oak and into the thick underbrush, ignoring the scrap of fabric. Before long, winter would claim the life of the natural covering that protected her hiding place. She must look for another soon.

She circled the area, gathering black walnuts that had fallen to the ground. The season for walnuts was drawing to an end but she found plenty that had not yet molded, and soon her basket was full. Her senses on high alert for unusual sounds, she turned toward her house. Tension gripped her shoulders as she retraced her steps through the woods. She stopped at the base of the twisted oak and knelt while pretending to inspect something on the ground. Moving quickly, she reached into an indentation in the trunk and removed a slip of paper from beneath the rock. With another cautious glance around, she read the note. Heart racing, she buried it in her basket beneath the walnuts.

Dry goods, clearly marked. That would be a woman with distinctive features. And a small package? Prudence's mouth went dry. A young child.

Jason would not be happy about this.

CHAPTER TWO

The café supported a good crowd on Saturday, thanks to Winnie's peanut soup, no doubt. Janice pitched in to help Taylor deliver steaming bowls from the kitchen to the diners seated around the café. She nodded a greeting toward Ruby Meyers over by the window as she placed a brimming bowl in front of Charlotte Bickerton.

"There you go. Can I get you anything else?"

Charlotte inhaled the fragrant aroma wafting from her bowl and spoke in her whispery Marilyn Monroe-wannabe voice. "This will be more than enough. I swear this place is gonna be the death of my figure."

Janice eyed her size-two frame. "You have nothing to worry about."

A voice from the next table called her name. She wished Charlotte a bon appétit and turned to smile at Brad Grimes, the Inn Crowd's one-time Realtor and full-time friend.

"Any chance for a refill?" He held his coffee cup aloft and flashed his charming little-boy grin.

"Coming right up." Janice crossed to the server station in the back of the café and returned with the carafe. "How are things down at Grimes Realty?"

He gave a casual shrug. "So-so. Realty slows down in the fall."

Janice grimaced and leaned close so she wouldn't be over-heard. "As does the hotel business, apparently."

The bell sounded when the front door opened. Janice looked in that direction and watched Marla float into the room as if she was rolling to shore on high tide. At least she wasn't bouncing on her toes today. A second later, a man entered, and Janice instantly recognized him as Byron Wickham, Marla's Canadian fiancé. He reached down and took Marla's hand when he crossed the threshold. There was no mistaking the happy glow on her face. Janice studied Byron closely looking for signs of insincerity, and then chided herself. She'd spent the evening in her sitting room praying about the upcoming wed-ding. Or more precisely, about the marriage. Though she had felt no sense of the divine reassurance she sought, she'd come to the conclusion that Marla was old enough to make her own mistakes. Why look for trouble where there may not be any?

A third person followed the couple into the room, a white man of about the same age as Byron. His friend, apparently. She hurried across the room to greet them.

Marla caught sight of her and stepped forward with an out-stretched hand, though she did not release her hold on Byron. "Here she is. This is Janice, the one I was telling you about."

Byron gave her a friendly smile. "We've met, though you might not remember me."

Janice returned the smile. "I certainly do. I think of you as the Gumbo Man."

He threw back his head and laughed, a deep, rumbling sound that fell pleasantly on her ears. "I see you do remember me. I'm hoping Miss Winnie will make some gumbo while I'm here. She gave me her recipe, but she must have held a secret back. Mine doesn't come close to hers."

Brad joined them from the café, his hand outstretched. "Hello. Bradley Grimes. Welcome to town."

Marla hugged Byron's left arm while he shook Brad's hand with his right. "Brad is the Realtor I mentioned. If we decide to look for a bigger place, he's the one who'll help us."

"Glad to be of service." Brad smiled at Marla. "We've known each other a long time."

Janice switched her gaze to the second man who had entered behind the couple. "Hello."

Marla spoke up. "This is Lucas Newsome. He and Byron's brother are going to stand up with Byron in the wedding. And Byron's nieces are gonna be in it too."

Lucas shook Janice's hand with a firm grip. "It's nice to meet you Ms. . . . "

"Eastman. But please call me Janice. We've been expecting you and have your rooms ready." She included Byron in the statement with a glance. "How long will you be with us?"

"All the way till the wedding." Byron covered their clasped hands with his second one and grinned down at Marla. "My bride-to-be will probably need help getting everything ready for our big day."

"Oh, trust me, honeybun." Marla giggled as she spoke the endearment. "Janice has everything well in hand."

Dismay filled Janice. Did Marla intend to let her shoulder the entire responsibility for planning the wedding? She schooled her expression. "I'm sure we can find plenty for the groom to do, especially since we have so little time." Did that comment sound snarky? She hoped not. "Remember, we have a belfry to clean out. We may have some heavy lifting to do. There's a ton of furniture and boxes stored up there."

Brad's eyebrows arched. "You're going to tackle the belfry?"

"Not alone," Janice assured him with a meaningful glance at Marla.

"A belfry?" Byron looked down at Marla, who nodded.

"Years ago we used to ring those bells all the time, every Sunday. And especially at every wedding. Ours will be the first time they've chimed in a long time."

"About twelve or maybe fifteen years ago we had a complaint from a neighbor who claimed to have chronic inner ear problems," Janice explained. "He said the bells exacerbated his condition and got up a petition. Though most people in town loved hearing the bells, we ended up with quite the controversy on our hands. The church elders finally decided it was better not to ring the bells every Sunday, rather than defend ourselves against charges of violating the Americans with Disabilities Act. So we pulled the bell ropes up to the belfry."

"The whole thing was downright shameful." Marla scowled. "But that old man died a few years back."

"True, but by then the belfry was full of junk and the bell ropes are coiled up and buried under the mounds. We always

25

intended to clean it out, and then after my husband passed away..." The old familiar grief squeezed her heart.

"Janice's husband was our pastor back then," Marla said.

Drawing in a deep breath, Janice banished the pain and continued with a quick smile. "Anyway, we never got around to it. What we really ought to do is have the owners of all that junk come get their stuff."

"The owners?" Lucas asked.

Brad nodded. "Every few decades or so the Ohio River floods."

"Of course, the church is on higher ground," Janice explained, "so we've never had a flooding issue there, but many in our congregation did during the last flood. My Lawrence opened up the church, not only to the people whose homes were flooded, but also to store some of their belongings. Most took their stuff back when they returned to their homes, but a lot was left over. Forgotten or abandoned." She shrugged. "We moved it up to the belfry to get it out of the way since that space wasn't being used, and over the next few years that became a kind of dumping ground for anything we didn't know what to do with."

Marla spoke up. "I stored some stuff up there myself. I took most of it back home, but I do believe I still have a few boxes up there. I've been meaning to get over to the church and go through things, but I never got around to it. I think it's mostly old papers and books and stuff like that my daddy had stored down in our basement."

Lucas straightened, interest sparking in his eyes. "Like family papers?"

"Maybe." Marla shrugged. "I don't rightly know."

"I'll be happy to help clean out the belfry," he offered.

Janice awarded him a grateful smile. "And how long will you be staying with us?"

"Luke is staying as long as I do," Byron said. "Up until the wedding. Then he'll head back home while Marla and I are on our honeymoon."

Suspicion pinged in the back of Janice's mind. What kind of jobs did they have that would let them take off on such short notice? Of course, she didn't have much experience with corporations and so on, but didn't most jobs require their employees to request vacation time in advance?

She ran a hand through her platinum-tinted curls, no doubt rendering them more unruly than usual. "How nice for us to have the pleasure of your company for such a long time. And how wonderful that you were able to get off work." She left the statement hanging, an invitation for an explanation.

Byron supplied it. "I'm an accountant up in Toronto. Business is slow this time of year, so my boss didn't have a problem with me taking a couple of weeks off. I have a ton of vacation time accumulated, since the Sternwheel Festival was the first trip I've taken in years. Never had any reason to take a vacation." He grinned down at Marla. "Until now."

Marla beamed.

He continued. "And Luke here is a writer, so he can work just about anywhere."

Brad turned toward Lucas. "A writer? How interesting."

The man shrugged. "I write a column on business and finance that's carried in several Canadian newspapers. As long as you have access to the internet here, I can work."

"We certainly do," Janice assured him. They'd had some trouble with the inn's internet connection after they opened, but Thorn had installed devices on every floor to boost the signal. Since then they hadn't received a single complaint.

The door dinged open, and Maybelline Rector entered. She smiled a greeting at Janice and headed for the café.

"Let's get you checked in." Janice led Byron and Lucas toward the check-in desk. "We've put you in two nice rooms across the hall from each other on the third floor. I think you'll be comfortable there."

"You'll love it here," Brad called after them, and then gave Janice a playful wink. "The proprietors are personal friends of mine." He touched a finger to his head in a farewell gesture and left.

"I'll be satisfied with a cot in a closet." Byron lifted Marla's hand and placed a kiss on the fingers entwined with his. "I'm happy as a clam as long as I'm in the same town as my bride-to-be."

A schoolgirl blush rose on Marla's cheeks, and she giggled. Janice peered closely at Byron's face while trying to pretend she wasn't studying him. He certainly *looked* sincere. Then she caught sight of Lucas. Deep crevices marked his brow as he watched the couple.

So, the best man has a few concerns of his own.

For some reason, that made Janice feel better.

When Byron had been installed in the Woodsmoke and Pine room, with Lucas across the hall in Woodbine and Roses, Janice headed for the kitchen. Her heart grew heavier with every downward step. Which was ridiculous. Byron seemed like a perfectly nice man, and as far as she could tell, he was genuinely fond of Marla.

Fond of. Fondness was not a good basis for marriage.

In the kitchen, she found Tess at the sink washing a stack of soup bowls while LuAnn sliced thick slabs of crusty sourdough bread and placed them on small plates to be delivered to the café guests. Stationed at Big Red, Winnie stirred a giant kettle of soup.

"Marla's fiancé just arrived," she told them.

Tess turned, her hands still immersed in soapy water. "You sound as if you're announcing a funeral. Didn't you like him?"

"Oh, I like him fine. He's very friendly, and he's every bit as handsome as Marla claimed."

"But?" LuAnn asked.

Janice shrugged. "I still think they're moving too quickly."

Winnie tapped her spoon on the edge of the pot before setting it on a spoon rest on the counter. "I'm happy for them.

Marla's been alone her whole life. She deserves to spend the rest of it with someone who loves her."

"But how can they possibly know if they really love each other?" Janice crossed the room and extracted a clean dishtowel from a deep drawer. "Lawrence and I dated for four years before we got engaged, and then we spent a whole year planning our wedding. And not just the wedding either. We talked about everything. The kind of life we would live. How our finances would work. How we'd raise our children when they came."

"Well, Marla and Byron won't have to worry about raising children." Tess chuckled as she dipped a clean bowl in the tub of disinfectant before rinsing it.

LuAnn went to the giant refrigerator and removed a container of preformed butter pats. "I agree with Winnie. I think this is a terrific blessing for Marla and Byron."

"How can you say that? They're each marrying a stranger." Janice rubbed extra hard at a wet bowl.

"Not necessarily," LuAnn said. "These days, with the internet and free long distance phone calls they've probably spent more time getting to know each other than most people who dated for years back in our day. Besides, we can't judge the depth of someone else's feelings."

The truth of the statement resonated with Janice. Perhaps the couple truly loved each other enough to overcome the challenges of a hasty marriage. She certainly agreed that Marla deserved happiness, and if Byron was the one God had selected for her, everything would work out beautifully.

If being the critical word.

What's the matter with me? Why am I so negative about this, Lord?

The answer came almost as quickly as she had formed the mental question.

I'm being a mother hen.

The realization almost made her laugh. Marla wasn't that much younger than she was, but for some reason she'd stirred Janice's motherly instincts. All those years of being the pastor's wife, of shepherding and counseling the women of the congregation, had turned her into Hover Mother, a term Stacy coined during her teenage years. But that was a different life, one she had left behind when Lawrence passed. Her job now was simply to be a friend. Marla's friend.

She drew in a deep breath and let it out slowly, willing her pent-up worries to leave with the expelled air. "I guess you're right. Marla is capable of making her own decisions. The only thing we can do is pray that she'll make the right ones."

Tess handed her another rinsed bowl. "Prayer isn't simply the *only* thing we can do. It's the *best* thing we can do."

"Amen," Winnie said, reaching for a clean bowl and her soup ladle.

CHAPTER THREE

J ust look at all this junk." With her hands planted on her hips, Janice stood in the doorway of the belfry and gazed at more than a decade's accumulation of stuff. They could barely move for all the clutter.

LuAnn sneezed. "Have you ever seen so much dust in your life?"

A thick layer coated everything—boxes, books, crates, and a million miscellaneous items that had been tossed on the pile in a haphazard manner. At the tip-top, the crook of a cane protruded from a dilapidated plastic tote.

Actually, now that she looked closer, a few of the items appeared to be almost dust-free. A stack of old *Guideposts* magazines looked as if the one on top had been swiped with a hand, and a cardboard carton next to it had barely any. New additions to the pile, maybe?

Janice leaned sideways and peered beneath the rubble. "Are those beanbag chairs under there?"

Tess stepped forward and reached through the legs of an upside down end table to poke at a cushion. "I think it is. I wonder who they belong to?"

The vaguely familiar pattern elicited a memory. "I think those used to be in the youth room," Janice said. "I haven't been down there since..." She'd almost said *since Lawrence died,* but at the last minute changed the words. "...since Pastor Ben and Paige arrived. Maybe they replaced them with something else."

"Well at least we don't have to find out to whom they should be returned. Looks like a Goodwill contribution to me." LuAnn shoved a nearby box with the toe of her tennis shoe. "Assuming a lot of this stuff belongs to church members, it's going to take forever to identify the owners. And where can we put it in the meantime?"

"Do we have to completely empty this belfry?" Tess propped her hands on her hips and eyed the pile. "Maybe we could just rearrange things enough to access the ropes."

Not a bad idea. Janice stood on tiptoe and craned her neck to see around the mountain of clutter that seemed to fill the entire room. There was barely enough space to maneuver while they sorted through the junk, but perhaps if they relocated the best part of it to the perimeter of the room the bell rope would be able to swing free.

"I hate to leave this mess for someone else to deal with," she said.

"I don't." Tess slapped a piece of faded fabric that Janice recognized as an old choir robe. "This looks like a job for the youth group, if you ask me. Maybe in the spring they could haul all this stuff outside and let the members of the church pick through and cart off their own junk."

LuAnn pointed at her. "I like that."

"Sounds like a plan." Janice reached for the broken tote. "Somebody give me a hand here."

They spent a dusty couple of hours with much coughing and sneezing. A few treasures did lay hidden amid mounds of trash. A garment bag stuffed full of shepherd and angel costumes that were still in great condition. A completely unused container of white altar candles, perfectly preserved and sealed in plastic wrap. The real treasure, in Janice's opinion, was a folder of piano music, classic arrangements of some of her old favorites. Those she set aside to take back to the inn.

By the time the light filtering through the narrow windows began to fade, they'd made enough progress to feel hopeful.

"We could go downstairs and try to scrounge up a couple of lamps if we want to continue," LuAnn suggested.

Tess rubbed her eyes. "I don't know about you two, but I'm about ready to call it a day. I vote we come back Monday afternoon and bring some muscle. It'll probably take another two or three hours to finish."

Janice had finally unearthed the end table. She grasped two spindly legs and lifted it. Beneath the scarred surface lay a cardboard box, the four flaps folded at the top. Her own handwriting was scrawled across the front, and her heart caught in her throat at the words she had written years before.

Lawrence J. Eastman
Awards and Recognitions

"Look what I found." Her voice came out choked.

Tess and LuAnn stopped what they were doing to watch as she unfolded the flaps. She'd forgotten about this box, but when she lifted out the first framed certificate, memories flooded back.

"It's Lawrence's diploma from divinity school," she whispered.

The words on the document blurred as tears filled her eyes. Tess laid a comforting hand on Janice's shoulder and squeezed while she battled a lump in her throat.

"I boxed up all the stuff from his church office before Pastor Ben arrived. But I couldn't take it to Stacy's house when I moved out of the parsonage. I couldn't make myself. So I stuck it up here."

So vivid was the memory, she could still feel the weight of the box dragging against her arms as she forced her legs up four flights of stairs to the belfry. Thrusting away the thought, she set the diploma to one side and withdrew a thick bundle of letters held together by a bright red rubber band. When Lawrence celebrated his thirtieth anniversary as a pastor, most of the congregation had written to express their gratitude for his service. Many of those letter writers still attended this church.

"Do you want me to put the box over against the wall?" LuAnn asked in her most gentle voice.

Janice shook her head. "I think...I want to take it home." She placed the letters back inside and refolded the flaps.

Tess picked up the box. "I'll carry it down to the car for you."

When she turned away, Janice spied a second box beneath that one. Different handwriting identified the owner of this one as Marla Still.

LuAnn glanced at it. "She said she thought she had more stuff up here."

"I might as well take this one too." Pleased that her voice sounded normal once again, Janice lifted the second box. "I'm supposed to meet with her and Byron tomorrow after church to go over wedding plans. I can take it to her then."

LuAnn followed Tess, and Janice fell in behind her. Before she descended the steep stairs, she turned to survey the belfry. They'd made progress. It wouldn't take too much longer to clear the way for the bell ropes to swing freely. Her arms tightened around the cardboard box she carried. But what else awaited discovery in that dwindling pile of debris?

Most of the time, Janice stayed up for a couple of hours after retiring from the common room on a weekend night. But this Saturday night was a different matter. She was exhausted, both mentally and physically, from the work they'd done in the attic that afternoon. Even though it was just a little after eight, she decided to get ready for bed. She padded around her quarters in pajamas and slippers, enjoying the feel of the soft flannel. Not until recently had she switched from the feminine nightgowns that Lawrence favored to more practical pajamas. Though she still felt a tiny bit guilty, as though ignoring her nightgowns was laying to rest another small piece of her life with her husband, flannel kept her a lot warmer at night.

But then she found she couldn't settle down. The box of Lawrence's things rested in the corner by her reading chair and drew her attention like a magnet. Perhaps bringing it home had been a mistake. Was she really ready to dredge up all those memories? Maybe she ought to give the box to Stacy or Stuart to deal with.

No. It was her place to go through the contents first, and then she could parcel out items that the kids might wish to keep as mementos of their father.

But not tonight.

That decision made, she picked up the box and carried it through the doorway to her sitting room. She'd sleep better with those things in the other room.

After she set it down in the corner, her eyes fell on the second box she'd brought home, the one belonging to Marla. With thoughts of tidying up the space, she lifted Marla's box to stack it on top of the other. When she did, the bottom of the warped old cardboard box opened, spilling its contents on the floor. She managed to refold the flaps and secure them with a strip of packing tape she retrieved from the desk. Then she began to repack the assortment of file folders, papers, and books back into the box. One leather-bound book had been carefully sealed in a plastic bag. The worn binding had the unmistakable look of a Bible. Feeling only a little guilty—after all Marla had left these things in the belfry for years—Janice slipped the book out of its protective casing. Yes, definitely a Bible. And old, by the look of it. She ran a hand over the cracked leather cover. The edges were well worn, which meant this Bible had been used often by someone. Careful of the brittle binding, she opened the cover. A beautifully scrawled script on the inside page identified the owner. Janice's breath caught in her throat.

This Holy Bible presented to
William Still
By
Letitia George Still
August 1, 1847

The impact of the discovery of the owner of the book she held in her hand struck Janice like a slap. This Bible had belonged to the Father of the Underground Railroad, Marla's great-great-great-grandfather. William Still had led over two hundred slaves to freedom. The only person who had freed more slaves was Harriet Tubman. Unless Janice was mistaken, Letitia had been William's wife.

She turned the page to find a record of the marriage between Letitia George and William Still on August 1, 1847. So the Bible had been Letitia's wedding gift to her husband. Recorded on the following pages were the births of their four children—Caroline Virginia Matilda, William Wilberforce, Robert George, and Frances Ellen—and the deaths of Charity Sidney Still and Levin Still.

A sense of awe crept over Janice. She was holding William Still's family Bible. The historical significance was incredible. A treasure Marla obviously didn't know she possessed, tucked away in her father's old papers.

Why, this book could be worth a fortune!

She should call Marla right now. When she reached for her phone, she glanced at the clock. Past midnight. Probably not a good idea to make a call this late. If Marla hadn't known of this prized keepsake all the years of her life, tomorrow would be soon enough to reveal its discovery.

Instead, Janice carried the Bible into the bedroom and set it on her bedside table. Marla wouldn't mind if she peeked inside, as long as she was careful. Once she'd settled in bed, her back propped against a pile of fluffy pillows, she laid the Bible on her lap. Fanning through the pages brought a smile to her face. Mr. Still had made copious notes in his Bible, just like her Lawrence. Many verses were underlined or circled, and cramped handwriting crowded the narrow margins. She turned to one of her favorite verses. Lawrence had intoned Mark 10:9 in his deep voice at the end of every wedding he performed. Apparently, it had been a favorite of William's too. He'd drawn a circle around it.

What therefore God hath joined together, let not man put asunder.

Beside the verse was written *E.B.* Initials? Perhaps, or maybe an abbreviation that made sense to William and no one else. She turned several pages, noting many initials, and a few cryptic notes. The margin beside Romans 6:23, another one of Lawrence's favorites, bore a date—10/15/1857—below the letters *L.T.* Whatever that meant.

In the distance, a siren sounded in the night. At first, she barely noticed, but then it was augmented by a second siren, and then a third. She glanced toward the window, though she could see nothing beyond the drawn curtains. Oh, dear. There must be a big fire somewhere in town. She closed the Bible and put it in the drawer in her nightstand. As she turned out the light and snuggled beneath the covers, she whispered a prayer.

Lord, please be with the firefighters and keep them safe. And be with whoever's house or business is burning.

Sleep had almost overtaken her when a loud pounding on her apartment door jarred her awake.

"Janice! Janice, wake up." LuAnn's voice, full of urgency.

Janice jumped out of bed and hurried toward the door. She opened it to find LuAnn and Tess, their hair tousled and their expressions wide-eyed. Her heart sped up.

"What's wrong? What happened?"

"You're not going to believe this." LuAnn clutched at the neck of her bathrobe. "Somebody set the church on fire."

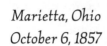

Marietta, Ohio
October 6, 1857

Thank thee, Lord, for a cloudy night. Prudence tied her skiff on the usual branch and climbed up the muddy bank on the Virginia side of the river. She hurried to the cover of the trees, peering in the darkness all around her for signs of movement. Her heart pounded like a drum inside her chest. It always did when she conducted. At this moment Jason was back at home, maintaining a constant, fervent prayer for her safety and the safety of the precious cargo she would soon receive.

The crack of a branch to her left sent blood roaring in her ears. She froze. A figure emerged from behind a tree.

She released a pent-up breath when she caught sight of the familiar face.

"You're on time. Good." The man spoke in the hushed tones of one accustomed to making as little noise as possible. "We ran into some trouble a few miles back."

Fear gripped Prudence by the throat. "Is thee well?"

He nodded. "This package needs to be stored for a while, maybe two weeks."

Stored. Meaning Prudence would need to keep them at the Riverfront House instead of sending them on to the next station within a day or two, as she usually did.

"How will I know when it's safe?"

"Someone will come for them."

His eyes darted everywhere. Prudence scanned the area as well. The forest around them was silent, the nighttime animals aware of their presence.

Hopefully no one else was.

Apparently satisfied they were alone, the man took her arm and led her a few yards deeper into the woods. A dark shadow separated itself from the cover of a tree just ahead. Prudence made out the figure of a woman carrying a bundle.

In a hushed voice, the man explained that Prudence would take her to a safe place. The woman turned toward Prudence, the whites of her eyes the only discernible feature in the dim light. The bundle propped on her hip whimpered and moved, revealing itself to be the child referred to in the note.

The man, whose name Prudence did not know and would never ask, whispered, "He cries. Almost got us caught."

The woman added a quick, "He was a'-sceered."

Prudence instinctively placed her hand over the woman's mouth. Though she'd spoken quietly, the s sounded with a hiss that easily pierced the silence in the woods. Smiling, though the woman probably couldn't see Prudence's expression, she reached into her pocket and pulled out a stick candy. Though she had no idea how old this child was, she had come prepared to quiet a restless little one. She extended the candy, and chubby brown fingers brushed hers as the child took the sweet.

Taking the woman's arm, Prudence guided her toward the skiff. The man disappeared silently into the woods behind them. Once in the boat, Prudence gestured for the woman to crouch low on the deck, and then she covered them both with a dark blanket she kept for that purpose. The child made no noise except the occasional sucking sound as he enjoyed the candy.

Prudence loosened the tether, climbed inside, and picked up her paddle. This was the most dangerous part of the transfer. Even with no moon, anyone scanning the area could identify the skiff as an unusual object paddling against the current as she crossed the river. As always, she maintained a silent plea to the Almighty for protection and cover.

Though the time was closer to morning than night, a single light flickered in one of the guest room windows at the Riverfront House. Someone was awake. Would that person glance out the window and spot them? Prudence fought a rising panic and paddled as quickly as she dared.

The little boat finally reached its destination, and she hopped out onto yet another muddy shore. Wordlessly, she assisted her passengers onto land and then pulled the skiff out of the water. She glanced at the hotel looming over her. The candlelight still glowed. Moving as quietly as she could, she dragged the boat up onto the grass where it would leave no trail, and then, behind a trio of scraggly evergreen bushes that hid the entrance to the tunnel. Only when she and her charges were inside did she breathe more easily.

The boat now safely hidden from a casual observer, she left it in its usual place just inside the tunnel and took the woman's arm. The bare skin beneath her fingers felt icy. The child whimpered when they plunged into an ever-increasing darkness, but Prudence could not risk a light being seen from outside. She ran her hand along the damp brick wall, feeling her way down the familiar path.

Only when they reached the first of the hidden rooms did she release the woman's arm. She felt along the wall for the shelf where they kept a candle. The tiny flame she struck took hold of the wick and chased the darkness into the corners. The meager contents of the room came into focus. A narrow quilt-covered cot. A sturdy wooden stool. A chamber pot. Prudence turned a smile on her charges.

She had become practiced at keeping her emotions from displaying on her face. Even so, she could not stop a rush of tears when she caught sight of the passenger she would help to freedom. Dark, frightened eyes peered at her from a dainty, heart-shaped face. The skin of one cheek was smooth and brown. But the other? Prudence swallowed against a hard lump that lodged in her throat. The young woman's other cheek bore an ugly, raised scar in the shape of a D.

The fugitive slave before her had been branded.

CHAPTER FOUR

No one was surprised the next morning when Fire Chief Kevin Franklin arrived at the inn. Breakfast preparations were fully underway in the kitchen, and the front door had not yet been unlocked. When the buzzer sounded, Janice hurried through the empty café to let him in.

"Good morning, Kevin." She'd known the fire chief practically his whole life, since he and Stuart had attended grade school together.

"Mrs. Eastman." He nodded his greeting. "I know it's early, but I wonder if you and your friends would mind talking with me a few minutes."

"Oh, we've been up for hours." She stifled a yawn. The truth was, none of them had been able to sleep much after hearing about the fire. "Come on back to the kitchen and have some coffee."

"Don't mind if I do."

LuAnn had anticipated her offer and set a coffee mug on the table. She stood beside it with the carafe in her hand. "Do you take cream and sugar?"

Kevin refused the condiments but accepted the offer of a fresh apple bran muffin. While Winnie worked at Big Red, the Inn Crowd joined Kevin at the table.

"I take it you've heard about last night's fire." He tore the muffin in half and inhaled appreciatively of the fragrant aroma.

LuAnn nodded. "Brad Grimes called last night to tell us about it. I hope no one was hurt?" She turned the statement into a question.

Kevin shook his head. "The church was empty."

"Thank the Lord," Janice whispered.

"Was there much damage?" Worry lines lay heavy on Tess's brow.

"A bit of smoke and a few items burned but very little structural damage. The old stone that the church is made of has lasted hundreds of years, and the belfry is sturdy."

Janice leaned slowly back in her chair, her gaze flying to her friends' faces. "The belfry?"

"That's right," Kevin said. "The fire started in the belfry. Thankfully our team arrived in time to contain it to that area."

"But…" LuAnn swallowed and tried again. "But we were in the belfry last night."

Kevin focused his attention on breaking his muffin into bite-sized pieces. "That's what I understand from Pastor Ben. And that's the reason for my visit this morning, obviously."

"When we left the church, everything was fine." Janice looked at Tess for confirmation.

"Absolutely fine," Tess agreed.

"About what time was that?"

"I can tell you exactly what time it was." LuAnn slipped her cell phone out of her pocket and tapped on the screen. "It was

5:56 p.m. I got a text in the car as we were pulling out of the parking lot."

Janice remembered. Winnie had texted with a question about next week's soup menu.

Kevin extracted his cell phone from his breast pocket. "Sunset was officially at 6:49 p.m. last night. So it must have been starting to get dark when you left. Right?"

Tess nodded. "That's why we left. Those skinny windows don't give much light to begin with, and there's no lighting up there."

"How did you get into the church?"

"I have a key." Janice shrugged. "I've had a key for years."

"And what door did you use?" He paused in his note-taking to look up at her.

"The back door. The one leading from the hallway by the pastor's office out to the rear parking lot." She paused, and then offered a further explanation. "I always park in that back lot rather than on the street."

"And was there anyone else in the church, either when you arrived or when you left?"

All three women shook their heads.

"Not a soul," Tess said. "We were alone the whole time."

"And how long was that?"

"About two-and-a-half hours," Janice told him. This was starting to feel like an interrogation. Surely, no one thought *they* had set the fire.

Kevin fiddled with a corner of his mustache, his brow furrowed. "And you spent the whole time in the belfry? What were you doing up there?"

"Cleaning," Tess and LuAnn answered at the same time.

Janice explained. "A friend of ours is getting married in a week, and she requested to have the bells rung at her wedding. But they haven't rung for years because of all the junk piled up in that belfry, so we were cleaning it out."

He considered that, and tapped something on his phone. "If you were in the belfry that long, is it possible someone came into the church below you? Maybe hid there until after you left?"

A relieved breath escaped Janice's lips. So, they weren't suspects after all. "I don't see how. We locked the door behind us when we arrived, and it was still locked when we left."

He held her gaze. "And you're positive you didn't leave it unlocked? Not intentionally," he hurried to add, "but maybe it slipped your mind?"

Janice returned the stare steadily. "Absolutely positive. I was carrying a box, and I remember balancing it on one arm while I used my keys with the other hand."

Tess leaned forward, her hands folded and resting on the table before her. "Do you have any idea how the fire started?"

"Actually, yes. My investigators found the source almost immediately. It was a candle."

Janice gasped, drawing Kevin's quick gaze toward her. "Yes?"

"We found a box of candles up there," she told him.

LuAnn agreed. "They were altar candles, still wrapped in cellophane. They'd never been used."

Kevin grimaced. "Well, one of them has been used now."

Tess had a narrow-eyed gaze fixed on him. "You don't think we set the fire, do you?"

He looked surprised. "No, of course not. I'm merely trying to put all the pieces of this puzzle together, and you ladies"–he included Janice and LuAnn in his glance–"have one of the critical pieces, since you were in the exact location a few hours before the fire started. Besides, none of you fit the description of our suspect."

Janice's spine stiffened in her chair. "You have a suspect?"

Kevin cocked his head. "Nothing solid, but we have some ideas. And we have a witness. A man was seen running away from the church at around 8:45 last night. That's when the fire was discovered, and we were called."

Relief loosened the last of the knots that had pulled tight in Janice's stomach.

"A man, you say?" Tess asked. "Did you get a description?"

At her question Kevin's expression became brittle. He hesitated a moment and then popped the last bite of muffin into his mouth. He took his time chewing before voicing an answer. "Tell you what. You leave that to us. We'll get the guy, don't worry." He placed his palms on the table and rose from the chair. "You've been very helpful, and I sure do appreciate the breakfast and the coffee."

In other words, mind your own business. Janice and the others followed his lead and stood as well.

Winnie, who'd been uncharacteristically quiet during the interview, turned from the stove. "I bet it was kids. Sounds like a prank a teenager would pull. Meaning no mischief, just poking around where he shouldn't be."

Kevin's smile broadened. "That is one theory, and we're looking into it. Again, thank you, ladies."

"I'll see you out," Janice said.

She walked beside him to the front door, thoughts spinning in her head. Though she would love to push for more details, she sensed from his manner that none would be forthcoming.

The bell chimed when she opened the front door. "I'm curious about one thing. Who called in the fire?"

Kevin studied her for a minute, as though trying to decide whether or not to answer the question. Then he gave a small shrug. "It'll be in the newspaper today. Harry Olson. He saw the flames and called from his cell phone. Good thing too. Otherwise the fire might have spread to the lower part of the church where it could have done a lot of damage."

Harmless Harry, owner of the Antique and Salvage Mall and a longtime friend. He'd been entirely supportive of the Inn Crowd and their vision to open Wayfarers Inn.

"Thank the Lord." She pulled open the door. "If you think of any other questions we can answer, please don't hesitate to call or stop by."

"I won't. And thank you, ma'am."

Janice stood leaning against the door as he descended the porch stairs and got into his car. She stayed where she was, watching as the car disappeared down Ohio Street. If there was anything she disliked, it was unanswered questions, especially when it came to something surrounding Christ Fellowship church.

Janice had barely returned to the kitchen when the morning's second visitor burst in.

"Did y'all hear the news?" Marla demanded. "Somebody went and burned down the church. Now I'm never going to have my dream wedding." Tears streamed from her eyes.

LuAnn hurried across the room to pull the woman into an embrace. "Don't worry. The church is fine. The fire chief just left here, and he assured us that the damage was contained to the belfry."

"Belfry?" Marla's gaze sought Janice's. "Does that mean the bells burned up?"

"I doubt that," Janice assured her. "Those things are heavy cast iron and wouldn't burn. But we don't know what shape the actual belfry is in." Her tone became apologetic. "The support structures may have been damaged,"

A wail rose from the sobbing woman. As if on cue, Byron rushed into the room followed by Lucas.

"What's wrong with my sugarplum?"

LuAnn stepped back, and Byron wrapped Marla in a bearlike embrace.

Marla's answer was muffled against his shirt. "Somebody is trying to sabotage our perfect wedding."

Lucas gave a surprised exclamation.

Byron looked up at Janice, clearly startled. "Sabotage?"

"I doubt seriously if anyone is attempting to sabotage the wedding." She poured as much comfort as she could into her tone. "However, there was a fire in the church belfry last night."

Byron tightened his embrace around Marla. "Don't you worry about a thing. We're getting married, bells or no bells."

Marla's sobs grew quiet. Finally, she lifted her head. Lucas hurried forward with a crumpled tissue he extracted from his pocket.

She accepted it and blotted her eyes. "Y'all think I'm being silly. But you know how girls are. They daydream about their wedding day. I had mine all planned out by the time I was fourteen, and I always dreamed of hearing those bells ring out." She sniffed. "Of course, I gave up on that dream many years ago. Till I met you." She lifted a trembling smile to Byron.

Indulgence softened his features. "If you want bells, we'll have bells. Even if I have to climb up there and fix them myself."

The joy that lit Marla's face sent an answering shot of warmth through Janice's heart. Her friend certainly was head over heels in love with this man. Janice shifted her gaze to Byron, who continued to look down at his bride-to-be with a soft smile. A genuine smile? She didn't know him well enough to judge the sincerity. The warmth in Janice's chest cooled a bit. His intentions had better be honorable.

Then she noticed Lucas, who stood slightly behind and off to one side of the couple. His expression was easy to read. He looked more than a little troubled.

Behind them, Winnie opened one of the huge oven doors and pulled out a breakfast casserole. She slid it onto a cooling rack before turning toward them and planting her hands on her hips.

"What I'd like to know is, what are all these people doing in my kitchen? We're probably violating some health code or other." She lifted her hand and waved toward the café. "Guests belong out front where they can be served proper. Go on. Git."

She took exactly the right tone to break the tension of the moment.

Byron laughed in his booming voice. "You heard the woman. And I always say, if there's one person you want to keep happy, it's the cook."

He guided Marla with an arm around her shoulder toward the front of the inn, with Lucas in tow.

When they were gone, Tess opened the cabinet and began pulling out breakfast plates. "I like that man."

"He certainly seems to care about Marla," LuAnn stated.

Janice's thoughts leaped to the Bible upstairs in her dressing table. "Oh! I forgot to tell Marla what I found. You remember that box of her things we discovered up in the belfry? You'll never believe what was tucked inside."

She described finding William Still's Bible and his scribbles in the margins on practically every page. As she talked, she became more and more reluctant to turn the Bible over to Marla. Or more specifically, to Byron.

LuAnn slid into one of the chairs around the kitchen table. "You know how proud Marla is of her famous ancestor. That Bible would have a lot of sentimental value to her."

"I'll bet it's worth a lot of money too," Tess said.

Janice rounded on her. "Exactly. And that's why I don't think it's a good idea to give it to her yet."

Tess looked puzzled. "Why not?"

"Well, because she's distracted right now with all the changes in her life. She probably wouldn't truly appreciate it." Janice flinched. She didn't realize how lame that excuse would sound until she voiced it.

"Nonsense." LuAnn studied her closely. "There's another reason. Spit it out."

She struggled to find words that wouldn't make her sound like a suspicious fool. But these were her friends. If she sounded like a fool, so be it. "What if the Bible is worth a lot of money? Gold diggers have been known to take advantage of people for far less money than that Bible could be worth."

"Gold diggers?" Tess circled the table, setting four breakfast plates in place. "You don't mean Byron?"

"Well, we don't know him, do we?" Janice answered, feeling a bit defensive. "And neither does Marla, no matter what she says."

With a stubborn expression plastered on her face, LuAnn opened her mouth to speak, but Winnie preempted whatever argument she was about to voice.

"I don't see any rush in giving it to her." She set the casserole dish on a hot pad in the center of the table. "Not that I think Byron's intentions are anything but honorable, but those two have enough on their plates right now. A lot of details to think about, what with combining two sets of furniture and all. They don't need a box of old papers to deal with on top of it."

Janice flashed her a grateful smile. "I'm not planning to keep it from her forever, but I'd like to hold on to it a little bit longer. Just to be on the safe side."

Tess and LuAnn exchanged a long look, and then Tess shrugged.

"It won't hurt to keep it for a few days, until we all get to know Byron a little better."

From the look Tess shot Janice, by *we all* she meant Janice.

LuAnn didn't look completely convinced, but she did nod. "I've always assumed if I feel hesitant about a decision, that means I should wait before deciding."

Relieved, Janice let out a breath before taking her seat.

CHAPTER FIVE

A small crowd stood on the sidewalk in front of Christ Fellowship when Janice, Tess, and LuAnn arrived at the church a few minutes after ten thirty. Janice recognized Pastor Ben and Paige surrounded by a half-dozen or so church members. Her eyes were drawn to the belfry, a castle-like tower that rose five floors above the front entrance. Four majestic stone columns reached high into the sky, directing viewers' eyes to the heavens. Between them, narrow tracery windows revealed the only visible damage from this viewpoint. Janice winced at the sight of smoke-scorched stone, well over two hundred years old. Apparently, the glass on the inside had been broken, by either the fire or the firefighters.

Instead of driving around to the back lot, Tess pulled into one of the diagonal spaces near the arched front door. The three exited the car and then paused for a moment, their gazes drawn upward.

"It doesn't look so bad from here," LuAnn said.

Tess shook her head. "Whoever cleans that stone better have a big ladder."

A woman standing in the group near Pastor Ben caught sight of them. Gloria Bellamy, a longtime member of Christ

Fellowship who had made no secret of her disapproval when the staff-parish committee hired Pastor Ben, hurried toward them.

"Can you believe it?" Her spiky gray hair stood straight on end, giving her the appearance of one who has just stuck her finger in a light socket. "Our church nearly burned to the ground."

"That's a bit of an exaggeration, isn't it?" LuAnn asked in a soft but slightly chiding tone.

Janice agreed. "The fire chief told us they arrived in time to confine the fire to the belfry. The only thing up there was a bunch of junk."

The woman's lips tightened. "Junk that had no business still being there, the way I hear it." She turned her head slightly and raised her voice, which easily carried to the nearby group. "Pastor Lawrence would never have allowed the church's belfry to remain a dumping ground for people's trash. It was a fire hazard, and somebody"—she emphasized the word—"should have taken care of it before now."

Janice saw Pastor Ben wince, and beside him, Paige's expression became troubled. Though the young couple had been accepted by the vast majority of the congregation, a handful of longtime church members still seemed to look for reasons to complain about the new ideas Pastor Ben was introducing. Lawrence used to say, "Resistance to change is an excuse to find reasons to criticize."

"Excuse me." LuAnn stepped away and headed down the sidewalk, where Janice spied Brad's car pulling to a stop. Tess followed, but when Janice went to join them, Gloria grabbed her arm.

"It's the pastor's place to look after the church building. That means when something like this happens it's his responsibility."

Janice considered physically removing the woman's fingers from her arm, but longtime training prevented it. Instead, she patted the pudgy hand in a motherly manner. "Now, Gloria, that's not fair. A lot of that stuff was stored up there when Lawrence was still alive."

"Stored is one thing. The way I understand it, there was junk piled all the way to the rafters, and it wasn't that way a few years ago."

Unfortunately, she was correct. The beanbag chairs, for instance, and many other things, had been added fairly recently.

Gloria continued, her tongue dagger-sharp. "I knew the minute they brought those projectors into the sanctuary that things were going downhill. Pastor Lawrence would never have stood for it."

The projection system had been installed months ago and had polarized the congregation of Christ Fellowship. Most everyone loved it and hailed the purchase as a step into the modern world of worship. Unfortunately, a small number of change-resistant congregants like Gloria claimed the screens detracted from the reverence of the service. Janice tugged her arm slightly, but Gloria didn't release her grip.

"I think I can speak for Lawrence. He loved the old hymns, but I know he would have approved of the projection system.

The church simply never had the money to buy one until Pastor Ben came and started attracting so many young people."

She might as well have saved her breath. Gloria went on as if she hadn't spoken.

"Hymnals have the musical notes, not just words. Young people these days have no respect for traditions. And what does it lead to?" She threw her hand toward the tower.

At least the gesture freed Janice, who took a backward step. She used her most reasonable tone, cultivated during years as the pastor's wife. "Now, Gloria, I hardly think our new projection system led to the fire. To my understanding, it might even have been kids playing with matches up there." No need to mention the locked doors. "We can be thankful there was no permanent damage to the church."

"But there could have been," Gloria said ominously. "There could have been."

Another car pulled into a parking place across the street. Catching sight of the occupants, Gloria hurried toward them, no doubt in search of a friendlier ear for her complaints.

Janice approached Pastor Ben and Paige. "I'm so sorry."

The pastor gave her a genuine smile, though Paige looked nearly ready to cry. Janice's heart went out to the young woman. Such a bubbly, cheerful person with an incredible desire to fit in at Christ Fellowship. Janice put an arm around her and squeezed.

"They'll come around," she whispered.

Tears glistened in Paige's eyes. "Don't mind me. The pregnancy hormones are raging lately." She gave a little laugh.

Though she was about four months along, her slender waist had barely begun to thicken. Janice squeezed again before releasing her. Her gaze strayed toward the bell tower. "Was there much damage?"

Pastor Ben grimaced. "It's a mess up there. Charred furniture, melted plastic, and everything covered in CO_2."

Janice raised her eyebrows. "CO_2? So they were able to put it out with fire extinguishers?"

He nodded. "Thank goodness. If they'd needed to use a fire hose they would have had to bust through the stonework in those skinny windows."

"Can I go up there and take a look?" she asked.

He shook his head apologetically. "The fire department has it taped off at the bottom of the stairway. The fire was pretty much contained to that stone area, but there's a lot of cleanup that needs to be done before anyone can get up there safely."

Not good news. "Has Marla Still spoken with you about her wedding?"

Pastor Ben's face cleared. "She asked me to officiate. And I understand you're helping her put it together." His quick glance at his wife, and the slight pained expression that crept over Paige's face, told Janice a lot. But surely the young couple understood that she and Marla had been friends for decades before they came along.

"Yes, she did ask me to help." Janice refused to feel guilty for something that was not her fault. "And she has her heart set on those bells ringing at her wedding."

His expression became doubtful. "I don't know if that's going to be possible." He chewed on his lower lip for a moment. "But I'll see what I can do."

Janice patted him on the arm. "That would mean a lot to Marla, Pastor." Her gaze strayed over his shoulder, where Gloria stood with two older church women, their heads together and Gloria's jaw flapping. "Just do what you can. That's all anyone can expect of you."

The friends retired early Sunday night. Since no one had gotten much sleep the night before, they did not linger in their fourth-floor common room as had become their custom. Janice bade her friends good night and hurried to her apartment, eager to slip into a fresh pair of pajamas and slide between the sheets.

Forty-five minutes later, she still stood at the sink running a brush through her unruly hair. Why did it always seem that the more tired you were, the longer it took to get ready for bed? She used a comb to strip a few platinum hairs from the brush before tossing it back in the vanity drawer. Stifling a yawn, she turned out the light and headed for the bed.

The minute her head hit the pillow, she knew it was no use. Thoughts spun like a twister in her mind. What possible reason would anyone have for setting fire to the church? Gloria's spiteful comments surfaced. Did anyone in the congregation dislike Pastor Ben enough to want to cause mischief for him? Congregational loyalties ran deep, that's for sure. The fact that nearly two years after Lawrence's death, people still thought of Ben as a usurper proved that.

The box of Lawrence's mementos in her sitting room tugged at her. With only a moment's hesitation, she switched on the lamp and slipped out of bed.

The stack of letters lay on top of the rest of the contents. She lifted the bundle out and fanned through them. Did she dare read them tonight, or would that merely make her melancholy? The one on top bore Lawrence's name scrawled in a familiar script. A tender smile curved her lips. She remembered that letter vividly. She slid it from beneath the rubber band and opened it up.

Dear Daddy,

Not only are you the best preacher in the world, you're the best father too. The Bible says we love God because God first loved us. You are the one who showed me first what God's love really is.

The letter was signed "Love, Stacy."

Smiling through her tears, Janice refolded the letter and slipped it beneath the rubber band.

When her fingers lifted the rubber, her hand hesitated. She gave the band an experimental tweak. It snapped back against the papers with force.

Odd. She would have sworn... Setting the bundle aside, she proceeded to empty the box. Framed diplomas, an engraved plaque from the Marietta Pastors' Association, a photograph of

Lawrence with the Rev. Billy Graham snapped at one of the famous preacher's crusades. More photos of Lawrence with various church and civic leaders. And then—

"I thought so."

Janice lifted out the mangled remains of a nondescript tan rubber band. Much older than the red one, the rubber was brittle and had snapped in two. That was the band she'd used when she packaged up these letters, she was sure of it. In her mind's eye rose an image of Lawrence's desk drawer in the church office, every item neatly segregated. Paper clips in one tray. Thumbtacks in another. Pencils stored separately from the pens. And rubber bands. All of them this light brown color.

She picked up the letters again and fingered the red rubber band. Someone had put that there, and it wasn't her. Which meant someone had read these letters. But who?

A suspicion wormed its way into her brain, and her face heated with a guilty flush. Who had access to this box of memorabilia? Well, to be honest, practically everyone in the church. But who spent the most time in the church alone?

She began piling the stuff back in the box with quick, jerky movements. And why wouldn't Pastor Ben glance through these letters? Why wouldn't he open this box? After all, it was stored in his church. It would be only natural for him to glance through them.

She dumped the letters on top of the other things and folded the flaps shut. Then she went to the bathroom and washed her hands, scrubbing away traces of dust. Only when she was back in bed, her head resting on her pillow, staring at the darkness around her, did she give her thoughts rein to travel in the direction they wanted to go.

Just because Pastor Ben had received a sharp reminder of how beloved his predecessor had been and still was, didn't mean he set the fire.

Tess eyed Janice over the rim of her coffee cup. "That's too big a stretch. I don't believe it for a minute. And I don't think you do either."

After more than an hour of fretful fighting with her bed-sheets, Janice had finally managed to drift off. But her sleep had been full of anxious dreams where she raced up and down the aisles in the parking lot at the supermarket looking for her car. Her reflection in the mirror this morning betrayed her restless night, with dark sagging pouches beneath her eyes that no amount of makeup would conceal.

"Of course Pastor Ben did not set that fire." LuAnn smeared a spoonful of strawberry-rhubarb jam on a piece of wheat toast. "Even if he were upset by those letters, why would he set fire to everything else in the belfry? It makes no sense. If he really wanted to torch the memories of Lawrence, he would have taken the box out back to a trash bin or something."

"I don't think he would even do that," Tess said. "That young man sincerely loves the Lord and loves Christ Fellow-ship. I don't think he's capable of such a spiteful act."

Janice completely agreed. And yet, a shred of doubt remained. "But what if it was an accident? What if he went up in the belfry after we left for some perfectly innocent reason?"

LuAnn looked thoughtful. "I can see that he might want to check how much progress we'd made."

"Exactly. And we know it was dark up there. And those candles were sitting out in plain sight. So, he lit one, just to have a look around. And then maybe he dropped it or something."

They sat in silence while the scenario ran through their minds.

Then Tess spoke up. "Highly unlikely. Besides, if that happened he would have run downstairs and grabbed a fire extinguisher himself. He certainly wouldn't have run away and left his own church burning."

This morning, in the light of day, the idea certainly did seem silly.

"You're right," Janice agreed. "I'm sorry for suggesting such a thing. I guess I was just tired and a bit emotional last night."

LuAnn reached across the kitchen table to pat her hand. "We've all had an emotional few days."

Janice smiled her appreciation at her friends. Not everyone was fortunate enough to have friends who would listen to her ravings and not think worse of her for them. She stirred a splash of cream into her coffee and watched as the liquid swirled in her cup. Of course, they were right. Even if Pastor Ben had caused a fire accidentally, he would have kept his head and put it out himself.

But what about Paige? Janice's hand froze. In Paige's highly emotional state, would she have read those letters and interpreted them as a threat to her husband's position at the church? If she dropped a lit candle, might she have panicked and run away?

I'm being ridiculous. Under no circumstances could she see Paige panicking to that degree. Bursting into tears, yes. Still, the idea was worth considering. The fire might have been an accident, and the culprit may have run away in a panic.

But who?

Marietta, Ohio
October 8, 1857

"Prudence, may I have a word with you?"

Prudence's hands trembled as she set the dish on the shelf, but she turned a calm countenance toward the man all the inn employees knew as Howard Bickerton. "Yes, sir."

He glanced around the kitchen, where several of the hotel staff were cleaning up from breakfast. "Let's step into the other room for a moment."

Prudence wiped damp palms on her apron as she followed her employer out of the kitchen and into the bookshelf-lined room he called his den. Though this man had been nothing but kind to her, she had never felt entirely comfortable around him. He played an important part in the Cause, and as such was a man of secrets. Her most fervent prayer was that he would never discover she knew one of them.

She followed him into the den, where he turned to face her, but did not suggest that she sit down. Instead, he spoke in a tone just above a whisper, his gaze focused on the open doorway behind her.

"Our latest passengers have posed something of a problem. I've had a guest complaint."

Prudence guessed the nature of the complaint before he spoke it but held her tongue and waited for him to continue.

"It appears the little one has a piercing cry which disturbed Mr. Faulkner's sleep. I explained that the baby"—his eyebrows arched high on his forehead—"is the child of one of the maids and sickly, but Mr. Faulkner was not inclined to be understanding." He lowered his voice even more, so that Prudence was required to lean closer to hear his words. "He is an influential man from Georgia. A landowner, with quite a bit of, ah, property."

The meaning became clear. Mr. Faulkner owned slaves, which meant everyone at the Riverfront House who knew of its dual purpose must do all they could not to arouse his suspicions. Prudence nodded to indicate that she understood.

He cleared his throat. "I wonder if it might be possible for this maid to find employment elsewhere."

Clearly Mr. Bickerton had not met their newest passengers.

Prudence shook her head. "I fear she is unsuited for any other location." She held his gaze and poured meaning into her voice. "Particularly employment which would require her to serve the public."

He drew in a long, slow breath. "I see. And how long should we expect her to stay on here?"

Prudence clasped her hands together at her waist. "Thee might give her notice, sir, but I fear it would take her at least two weeks to find a suitable job."

He lifted a finger and rubbed it across his mustache while thoughts played across his face. "Very well. Please speak with her and explain that the comfort of our guests is of utmost importance. She must strive to teach her child restraint."

"Yes, sir."

After another long pause during which his eyes bored into hers, he dismissed her. "Thank you, Prudence."

She hurried back to the kitchen, her head bowed and her thoughts troubled. One of the other maids had delivered breakfast to the hidden room in the basement. Prudence had not yet spoken with the young woman she had ferried across the river early this morning. But she must do so at her earliest convenience.

The dishes cleaned and stored, the staff of the Riverfront House left the kitchen to perform their various duties. Prudence gathered a handful of dried cherries from the larder and, after checking to be sure no one lurked about, ducked behind the secret doorway and crept down the hidden stairs. She hurried across the dirty brick floor without lighting a candle, and by feel located the catch that would let her into the hidden rooms.

When she pushed open the last door on the right, the woman inside leapt to her feet. Fear showed plainly on her face. On the narrow cot sat a baby. Sensitive to his mother's emotions, his face scrunched and he began to wail.

"Shh. There now." Prudence shut the door behind her and closed the short distance between them in a hurry. "Do not cry, little one. Look what I have brought thee." She extended her palm and showed him the dried cherries.

The wail receded to a whimper. The boy, who appeared to be around eighteen months of age, looked from the cherries to his mother, who stood rooted to her place at the head of the cot. He grasped a pudgy handful and shoved them all in his mouth.

Prudence chuckled and closed her hand on the rest of the fruit. "Thee must not be greedy. Take thy time, lest thee chokes."

She smiled at the child's mother and revised her initial opinion. Upon closer inspection, the woman was little more than a child herself. Perhaps no more than seventeen or eighteen. And clearly terrified. Spindly arms hugged her narrow waist, her fingers biting into the flesh on each side. The dress she wore hung in tatters from bony shoulders. The ugly scar Prudence had seen the night before showed starkly beneath protruding cheekbones.

"I am Prudence." She poured warmth into her smile. "What is thy name?"

"Becca." The word was spoken barely above a whisper.

Prudence transferred her smile to the child. "And this little one?"

"Ezra." The hint of a smile appeared on Becca's face. "Ezra Junior."

The boy looked up at his name but continued chewing the mouthful of cherries.

Prudence addressed the child. "Ezra Junior, thee must learn the art of silence. I have practiced it much." The Quaker community to which Prudence belonged considered silence a virtue to be treasured. Quaker meetings were conducted without words, but instead, hours of communal quiet contemplation of God's glory.

"He's a'-sceered of the dark," Becca said in her soft voice. "That stub of a candle burned out, and it's black as night in this room."

Prudence glanced at the candle that glowed inside a glass chimney. Well used, to be sure, but several inches of wax remained beneath the flickering flame. The maid who brought breakfast must have fetched a new one for Becca.

"Then we shall make sure thee has plenty of candles." She looked up, toward the ceiling and the rooms above them. "Thee must not disturb the guests. If thee is found..."

She need not finish the sentence. Terror showed plainly on the scarred face before her.

"I can't go back. I'll be kill't this time."

Prudence's heart ached with sympathy. "Thee has escaped before?"

Becca's jaw trembled. "Twice. The last time the man who catched me, he told Massa Duncan that this would stop me from running." She touched her scarred cheek.

Ezra Junior swallowed the last of his cherries and stuck out his palm for more. Prudence sat beside him on the cot and counted five into his hand.

"How far north did thee get the first two times?"

Becca shook her head. "I wasn't running for the north. I was heading to Kentucky. That's where my man is."

"Ezra Senior?" Prudence rubbed the baby's tightly curled hair.

"My husband. Massa Duncan, he told Ezra he was gonna sell him. Said Ezra gonna learn how to work tobacco over in

71

Kentucky. So we hurried up and got married." Tears welled in her eyes. "We only had three days for Massa Duncan did what he said. He sold my man off to Kentucky."

"Only three days?" Prudence gave the little head one more rub. "He never got to meet his son?"

"No, ma'am. Ezra, he didn't even know he had a son. That's why I's trying to find him. Ain't right, a daddy not even knowing. But that evil man caught me." She shut her eyes and shuddered. "He caught me once, then he caught me again, and told Massa to put this here on my face so everybody who sees me know I'm his property."

Bile churned in Prudence's stomach. Becca's story unearthed a nightmare buried deep in her memory. She, too, had met evil men.

"Thee is not property," Prudence told her. "Thee is going to be a free woman."

"That's what the man said."

Prudence peered at her, momentarily taken aback. "Does thee mean the evil man?"

Becca shook her head. "The man who came to see Massa Duncan. He came out where I was hanging laundry, puffing on a pipe, and told me he came from Kentucky and he knew my Ezra. He brought me a message. Me and Ezra Junior slipped away on the night that man told me to. And there was another man right where he said he'd be. He brung me to you, and he told me I'm supposed to wait here with you until Ezra comes." A different kind of tears sprang to her eyes, and her voice trembled with joy. "My Ezra knows he's a daddy. That good man, he carried the news back to him."

Prudence gazed at the boy, who had apparently eaten his fill of cherries. The pattern of the quilt on which he sat had caught his attention, and he traced the stitches with a stubby finger. How Jason would love this little boy. The joy of having a child might even soothe some of his pain. She closed her eyes against the wave of sorrow that threatened to drown her. They'd had a child once. Little Hope had lived long enough to teach Prudence the joy of motherhood and the agony of loss, all within the span of two infant breaths.

"We will see thee reunited with thy husband." She stood and glanced around the tiny hidden room. "And I will bring treats to keep this little one quiet."

CHAPTER SIX

Once her housekeeping duties were complete, Janice volunteered to run to the store and pick up a few things Winnie needed for the gumbo she planned to cook the following day. After her conversation with her friends this morning, she felt slightly guilty for coming up with an excuse to get out alone. They were the Inn Crowd, a team. Once before she'd kept something secret from her friends. A photograph. That had been because of pride, a desire to prove something to herself and to her friends.

But this was different. It wasn't pride that kept her silent, it was uncertainty. She felt awful for even *thinking* Pastor Ben was somehow involved. And yet, that nagging feeling that something needed to be explained would not be banished. If all three of them showed up to question him, he would feel ambushed. But one person asking a simple question about his whereabouts wouldn't be threatening at all.

Before she went to the market, she drove a short distance in the opposite direction, and parked outside the rear entrance to Christ Fellowship.

Inside, she smiled a greeting for Mary Beth, who had been the church secretary for more than a decade.

"Good morning." The woman paused her typing. "What brings you here on Monday morning?"

"I thought I'd take a chance and see if Pastor Ben has a moment to talk." She glanced at the closed door to the pastor's office.

"I think he's just reading his email in there. Go ahead and knock."

Janice smiled her thanks and rounded the assistant's desk. She rapped on the heavy wooden door with two knuckles.

A muffled voice sounded from inside. "Come in."

When she entered the office, Pastor Ben looked up from his computer and his face brightened. "Mrs. Eastman, what a nice surprise."

He left his chair and came around the big heavy desk— Janice refused to think of it as Lawrence's desk—with outstretched hands. Returning his hug, Janice battled another stab of guilt. What was she doing here? She did not believe this man was capable of setting fire to his own church. But he had to be convinced that openness was his best and only defense against vicious whispers.

"Have a seat." He gestured toward one of the comfortable armchairs near the bookshelves. "Would you like coffee?"

"No, thank you."

Before she took the indicated chair, Janice pulled the door closed behind her. Pastor Ben's eyebrows traveled up his forehead. Except in the instance of a counseling situation, it was considered appropriate for a pastor's door to remain open while meeting with a female parishioner. Tongues tended to wag, and a pastor must take care to remain above suspicion.

But no one would think anything inappropriate was going on between the former pastor's wife and this young man. Besides, Janice preferred that Mary Beth, who had notoriously sharp ears, not overhear the conversation.

"I hope everything's okay," he said as she seated herself.

"Everything's fine," she assured him. "Well, I hope everything's fine. It's only that I'm concerned about spiteful gossip spreading through the church." She battled a rising warmth and managed to stop it before it reached her face.

"About the fire?"

She nodded.

"I don't think you need to worry about that." A kind smile appeared on his face. "I'm sure no one thinks you and your friends had anything to do with that fire."

The comment startled Janice so that she almost gave a nervous laugh. He'd obviously misunderstood her intent. She decided not to correct him. That would be a much easier conversation than the one she came here to have.

"You don't think so? I heard a lot of whispering yesterday during the fellowship hour after church. I almost felt as if people were demanding that we tell them our alibi." She avoided his gaze. "And not just us but everyone who has access to the church."

Pastor Ben rested his elbows on the arms of the chair and steepled his fingers before him. "You know as well as anyone how dangerous it is to heed spiteful gossip."

"Yes, of course. But I also know the importance of clergy remaining above suspicion. And even though I am no longer in a position of leadership, people naturally assume an association." He tilted his head as he studied her. Janice rushed on. "I assured everyone that the three of us left before dark, and we could all vouch for each other. That put a halt to the talk." She cleared her throat. "At least about us."

They sat in silence a moment, and Janice resisted the urge to squirm beneath his steady gaze.

Finally, he spoke. "Are you suggesting that I or anyone else in church leadership should make a public statement about our whereabouts when the fire was set?"

"Nothing so formal as a public statement," Janice rushed to say. "But it might not be a bad idea if word got around that you were"—she arched her eyebrows—"at a meeting, perhaps? Or wherever you were?"

His expression became knowing, and Janice was unable to meet his gaze.

"I'm afraid I disagree," he said gently. "I think it's a mistake to acknowledge untrue accusations, especially when they take the form of gossip. Besides, sometimes a pastor's duties must remain confidential. I'm sure you, of all people, understand that."

Heat flooded her cheeks. In other words, she was being told politely to mind her own business. "Of course I understand. You're absolutely right."

She cast about for a way to bring up the rubber band. Could she ask to inspect the contents of his desk? No, of course not.

"I was recently reminded about the duties of pastors when we were going through the stuff in the belfry." Did that sound natural enough?

His expression stayed pleasant. "Oh?"

"I found a box of my late husband's things up there. Some certificates and awards." She glanced up. "Some letters of appreciation written by members of the congregation."

"I remember seeing that box when the youth were carting some things up there to store. I admit I glanced through the contents. He was very well thought of by this church. As are you." His fingers tapped together. "Mrs. Eastman, it would be a big help to Paige and me if you would help us put a stop to any malicious gossip about this fire. It's simply not healthy for the congregation."

"Yes, certainly. Whatever I can do to help." So great was the urge to squirm in her chair that she found herself jumping out of it, ready to escape this uncomfortable conversation. "In fact, if you would like me to spearhead a cleanup of the belfry, I'll be happy to do that."

He stood as well, and his smile appeared entirely genuine. "Thank you. I do appreciate that, but it's not necessary. Actually, Harry Olson stopped me after church yesterday and volunteered to see to the cleanup. He's accustomed to wading through the junk and dirt. If you want to help, you might give him a call."

Janice told him she would do that, and made her exit.

Out in her car, she sat for a moment with her eyes closed, letting guilt wash over her. What had she hoped to discover during that visit? She wanted to hear Pastor Ben's alibi, to lay to rest this nagging suspicion that he or maybe his wife was somehow responsible for the fire. Pastor Ben was no dummy. No doubt he knew exactly what she was after. All she'd managed to do was embarrass herself.

Worst of all, she had not gotten the information she was after.

Janice turned a page on the musical score with a practiced flip, her right hand not missing a beat on the piano keys. The haunting melody that filled the parlor reminded her so starkly of Lawrence that she had trouble swallowing past a lump in her throat. Strains of "Somewhere My Love" dredged up memories of their early years together and served to push away the unpleasant feelings from this morning's meeting with Pastor Ben. She vaguely heard the ding of the front door as someone entered but did not take her eyes off the music or her fingers from the keyboard until she reached the last stanza. As the music died away, a smattering of applause sounded from the lunch stragglers in the café.

She turned to smile her thanks for their appreciation and caught sight of a woman standing just inside the doorway. Tall, slender, and pulling a rolling suitcase behind her. But what struck Janice was the pained, almost agonized expression on the narrow face.

When the woman realized she'd been spotted, the expression disappeared, though a lingering sadness remained.

LuAnn emerged from the office and hurried toward the new arrival. "Hello. Can we help you?"

The woman tore her gaze from Janice and fixed it on LuAnn. "Yes. I have a reservation. I'm Pauline Richardson." She released the handle of her suitcase to cast a quick glance at her watch. "I don't know what time check-in is. I'm probably too early."

"Welcome to Wayfarers Inn." LuAnn's warm voice sounded in sharp contrast to their guest's nervous one. "We have your room ready. Let's get the paperwork out of the way, shall we?"

With another glance at Janice, Pauline followed LuAnn toward the registration desk, where she completed the check-in forms. Janice closed the piano lid gently and followed, her curiosity piqued, and for some reason, her compassion stirred. She stood beside LuAnn, behind the ornately carved bar that served as a registration desk, while Pauline Richardson's pen scratched across the paper.

"I understand you'll be staying with us for two weeks," LuAnn said when their guest slid the form and a credit card across the desk's surface.

LuAnn's chatty tone invited more information, but the only response she received was a quick, brittle smile.

Janice thrust a hand across the bar. "I'm Janice Eastman. And this is LuAnn Sherrill."

Cold fingers wrapped around hers and were withdrawn almost immediately.

"Since you will be here through the end of the month, we hope you'll join us for our first annual Harvest Celebration feast."

LuAnn gave her a sharp look. They had not discussed making the celebration an annual one. Janice shrugged an apology.

"Oh. I'm not..." Again, the brittle smile put in a brief appearance. "I'll see."

Janice and LuAnn exchanged a glance, and then LuAnn unlocked the desk drawer and removed a key. "We've put you in the Lilac and Sage room. It's one of our brightest, with an east-facing window. And it has a lovely view of the Ohio River on the south side."

Janice had tidied the room herself this morning and left the customary welcome basket of fresh fruit and granola bars on the bureau.

"I'm sure that will be fine."

"Breakfast is here in the café"—LuAnn gestured in that direction—"at eight o'clock. We serve soup and homemade breads to the public beginning at eleven. We don't serve dinner, but we can arrange for a sandwich or something light if you like. Otherwise there are several nice restaurants in the area."

Something about the woman's closed-in expression made Janice long to draw her out. She rounded the desk. "Let me get your bag for you."

She reached toward the handle, but Mrs. Richardson grasped it first and pulled it beyond Janice's reach. "That won't be necessary," she said quietly. "If you could just point me in the right direction."

Janice folded her hands in front of her. "Of course. It's on the third floor, right at the top of the stairs."

"We do have an elevator if you prefer," LuAnn said. "I'm afraid it's old and slow, but it's perfectly safe."

"The stairs will be fine."

Without further comment, she headed in that direction. LuAnn and Janice watched as she tugged the suitcase up the stairs behind her and disappeared around the corner at the first landing.

"I wonder what her story is?" Janice asked. "She looks so sad."

LuAnn agreed. "We'll pray for her tonight. I have a feeling the Lord sent her here for some sort of healing."

Janice glanced at her friend. LuAnn displayed an amazing sensitivity to others' needs. It was one of the things Janice had always admired about her. "What kind of healing?"

LuAnn shook her head. "I don't know. But He does."

When the café had closed for the afternoon and the kitchen had been cleaned, Janice went upstairs to her apartment. She needed to spend some time in prayer. Her suspicions surrounding Pastor Ben and Paige continued to worry her, mostly because she didn't really believe either of them had set the fire. So why did her thoughts keep traveling in that direction?

Settled in her comfy chair, she opened her Bible to the book of Philippians. The apostle Paul sometimes had a way of energizing her mind, but today she read the words that never failed to have the opposite effect.

"And the peace of God, which transcends all understanding, will guard your hearts and your minds in Christ Jesus."

She closed her eyes. "That's what I need, Lord. Your peace in my heart and mind."

A drowsy lethargy crept over her. She was getting too old to go very long without a good night's rest. Perhaps a nap would refresh her. She cleared her mind and drifted off.

The ringing of her cell phone jerked her awake. She snatched it up and glanced at the screen. Tess. She must be calling from downstairs, otherwise she'd tap on Janice's door. And she'd been asleep less than twenty minutes.

"Hello?" She assumed a chipper, fully awake tone.

"Can you come down here? Chief Mayfield would like to ask us a few questions."

The head of the Marietta Police Department.

"I'll be right down."

Janice hurried to the bathroom to run a comb through her hair and then trotted down the stairs to the main floor. She found LuAnn, Tess, and Chief Nelson Mayfield parked in the comfy chairs in front of the fireplace in the reception area.

The chief stood at her approach. "Thank you for joining us." He gestured toward the love seat. "I promise not to take too much of your time."

Janice settled on a cushion. "Whatever we can do to help."

Tess spoke up. "The chief was just telling us that the fire has officially been declared a crime."

"Arson." He settled a small notebook on his lap and clicked open a pen. "We found the point of forced entry yesterday afternoon."

Janice arched her eyebrows. "Pastor Ben didn't mention a break-in when I spoke with him this morning." Of course, he hadn't said much of anything.

"Apparently the culprit jimmied the lock on a window in the back," LuAnn told her.

"The one in that little room where they keep all the choir music," Tess added.

Janice knew exactly the one. That room was too small to be used for Sunday school classes, and the proximity to the choir room made it the perfect place for music storage.

"Those windows are old," she said. "I hope there was no damage to the music or the shelving in there."

The chief shook his head. "The arsonist even closed the window behind him. The only damage we've been able to find is to the contents up in that tower room. And I understand the three of you were up there a few hours before the fire was set."

They recounted the events of Saturday afternoon for the chief, the same things they'd told Fire Chief Franklin yesterday morning.

"And you didn't see anyone else?" He looked at each of them in turn. "Think hard. No one loitering in the area? Walking down the sidewalk? Anyone?"

They shook their heads.

"The paper reported that someone was seen running away after the fire was spotted," Tess said.

The fire had been all over the *Marietta Times* yesterday.

"Did Harry Olson recognize the person he saw?" Janice watched the man's face as she gave Harry's name.

Chief Mayfield had been at his job for too long to reveal anything accidentally. Instead of answering, he clicked his pen and shut his notebook.

"If you think of anything that might be helpful, anything at all, I hope you'll give me a call down at the station."

He stood, and the women did as well. Janice watched his retreat as Tess walked him to the door.

LuAnn turned toward her. "You spoke with Pastor Ben this morning?"

Janice fiddled with a lock of hair. "I did drop by the church for a minute on my way to the grocery."

LuAnn's eyes narrowed. "The church isn't on the way to the grocery."

Tess returned then, and both waited for an explanation.

"Oh, all right!" Janice couldn't keep quiet under the strength of her friends' stares. "I ran over there to ask him where he was Saturday night."

Tess's mouth pulled into a faintly disapproving frown. "I thought we agreed that Pastor Ben couldn't have set that fire."

"I know, but why won't he say where he was? I mean, he wouldn't have to make a public statement or anything, just tell someone who could vouch for him."

Tess narrowed her eyes. "By 'someone,' do you mean you?"

"Of course not," Janice hurried to say. "It wouldn't necessarily have to be me. It could be anyone with authority in the church."

"Janice, don't you think you're carrying this a little far?" LuAnn's voice held a gently understanding tone. "It seems as though you feel as if this fire was a personal attack against Lawrence's memory."

The idea shocked her. But in the next moment, she wondered if there was a grain of truth in the comment.

"I haven't considered that." She answered slowly, weighing her feelings as she spoke. Finally, she bit down on her lower lip. "Maybe that's part of why this mystery is bothering me so much. But that's silly, isn't it?"

"Yes." LuAnn leaned toward her and extended a hand, which Janice took. "I know Lawrence's memory is still very much a part of your life. But to everyone else, he's been gone a long time."

"She's right," Tess said in a kind voice. "Whoever set that fire wasn't doing it out of jealousy of Lawrence."

They were right. Janice knew it. And somehow, talking the matter over with her friends left her feeling better. But even though the fire had nothing to do with Lawrence, this crime still felt personal. Christ Fellowship was part of her life, both past and present.

"Maybe I've jumped to a conclusion that those letters praising Lawrence were somehow involved," she admitted, speaking slowly so she could piece together her thoughts. "But someone broke into the church just hours after we were there. Both the fire chief and the chief of police have shown up here to question us. That means we're somehow involved. Aren't you two the least bit curious to find out who did it?"

LuAnn looked thoughtful.

"Actually, I am curious," Tess admitted. "But I'm leaning more toward the teenager theory than anything. After all, Pastor Ben wouldn't have had to break in. He has a key."

"Good point." LuAnn sounded thoughtful. "That would also excuse anyone else who has a key."

Janice still held LuAnn's hand. She gave it a squeeze. This felt right, talking their thoughts out with each other. Three heads were better than one.

She grinned at her friends. "What would you girls think about a little shopping trip this afternoon?"

They returned her stare blankly.

"Shopping?" Tess asked.

Janice nodded. "I'd like to see if Harry has anything new at the Salvage Mall."

CHAPTER SEVEN

Half an hour later they entered the cheerful chaos of Harry's Antique and Salvage Mall. Janice paused to get her bearings. Everywhere she looked, her gaze settled on something interesting, items she itched to pick up and examine, or a picture that deserved closer consideration. Tables laden with dishes and figurines were scattered about the front room. Shelves lined the walls, crammed full of books and glassware and picture frames. Dust motes danced in rays of sunshine that filtered through the front window to rest on a small table and chairs that, with a little work and patience, could be restored to glory.

Alerted to their presence by chimes on the front door, Harry emerged from the back room. His smile broadened when he caught sight of them.

"My favorite customers," he exclaimed. "What a pleasure to see you today. Are you looking for something in particular, or just junking?"

LuAnn chuckled at his use of the term. "We had some extra time and thought we would come by to see if you've added anything new to your collection."

He waved a hand around the room. "I always have something new. Problem is remembering what's new and what's been here forever."

Janice picked up a porcelain cherub and turned it over to check the price. "I can't imagine where you find all this stuff. It must be a full-time job just keeping track of estate sales and so on." She glanced at Tess. "Or wherever else you find your treasures."

Tess cleared her throat. "And it must take a trained eye to identify the good stuff among piles of junk. We recently had some experience at that."

LuAnn smiled, her expression guileless. "Yes, we have. Up in the church belfry. But of course, that was before the fire."

The creases in his face deepened. "That was a shame, wasn't it? It's a good thing the fire department got there so quickly."

"Yes, it is," Janice said. "I understand you're the one who called them."

He nodded eagerly enough. "I saw a glow through those skinny windows up there. Kind of flickering. Could only be one thing. Flames."

"I know I speak for the entire congregation when I say thank you." Janice reached for his hand and squeezed it.

Flustered, he mumbled, "Anybody would have done the same." Then his eyes brightened, and he fixed them on her. "And you three were up there just a few hours before, the way I hear it. Sorting through the junk." He switched his gaze to Tess. "Did you find anything interesting?"

Eagerness saturated the question. A little too eager, perhaps? Janice watched his face while Tess answered.

"Oh, you know." She shrugged. "The usual stuff you would expect to find. Old magazines. A tattered altar cloth. Stuff like that."

"I heard tell you didn't get all the way through it." He looked to LuAnn for confirmation.

She nodded. "That's right. There's a lot of stuff up there. I'd venture to say we were a little over halfway finished when it got too dark to continue."

A wide grin appeared on Harry's face. "You never know what you might find piled up in old attics like that. I told the preacher yesterday I'd be happy to clear that stuff out of there. You know. Haul it off for him. I imagine a lot of it's scorched."

"I imagine it is," Janice agreed.

"And even if the fire didn't get it, smoke can do terrible damage." He eyed her. "Especially to fabrics and books and such like that."

Janice thought of the Bible they'd rescued. What would Harry make of it? She was on the verge of asking when LuAnn voiced a question of her own.

"We understand you saw the person who set the fire running away from the church."

"I don't know about that." He sucked his cheeks in for a moment and then released them. "I did see somebody running. He came out of the alley beside the church and ran up the street toward the mound."

Janice traced the path in her mind. The Mound Cemetery lay at the top of the hill, where the brick-paved Scammel Street ended at Fifth.

"He?" Janice cast a quick glance at her friends. "You're sure it was man?"

"It was a man all right. A big man, tall and with dark skin."

She started. "Dark skin? You mean he had a suntan?"

"No ma'am." He shook his head. "He was a black man. It was a clear night and the moon was out. I got a glimpse when he ran out of the alley and headed up the hill."

"Did you recognize him?" Tess asked quickly.

Harry shook his head again. "It was just a quick look as he turned the corner, and that's when I noticed the fire. I probably should've chased after him, but I was busy unlocking my car so I could get my cell phone."

A tall black man? Janice's mouth went dry. She knew many men in Marietta who could be described that way. So why did her suspicions immediately rest on Byron?

She gave her head a quick shake. What a ridiculous notion.

She focused her attention on Harry. "Out of curiosity, what took you to that part of town so late at night?"

The change in his appearance was sudden and remarkable. His expression slammed shut like a door. He half turned away from them and began straightening items on the nearest table.

"No reason in particular," he mumbled. "Decided to take a drive. That's all."

The friends looked at each other.

"Saturday night was a beautiful night for a drive," Tess said.

He pulled a handkerchief out of his back pocket and rubbed at a green glass bottle. "Yep."

Hadn't he just said he was trying to unlock his car to get to his cell phone? If he was out for a drive, what had made him park and leave his car long enough to lock it?

"And the temperature was mild for October," Janice prodded. "Perhaps you decided to take a little stroll as well?"

His head jerked toward her, his eyes sharp. She held her breath, awaiting his answer.

The shrill ring of a telephone from the back room reached them.

There was no mistaking the relief that wilted the tension in his shoulders. "Excuse me, ladies."

He hurried away from them and disappeared in the direction from which he had come.

"Well!" Tess planted her hands on her hips. "They say a guilty man always runs."

"Exactly." Janice stared in the direction he'd gone. "But guilty of what?"

Janice kept her suspicions about Byron to herself. She already felt bad enough pointing blame toward Pastor Ben. No doubt, her friends would accuse her of trying to find fault with Byron, especially after she'd been so outspoken with her hesitations regarding the wedding.

When LuAnn turned the car onto Ohio Street, Janice spied Marla's intended and his best man. They sat on a bench across the street from the inn, gazing out at the river. A puff of smoke rose into the sky above their heads. Did one of them smoke? Was it Byron? Did Marla know that?

And if he smoked, did he carry a lighter?

Stop it!

She was becoming a suspicious old woman. As long as he didn't smoke inside the inn, it was none of her business. Besides, if he did go to the church intent on setting a fire, he would have taken matches or a lighter with him even if he didn't smoke.

Tess and LuAnn came in through the rear entrance.

"I'm going to take my jacket upstairs," LuAnn said, heading for the front part of the inn. "And then I think I'll come back downstairs and have a cup of tea. Anybody want to join me?"

"Sounds good to me." Tess trailed after her.

"I'll join you in a bit. I want to talk to Stuart about something."

They left the kitchen just as the front door opened and Byron and Lucas stepped inside. Byron brightened when he saw them.

"Marla has been telling us about this building's history. She is quite the history buff."

"Yes, she is," agreed LuAnn.

"Luke and I were wondering if you would give us a tour of the basement. She said there's a hidden ladder or something that was used during the Underground Railroad."

Lucas's face bore an expression of mild interest, though Byron was clearly eager.

Tess glanced at Janice and LuAnn. "We are so proud of the role this building played in the Underground Railroad. We've talked about giving tours, but we haven't set up anything formally."

"We wouldn't want to put you to any trouble," Lucas put in hurriedly.

Tess shrugged. "Oh, it wouldn't be any trouble. But we certainly don't have a script prepared or anything."

Byron laughed. "All the better."

"All right. Just let me take my jacket and purse upstairs and I'll be right with you."

LuAnn's eyes turned upward toward the pressed tin ceiling. "I wonder if Pauline would like to go along."

An excellent idea, in Janice's opinion. An informal tour was a good opportunity to try to draw the sad woman out of her shell.

"Why don't you ask her," she suggested. "I'll join you after I make my phone call."

The plan made, Janice climbed the stairs to the fourth floor. Inside her apartment, she hung up her jacket and dropped into her comfy chair. Stuart served as the Washington County Coroner, and also maintained a small private practice in Marietta. Janice pressed speed dial number one and listened as the phone rang.

"Good afternoon, Dr. Eastman's office." Stacy's familiar voice sounded in her ear.

Janice's daughter handled the front office for her brother's practice, though Janice privately thought her capable of much more. Periodically Stacy mentioned returning to school to get her teaching degree but had not yet taken any positive steps toward that end. She would make an excellent teacher, in Janice's opinion.

"Hi, sweetie."

"Hello, Mother. What can I do for you?"

The words sounded clipped, distracted. Must be a busy day.

"I wanted to tell you about the Harvest Celebration the girls and I are planning." Though that was not the primary reason for her call, Janice might as well take advantage of the opportunity while she had Stacy on the phone.

"Oh? What's going on?" In the background, Janice heard fingernails tapping on a keyboard.

Janice fingered a loose thread on the arm of her chair. "Just that we're going to throw a huge dinner for our friends and family on the twenty-seventh here at the inn. Kind of a celebration of God's blessings."

A pause, during which Janice heard Stacy's slow intake of breath. "Okay, that sounds like fun."

Then why do you sound so cautious?

"And we thought we would invite others as well. You know, open the inn up to the community. Kind of a ministry thing."

"Let me make sure I understand. You want to run a soup kitchen at the inn?" Disapproval saturated Stacy's tone.

Janice had feared this kind of reaction. "Not a soup kitchen. A real Harvest Celebration dinner."

The keyboard sounds had ceased. Janice held her breath, awaiting her daughter's reply.

"If that's what you want to do, Mother," she finally said, her voice pinched.

Janice's fingers closed on the thread and, despite knowing better, she tugged. The weave unraveled another quarter inch.

"So, you and Larry will come?" A dinner celebrating God's blessings wouldn't be the same without her daughter and grandson.

"Of course we'll come." Another breath heaved, this one louder. Then Stacy went on in a softer tone. "I just don't want you to take on too much. I worry about you."

Janice relaxed. She'd known Stacy would come around. "Well that's only fair, since I spent so many years worrying about you." She laughed. "It will be fun. You'll see."

Stacy didn't reply. "Is that what you wanted to talk to Stuart about? Because if so I can give him the message."

"I did have one other thing I wanted to discuss with him. Is he free?"

"I believe he's just about to wrap up with a patient. I'll put you on hold and see if he has time to talk before he goes on to the next one."

"Thank you, sweetie. I love you."

There was no hesitation before her reply this time. "I love you too, Mom."

Classical music sounded in her ear, indicating she had been placed on hold. Janice inspected the fabric on her chair. A slight fraying, which she could fix in a jiffy with a needle and the right colored thread.

The music stopped. "Hey, Ma."

In her mind she pictured Stuart seated behind a cluttered desk in his tiny office. "Am I bothering you?"

"Never. What's up?"

Though she detected no hint of impatience in his tone, Stacy had said he was between patients. No chitchat today.

"I want to talk to you about Harry Olson."

"Harry?" He sounded surprised. "Is he okay?"

"He's fine. Well, I guess he's fine. The girls and I just came from his place and he seemed fine." Oh dear. She was blathering. Best to get right to the point. She drew in a breath. "Did you know Kevin Franklin came to see us on Sunday?"

An almost imperceptible note of forced patience crept into his answer. "Oh? Talking to you about the church fire?"

She pressed a finger over the tattered place in the fabric. "That's right. And he happened to mention that Harry called in the fire."

"I read that in the newspaper."

Of course he would have. "Yes, but today Chief Mayfield came by the inn, and he told us that Harry saw someone running away from the fire."

"Really?" Interest perked up his tone.

"Yes, so the girls and I went over to the Salvage Mall and—"

"Wait. You went over there to interrogate Harry?"

Janice shifted the cell phone to her other ear. "Not to interrogate him. Just to ask what he saw. He told us he didn't chase the man, because he was trying to get his car unlocked to get his cell phone so he could call in the fire. And then a few minutes later he said he'd been out for a *drive*."

A pause. "So?"

"So, if he was driving he would have been *in* the car. Obviously, he was outside. His car must have been parked. And when we asked him why he was over by the church, he got very nervous."

"Mom, are you seriously saying you suspect Harry of setting the fire? Harmless Harry?"

The reminder of Harry's nickname served to chastise Janice. She shifted on the soft cushion.

"No, of course not." Though the man's eagerness when discussing potentially valuable items stored in the belfry had raised her suspicions sufficiently to make this call. "I'm just saying there are questions he needs to answer. And I don't think I'm the one to ask them."

"Well at least we're agreed on that."

Janice launched herself out of the chair and paced to the window. "I thought since you and Kevin are friends you could mention it to him, and if he thinks it's important he could put a bug in Chief Mayfield's ear."

"I'm not going to do any such thing." His tone brooked no argument. I'm sure Harry had a perfectly reasonable explanation for being on that side of town. And I'm positive Chief Mayfield is intelligent enough to ask the question."

"Yes, but—"

"No buts, Mom. Harmless Harry is none of my business, and he's none of your business either. If there's anything to be found, the police will find it."

Janice's grip on her cell phone tightened. She thought at least Stuart would listen to her.

"Hey, I don't want to keep my next patient waiting any longer. Was there something else you wanted to talk about?"

She had already taken enough of his time. And been made to feel like a meddling old woman. "I did want to discuss our Harvest Celebration, but Stacy and I already talked about it. Ask her for the details, okay?"

"Okay. I love you, Ma. I'll talk to you later."

The call disconnected before she could answer. She stood there for a moment, staring at the dimming screen. Stuart was probably right. She should mind her own business. Back when Lawrence was alive that's exactly what she would have done too.

But she'd been a different woman then. Now she was a business owner, an entrepreneur. Well, she and LuAnn and Tess. And entrepreneurs didn't sit idly by while questions went unanswered.

CHAPTER EIGHT

Janice took the elevator all the way down to the basement. She typically used the stairs, but there was something about descending that last flight that gave her the creeps. Though they'd set traps everywhere, she was convinced that a herd of icky mice hovered at the bottom of the last one, ready to leap out and infect her with their germs.

Maybe we should get a cat.

The elevator came to a bone-jarring halt, and the door slid open. Several beams of light shown directly into her face, momentarily blinding her. She raised a hand to shield her eyes.

"Oh, sorry," came Tess's voice. "I was just getting ready to show them the ladder."

At least she had armed their guests with flashlights before descending to the dark depths. Janice herself had insisted on installing high-watt bulbs in the bare wire lights scattered about the cavernous room, but they served only to create bright pools in the dank darkness. No doubt the shadowy corners hid spiders and bugs and all kinds of insects. Someday, when they had extra money to spend, she would insist that they send Robin down here to do a thorough cleaning. And Thorn could install proper lighting as well.

But of course that would change the historical aspect of the basement, something they debated at length before any modification.

She slid the elevator cage open and stepped out while turning on her cell phone flashlight.

Tess aimed her beam at the wall on her left. Blinking, Janice saw four others follow their guide.

"Hello," Brad said. "I stopped by to see if you three had plans for dinner and got here just in time for your first official tour."

"Lucky you," Janice replied with a smile. She fell in beside LuAnn and spoke quietly, so as not to be overheard. "Pauline didn't want to join the tour?"

LuAnn shook her head. "She barely opened the door a crack to talk to me. I think she might've been crying when I knocked. Her eyes looked puffy."

Janice's heart twisted. "The poor dear. She's obviously suffered a tragedy of some sort."

Tess's voice drew their attention. "This ladder goes forty-nine steps from here all the way up to the fourth floor."

At her gesture, Byron stepped through the door and down into the four-foot-deep passageway to shine his flashlight up the ladder. "What was this used for?"

"We believe it was an escape route for runaways who were lucky enough to stay in one of the rooms upstairs." The dim lighting turned Tess's copper hair to an almost blood-red. "Prudence Willard's journal mentions using the ladder when she needed to access the upper floors unnoticed."

"Fascinating." Byron's voice held a note of awe. "Just think, Luke. My ancestors might have climbed this same ladder." He turned his head toward Tess. "May I?"

Tess glanced at Janice and LuAnn, who shrugged.

Brad, who stood off to one side with his arms folded across his white-shirted chest, said, "I wouldn't go farther than a few steps. They really need to have it looked at before they allow the public to access it."

"Good point," Tess said. "This ladder is more than a hundred and fifty years old."

Byron handed his flashlight to Lucas, who stood to the side while his friend climbed six or seven feet upward. His head disappeared, leaving only his shoes visible.

"This is incredible." The awe in Byron's voice struck a chord in Janice. Though she disliked dark, closed-in places, the ladder had the same effect on her. She sometimes wondered how many people had gone up and down, some with bare feet because they'd escaped without shoes. A shiver raced down her arms, as it always did when she considered those desperate slaves running from one hiding place to another in their escape to freedom.

Byron climbed down and took back his flashlight. "You want to give it a try?" he asked his friend.

Lucas shook his head. "I'm good, thanks."

The man sounded hesitant. Well, Janice understood that. Perhaps he disliked closed-in places as much as she did.

Tess shut the door and faced them. She gestured toward the row of washers and dryers. "Obviously we've made limited use of this basement, but we do have plans."

Brad grinned. "Are you still considering the hot tub idea?"

"Hey," she said, "it could work."

Byron turned in a circle looking around the huge space. "There is plenty of room. But not much in the way of atmosphere."

"We can take care of that." LuAnn gestured toward the wide-open space where the hulking, ancient wood-burning furnace used to stand. Now there was nothing left but a pile of ash, remnants from the last fire burned in it. "Naturally we'd clean it up first and relocate the nest of mice who take up residence here in the winter."

They all chuckled and followed Tess across the floor and around a short wall. A narrow corridor led them toward the southern edge of the building, four doors on each side.

Tess opened the first one and stepped back to allow Byron and Lucas entry. "When we first saw these rooms, we assumed they were quarters for staff when the hotel was first opened. Thanks to Prudence's journal, we now know they were also used by runaway slaves. The ones who could pass for free people occasionally even worked in the hotel cleaning rooms and cooking and stuff like that."

Byron and Lucas stood in the center of the room, which seemed to shrink around the two tall men.

"Not exactly spacious quarters, were they?" Lucas's question was more of a comment.

Janice had no trouble at all conjuring up the image of a nervous runaway cowering in the corner, jumping at every sound, terrified that any moment he would be discovered, shackled, and dragged back to captivity.

"I doubt if any of the people who stayed here cared," she said.

Byron's expression sobered. "I'm sure you're right."

The men left the room and returned to the narrow hallway. Tess squeezed by them sideways. "All eight rooms are nearly identical." She smiled. "Nearly."

She entered the last room on the left, followed by Byron and Lucas. Brad, LuAnn, and Janice stayed in the corridor to give their guests as much space as possible as they viewed the inn's most fascinating artifact.

Tess pulled the stool away from the wall to reveal a dark tunnel. A strong musty odor permeated the room. Janice couldn't help but shiver. Both men uttered exclamations when they caught sight of the brick-lined tunnel.

"This is how runaway slaves entered the inn." Tess shone her flashlight into the dark hole. "This tunnel goes beneath the street and ends down at the river. Slaves from West Virginia, which was a part of Virginia until halfway through the Civil War, would be transported by river usually and guided to the end of the tunnel. Prudence Willard and her husband were conductors in the Underground Railroad, and Prudence worked in this hotel."

"The slaves came from Virginia?" Byron asked.

Brad offered an answer. "From there, and even farther away. Kentucky, Tennessee, Georgia."

Byron turned toward his friend, excitement gleaming in his dark eyes. "My great-great-great-grandfather came from Kentucky. And my great-great-great-grandmother from Virginia. I know they came to Marietta in 1857 with their oldest son, who was just a baby at the time. They might even have come here, to this inn." He turned again to the gaping darkness beneath the floor. "This tunnel might have been part of their pathway to freedom."

Janice stuck her head farther into the room. "Your ancestors were slaves?"

"Yes, ma'am. That's what brought me to Marietta in the first place. I traced my family history all the way back here and beyond."

"There's certainly a lot of history in this town," Brad said.

Byron nodded. "Luke helped me a lot. He's got a knack for research, being a writer. He's pored through more of my family's records and official documents than I have."

Lucas gave an embarrassed shrug. "That's because you have a real job."

Byron ignored him. "He got so interested he's decided he might even write a book about my family and the Underground Railroad."

Tess faced Lucas with interest. "A book? How fascinating."

But the man shook his head. "I thought about it at one point, but there's been so much written already I'm not sure I could come up with a new angle to offer."

"We're still negotiating that." Byron nudged him playfully in the shoulder. "Anyway, he did a lot of research about Marietta, which is why I came here back in August. That's when I met Marla." A wide grin split his face. "I came looking for my past and found my future."

LuAnn rested a hand on her chest. "That is so sweet."

"Not only that," Byron continued, "but I know the Lord Almighty introduced us. With Luke's help."

Lucas's obvious embarrassment deepened.

"What do you mean?" Janice asked.

"My family stories talk about how my ancestors escaped from slavery with the help of Mr. William Still. He arranged for my great-great-great-grandparents to escape from their plantations and meet up on the road before going on to Canada. Luke here traced them back to Marietta at a time when Mr. Still was here. Imagine my good fortune to go into the very drugstore where William Still's great-great-great-granddaughter worked." His booming laugh filled the confines of the small room. "Who except God Almighty could work that out?"

LuAnn was grinning broadly. "Indeed."

But something in Janice's stomach reacted poorly to the comment. Was the Lord capable of arranging divine appointments? Certainly He was. But it would have been equally possible for Byron and Lucas to look up a Marietta resident who just happened to be a vulnerable and naively gullible descendant of William Still. The internet made finding people easy these days. And it wouldn't be too difficult, once Byron got to Marietta, to find out where Marla worked. He might have even followed her discreetly and then entered the drugstore with the flimsy excuse of looking for earplugs.

What if Byron's interest in Marla centered on his fascination with his own family history? Would that be a bad thing? After all, couples had been drawn together for less compelling reasons.

But what if that was all Byron wanted? She could almost see the way their relationship might have played out. He'd been so enthusiastic about tracing his family history's connection to the famous William Still, and then had found one of the man's real-life descendants. Naturally, he would be enthralled. Their relationship developed through all those phone calls, and he plowed full steam ahead. But was a shared fascination with the past a good basis for a future? What if, when Byron had satisfied himself about his family's history, his interest in Marla waned? The Bible that lay hidden upstairs in her nightstand weighed heavily on Janice's mind. What if the only thing Byron was looking for was an artifact from the person he credited with saving his family from slavery?

Janice shook herself. What was the matter with her? Tess and LuAnn had no problem with this man. And he was certainly likable, she admitted. Friendly. Intelligent. He had a good job.

Or did he? They only had his word about that, after all.

One thing was certain. She had been right to keep the Bible secret from him. She'd find a time to give it to Marla privately. After all, it had been tucked up in that belfry for years. What would a few more days or even weeks matter?

The women were relaxing in their cozy common area on the fourth floor that evening when Janice heard her cell phone ringing from her apartment. She hurried down the hall to catch it before the call went to voice mail. Glancing at the screen, she experienced a jolt of pleasure. There was Stuart, looking oh so handsome in his white coat with a stethoscope dangling from his neck—the picture she had attached to his name in her contact list.

"This must be my lucky day," she said when she had pressed the button to connect. "I get to talk to my son twice in one day."

"I wanted to get back with you because I felt kinda bad after we hung up. I think I was a little abrupt with you."

A tender smile curved Janice's lips. Stuart was not only intelligent, but he was also an extremely sensitive man. He would make some lucky young woman a wonderful husband one day.

"Thank you, but you don't have to apologize. I shouldn't have bothered you at work."

"You can call me anytime, Ma. You are never a bother."

Janice dropped into her chair by the window. "Did Stacy tell you about the Harvest Celebration?"

"Yeah. That sounds fine to *me*."

His emphasis on the last word told her a lot. Apparently, Stacy had shared her disapproval of their plans with her brother.

"We think it will be fun," Janice told him. "As well as an outreach opportunity."

"I think that's great," he said. "But listen, that's not why I called. I just hung up the phone with Kevin."

Janice bolted upright. So, he had a change of heart about contacting his friend. Out of guilt at telling her to mind her own business, perhaps?

"You did?"

"I told him everything you said about Harry. Kevin said when he spoke with Harry, he kinda noticed the same thing. Harry got evasive when he asked about his reason for being in the area around the church."

Janice shot to her feet. "Evasive. That's exactly right. That's just how he acted."

"Kevin had already talked to Chief Mayfield about it, in fact. And Mayfield told him that he had thoroughly checked out Harry's alibi. Apparently there's nothing whatsoever suspicious about his reason for being there."

Janice caught sight of her dim reflection in the window. She was scowling. She quickly changed her expression. "And what was that reason?"

"No idea. Mayfield didn't tell Kevin. But Kevin was satisfied. He says the chief is thorough and reliable, and if he says Harry's alibi is good, then it's good."

Frustration zipped along Janice's nerve endings. "It just doesn't seem right. If Harry has a good reason for being there, then why doesn't he just say so?"

"Apparently he did. To Chief Mayfield." Stuart spoke in a reasonable tone. "Ma, the Marietta police are good at their job. I've worked with them as a coroner long enough to trust them, and especially the chief. I think you can leave the investigation to them and be confident that they will get to the bottom of it."

Janice's right hand clenched into a fist. Stuart might not be as rushed as he was during their earlier conversation, but, basically, he was saying the same thing in a more polite tone. That she should mind her own business.

Further argument wouldn't accomplish anything. At least she had done what she set out to do—she'd voiced her concerns and her son had acted on them.

"I'm sure you're right," she said.

"So, you'll drop the matter? Leave the investigation to the police?"

Janice hesitated. She had never lied to her children, and she would not start now. But a mother didn't have to tell her kids everything, did she?

She gave a small laugh. "Well I can't think of any legitimate reason to pay another visit to the Salvage Mall. I've already got more junk in my apartment than I need." *There. How's that for evasive?*

Fortunately, Stuart took the comment for agreement.

"Great. So, is everything going okay? How's business?"

Janice returned to the soft chair and settled in. Her children were so busy it wasn't often she had the opportunity to enjoy a chatty conversation with either of them.

But even as she described the inn's recent business slow-down, a question lingered in the back of her mind. Everyone in town knew that Chief Mayfield and Harry Olson were long-time buddies. It would be natural for the chief to take his friend's word at face value and let the matter drop.

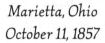

Marietta, Ohio
October 11, 1857

Prudence turned the small wooden dog over in her hand and ran a finger across the smooth surface.

"Thee is truly gifted." She pressed a kiss onto Jason's cheek, reveling in the warmth of his skin. "This will make the child happy, but not as happy as thee makes me."

He leaned into her kiss but dismissed the praise. "I have more than enough time on my hands for carving trinkets."

Prudence placed the toy in her basket alongside another wooden piece fashioned to resemble a barn cat. But it was the third that brought the biggest smile to her face. "'Tis the exact likeness of Patience."

She held the miniature wooden goose aloft toward its living model, who continued to groom the soft feathers beneath her right wing, entirely unimpressed. Laughing, Prudence set the goose beside the other toys and added a bundle of sweet cakes she had baked the night before. A homey aroma clung to the bit of cotton cloth that covered them. She did not have the money to continue buying Ezra Junior stick candy but prayed the molasses cakes would please the boy. Please him *and* keep him quiet.

As she covered the basket's contents with a checkered napkin, she did not bother to hold back a wistful sigh. "If thee could but meet him, thee would love him as I do."

Jason's features did not change, but his expression took on the stony appearance she identified with his most stubborn attitude. "I'm sure he is a winsome child."

A neutral comment that she did not acknowledge.

"The boy needs a strong hand. Becca is little more than a child herself, and though she loves him she becomes distraught when he cries."

Jason leaned forward to reach the Bible that rested in the center of the kitchen table. Frustrated, she busied herself with the wash bucket. Jason was known as a man who loved God's Word, and when he immersed himself in those holy pages, she might as well give up talking to him at all.

"What he needs is a man to take an interest in him."

"He will have one soon enough," Jason replied without looking up. "His own father."

She bit down on her lower lip. "What if tragedy strikes and Ezra Senior never arrives?"

"Then thee will see mother and child safely delivered to the next station."

Prudence wrung the excess water from the cloth. "They would be much more comfortable here."

There. She'd spoken the words that had grown inside her to the point of nearly choking her.

His expression patient, Jason closed the Bible. "Prudence, thee knows my wishes. Thee promised."

She abandoned the bucket and threw herself into the chair beside him. "And I have kept my promise. From the time the tunnel and the hidden rooms were completed, not one package has been delivered here."

"They are safer at the hotel." He spread his hands wide to encompass their home. "We cannot keep them as well hidden here."

"We have done so. Many of them," she reminded him.

He studied her for a moment, and Prudence did not look away. Let him see the emotions hidden in the depths of her soul.

"This mother and child hold a special place in thy heart," he said quietly.

Still holding his gaze, she nodded. "I see myself in the little one's eyes. He has been subjected to much that a child should not see."

"As is every child born into the horrors of slavery."

"Not just born," she murmured.

His features softened. "No, not just born. Perhaps it is even harder for those who know freedom and then are carried into slavery, as thee was." She averted her eyes, and he ducked his head to force her to look back at him. "Thee sees thyself in this family that has been torn apart."

A lump of tears lodged in her throat. "I do. Becca suffers the agony of being ripped from the arms of her husband, as my mother surely did. And when I think of Ezra, who did not even know he was a father..." She swallowed painfully. "Families should be together, the way God intended."

"Nor should people be enslaved. That is why we committed to the Cause." He leaned forward and grasped her hand. "But thee knows that they are more safely hidden in the secret rooms than here. And thee, my wife, is safer with them there."

"My safety is of little concern when compared to a family restored."

"Not to me. Prudence, thee is my family. Thee is my gift from God. Since the time of my injury, I have not ceased to pray for thy safety, as thee knows well. And God provided a means for thee to continue His work. He provided a sanctuary for those who seek freedom, a sanctuary that is more secure than the one we can offer here." He squeezed her hand hard. "I will hold thee to thy promise, Wife. It is the only way I have to keep thee safe."

She had promised that when the secret rooms were completed, they would no longer host runaway slaves in their home. She was bound by the bonds of marriage and by the depth of her love to keep that promise as long as he held her to it.

Nodding, she left the table to don her cloak. She must hurry, lest she arrive late for work.

CHAPTER NINE

The spicy scent of Winnie's gumbo filled the café. Normally Janice did not care for oysters. Even purchasing the slimy things at the market yesterday had turned her stomach. But simmered with the special spices Winnie used in her gumbo, the oysters were transformed into delectable morsels that bore no resemblance to the raw version. Gumbo days were always busy days at the café.

Today was no exception. Taylor had his hands full trying to take care of all the guests crowding the tables, while several others loitered in the parlor waiting for seats to clear. Tess divided her time between adding names to the waiting list and busing tables, while Janice circulated with a pitcher of iced tea in one hand and a coffee carafe in the other. LuAnn stayed busy in the kitchen.

Scanning the room for empty glasses, Janice zigzagged toward the front window, where Gloria Bellamy sat with Becky Eberly, a longtime friend from church. With them was Donna Pulliam, a woman Janice knew by name but not much beyond.

"More tea?" She held up her pitcher.

"Please." Becky pushed her empty glass forward, and Janice refilled it.

"How about you?" She indicated Gloria's half-empty coffee cup.

"A little," Gloria replied. "Just warm it up a bit."

Since Donna's water glass was still mostly full, Janice started to move toward the next table.

Gloria stopped her with a raised finger. "Do you have any idea what's going on back there?"

Janice followed the woman's gaze. At the table nearest the elevator, Byron and Marla sat with Pastor Ben. Lucas had come down earlier to devour a bowl of gumbo and then excused himself to go upstairs and work on an article. The three sat huddled around the table, their heads bent forward as they spoke quietly. To the right of the pastor's soup bowl sat a Bible, and every so often he rested a hand upon it as he spoke.

When Marla arrived earlier, she told Janice that Pastor Ben had suggested she and Byron meet with him privately for a few sessions of premarital counseling. An excellent idea, in Janice's opinion. Lawrence had insisted on similar meetings before agreeing to officiate at any wedding ceremony. The young pastor's suggestion went a long way toward putting Janice at ease about his dedication to the precepts of a Christian marriage and deepened her guilt for suspecting him of wrongdoing in the matter of the church fire. If he detected any insincerity in Byron's love for Marla, surely he would do something about it.

But she would say none of that to the women seated before her, who were far fonder of gossip than they should be.

She awarded Gloria a bright smile. "I believe they're discussing the wedding."

Donna actually twisted in her seat to eye the trio. "I never thought Marla would get married. And to such an attractive man too. I guess miracles do happen."

Janice's spine stiffened. If there was anything she could not tolerate, it was a sniping comment about someone she considered part of her flock. "And why wouldn't a nice-looking man be interested in Marla?"

The woman reversed in her seat and cast a quick glance up at Janice's face. Apparently she could tell she was close to crossing a line, because she backpedaled. "No reason in particular. The whole thing just surprised me, that's all."

Becky leveled a slightly disapproving look on Donna. "I'm not surprised at all." She halted and then corrected herself. "I mean, I was surprised about the marriage because I've always considered Marla to be a confirmed spinster and happy about it. But if she does want to marry, I say go for it. The world is full of handsome men. I'm glad she found one."

Donna had the grace to look embarrassed. She snatched up her water glass and took a long drink.

"I'll tell you what surprises me." Gloria emptied a sugar packet into her coffee. "Nobody has questioned Pastor Ben about that fire."

Janice stopped in the act of turning away. "What do you mean? Why would they?" She did her best to keep her voice level.

"I told you on Sunday." Gloria gave her a disapproving look. "He must know something about the fire. And if he doesn't, then the staff/parish relations committee needs to find out why he is not aware of everything that goes on under the roof of his own church."

Becky ran a distracted finger around the rim of her glass. "I have heard talk about that. I've even spoken with several people who asked the pastor point-blank where he was Saturday night."

She kept her face impassive, but inwardly Janice cringed. She was one of those people, though only her close friends knew it.

Gloria leaned forward. "And what did he say?"

"That's just it. He wouldn't." Becky's lips pursed into a tight bow. "If he has nothing to hide then why be so secretive?"

Gloria extended a manicured pointer finger in her direction. "That's precisely my point."

It was all Janice could do not to squirm in her sneakers. How disturbing to have her own thoughts echoed in such an unpleasant manner.

"Pastors often have duties they can't discuss with other people for confidentiality reasons." She parroted Pastor Ben's explanation to her, all the while feeling like a hypocrite.

"Well that certainly gives him a convenient excuse, that's all I have to say." Donna, who did not even attend Christ Fellowship, dabbed at her mouth with the corner of a crisp linen napkin.

Janice found herself actively disliking the woman, a position in which she rarely found herself, since she got along with almost everyone. "Surely you're not suggesting that Pastor Ben started a fire in his own church."

"I'm not suggesting anything." Donna folded the napkin and replaced it in her lap.

"Well, I'm suggesting it." Gloria leaned back in her chair and stared across the room. "It wouldn't surprise me if he sloshed gasoline on the mess up there and set it on fire just to be rid of it. Nothing about young people surprises me these days."

"I don't think you're giving the younger generation enough credit." Janice spied an empty tea glass across the room. "If you ladies will excuse me, I need to get back to work."

With haste, she made her exit, grateful to abandon the conversation that left her feeling distinctly uncomfortable.

Janice was clearing the last table when the trio in the corner finally ended their conversation. She had been hovering at a distance so she would not miss the opportunity for a word with Pastor Ben. She stood near the door holding a damp rag in one hand and a bottle of spray cleaner in the other while the pastor hugged first Marla and then Byron.

When he headed toward the exit, Janice intercepted him.

"I hope you won't think I'm being presumptuous." She had rehearsed the conversation in her mind while she worked.

Surprise appeared on his face, but his smile remained. "Mrs. Eastman, I would never think you presumptuous. I know you to be an honest woman, and I hope you know you can talk with me about anything."

Her eyes slammed shut for a brief moment. Salt in the wound. "I'm not sure if you saw Gloria and her friends having lunch an hour ago."

"I did. In fact, I intended to go over and greet them, but we got so involved in our conversation that I never had the chance. One minute they were there, and the next time I looked they'd left."

"That might not necessarily have been a bad thing," she commented in a dry tone.

Creases appeared in his forehead. "Oh? Nothing wrong I hope?"

"Nothing except a little gossip-fest going on."

The lines cleared and a knowing look shone in his eyes. "I figured as much. And was I one of the juicy tidbits on today's menu?"

In spite of herself, she chuckled at his joke. "In the part I heard, you were the main course. But I didn't stick around long enough to listen to the rest of the menu."

"I'm not sure I want to know what was being said. Do I?"

"Probably not. Just old ladies with old-fashioned ideas flapping their jaws." She averted her eyes. "But there is one piece of advice I hope you'll let me offer."

He splayed his hands wide. "Go ahead. I'm always open to wise counsel."

"If there is any way you can make your whereabouts Saturday night known, I think it would go a long way toward shutting down the gossip."

A cloud settled over his features. "Like I said the other day, I'm afraid I can't do that."

Disappointment stabbed at her. Because he refused to do whatever he could to put a halt to vicious gossip? Or because he refused to satisfy her curiosity? Janice wasn't sure which, and at the moment, she really didn't want to consider his motives. Or her own.

Instead, she merely nodded. "It was just a suggestion."

"I understand." The smile widened. "I do appreciate your thinking of my reputation. If I could impose on you enough to ask a favor?"

"Of course."

"Pray for us. The church, I mean. Situations like this one have torn congregations apart." His eyes drew Janice in. "I don't want to see that happen at Christ Fellowship."

On that, at least, they were in agreement, 100 percent.

"Neither do I," she assured him.

When the door closed behind Pastor Ben, Janice turned to find Byron and Marla watching her. The couple held hands, as usual, and met her halfway across the floor.

"Could I have a word with Miss Winnie?" Byron rubbed his stomach with his free hand. "That gumbo was as good today as I remember. Maybe even better. I'd like to thank her."

"I'm sure she'd appreciate that."

Janice led them into the kitchen, where Winnie, Tess, and LuAnn were just finishing their cleaning chores.

When LuAnn caught sight of them, her face brightened. "Don't go anywhere," she told the couple. "I have something to show you."

She scurried past them, and not a second went by before the room filled with Byron's booming voice. "Miss Winnie, you've been holding out on me."

The willowy woman eyed him with surprise. "I'm sure I don't know what you're talking about."

Because Janice knew her well, she detected the trace of a secret smile hovering about behind the calm expression.

"Your gumbo is about the best stuff I ever put in my mouth. And mine isn't." He dipped his head to spear her with a look from the top of his eyeballs. "I followed the recipe you gave me down to the last oyster."

"Can I help it if I'm a better cook than you?" Winnie turned her back on them and began brushing at invisible crumbs on the sparkling clean counter.

"Come on now. Don't give me that. What's your secret ingredient?" Byron held up three fingers, Boy Scout style. "I'll take your secret to the grave with me, I promise."

"Go ahead, Winnie," Marla urged. "He's talked of practically nothing else since he got here."

"No secret ingredient," Winnie insisted. "I told you everything." Then the smile widened. "But I might not have told you my personal technique."

"I knew it!" Byron gave a triumphant shout. "What is it? The order you add the ingredients? A certain brand of chicken?" He snapped his fingers. "I know. You only stir clockwise, right?"

Winnie's delighted laughter bounced off the ceiling. "Now you're just being superstitious." She fixed an amused stare on him. "You really won't tell anybody?"

"You have my word." His expression became eager. "Do I need to take notes?"

"Nah." She glanced around the room and lowered her voice. "It's the filé."

She pronounced the word *fee-lay*. Janice had never heard the term before.

"You buy a certain brand?" Byron's eyes narrowed slightly. "I asked you about that when you gave me the recipe, and you said I could find it on the internet."

"You did, didn't you?" When he nodded, she continued in a near whisper. "I make mine fresh."

Winnie held the attention of everyone in the room by this point. Tess hung her dishtowel on a hook and joined Janice beside the table.

"What is filé, anyway?" Tess asked.

"It's sassafras leaves, dried and ground fine," Winnie answered. "You can't make a proper gumbo without filé, and you've gotta have sassafras for filé."

"You sneaky woman." Byron wagged a finger at her and then demanded, "Where can I get some?"

"You gotta find somebody with a sassafras tree." Winnie grinned at him. "Just so happens I have a cousin down in South Carolina who has a bunch of trees right there on his property."

Byron looked down at Marla. "Have you got any pull with this woman?"

Marla laughed. "We've been friends a long time. I reckon I might be able to ask a favor every now and then."

Winnie's grin widened. "Well now, could be I just stumbled on what I might give you as a wedding present."

Byron rubbed his hands together. "Now that's what I'm talking about."

LuAnn entered the room with Lucas in tow. "Look who I found trying to escape."

Lucas gave her a startled glance. "I wasn't escaping. I was just going to step outside for a minute, I promise."

"I'm kidding," LuAnn told him, her tone gentler. "But since you seem to have an interest in history, I thought you might appreciate seeing this."

She placed a stack of papers on the kitchen table. Janice recognized them instantly as LuAnn's copy of Prudence Willard's journal.

"Byron, when you said yesterday that your ancestors escaped to freedom through Marietta with a baby, I was reminded of an entry I read some time ago." She turned pages as she spoke. "You said 1857, so it didn't take long to find what I was looking for."

Everyone moved closer to the table. Janice stood on the other side, so Prudence's sprawling script was upside down. She squinted to decipher the date. October 6, 1857. Byron and Marla crowded close on one side of LuAnn, and Lucas on the other. A deep interest showed on Lucas's face, which made him appear far more animated than Janice had yet seen. LuAnn stepped backward and the three pressed together, intent on the page before them.

Tess glanced at the journal. "I remember that one. We wondered what she meant by *special handling.*"

Byron lifted tear-filled eyes to answer. "I know exactly what this means." He exchanged a sideways glance with Lucas, who appeared equally moved. "My great-great-great-grandmother's name was Becca. She married my great-great-great-grandpa, Ezra, when they lived on a plantation in Virginia. Then the owner sold Ezra to a tobacco grower in Kentucky."

Through their research of the Underground Railroad, Janice had heard many similar stories. They never failed to twist her heart. "That's just horrible."

Byron nodded. "She tried to—"

Tears choked off the words, and he closed his eyes. Marla slipped her arm around his waist and squeezed as salty drops slid down his brown cheeks. LuAnn leaned forward and grabbed a napkin from the holder in the center of the table and handed it to him. He took it and then gestured toward Lucas, who continued the story.

"She escaped several times. Or tried to. But instead of running to freedom, she always went west."

"Heading to Kentucky," Tess whispered.

He nodded. "When Ezra was sold, he didn't know she was pregnant, and she wanted to tell him. But the second time she was caught, her owner branded her." He rubbed his cheek with two fingers. "On her face."

Marla gasped, and nausea swirled in Janice's stomach. "That's horrible," she managed to say.

"That's what Prudence meant when she said the dry goods were *clearly marked*," Winnie said.

Byron scrubbed his face with the napkin and, with a visible effort, recovered his composure. "And the small package must have been Ezra Junior, my great-great-grandfather. According to my grandpa, his grandfather was eighteen months old when his mama left the plantation for the last time."

"Hiding a baby would definitely have required special handling." Janice tried to imagine a toddler confined to the small rooms in the basement.

Lucas reached for the page and then hesitated. He looked up at LuAnn. "May I?"

LuAnn splayed a hand toward the journal. "Of course. This is a photocopy. We donated the original to the Underground Railroad Museum."

"I saw that yesterday." He slowly turned one page and then another. "I didn't know what I was looking at."

"This is it." Byron spoke in a reverent, hushed tone. "This is what we've been looking for."

Janice exchanged a glance with Tess. Naturally, Byron would want to find proof of his ancestors' escape to freedom. And apparently Lucas was just as interested in Byron's family history as Byron himself. She supposed that was natural for a writer and researcher. But was their quest for historical documentation their primary reason for being here in Marietta?

Tess was watching her through slightly narrowed eyes.

Please don't say anything about the Bible. Please don't.

Janice felt even more hesitation than before about revealing William Still's Bible. She absolutely would not turn it over to these two men, not until she was positive that Byron truly loved Marla for herself, and not just for her possible link to his family's past.

Lucas, who had been bent over the journal, scanning as he turned pages, straightened. He replaced the loose-leaf papers and straightened the stack.

"I hesitate to ask, but would you let us borrow this?"

Janice would have said no. She even opened her mouth, but LuAnn spoke first. "Of course. It's a photocopy, as I said." She smiled. "I think you'll find some fascinating nighttime reading in that journal. We certainly have."

"Thank you." He wasted no time in scooping up the pages and hugging them to his chest.

"This has been a fabulous day." Byron gestured toward the journal and grinned broadly at Winnie. "And a productive one."

Marla ran a hand down his arm and then intertwined her fingers with his. "And it's not over yet. We still have to go pick out flowers and a cake." She looked across the table at Janice. "You haven't forgotten, have you?"

In fact, Janice had forgotten she'd agreed to accompany the couple this afternoon. Flowers and cake, two essential ingredients for any wedding. Normally Janice loved this part of planning a wedding, but she rather dreaded spending the afternoon with Byron. The problem was, she was beginning to really like the guy. If only she could rid herself of her suspicions regarding his true intentions for Marla.

She slid her gaze from the happy couple to Lucas, who stood hugging the pages of Prudence's journal as if they were Moses's stone tablets. What was his part in this? Was he truly Byron's friend, there to support him as he married the love of his life? Or was he in Marietta to help Byron find and steal documents of historic or even financial value?

CHAPTER TEN

O range?" Janice kept her expression carefully bland. "You're sure?"

Marla nodded without hesitation. "Orange and purple. I can already see them in my mind."

Though Janice personally wouldn't have chosen those colors, Nancy, the owner of Tie the Knot Wedding Designs, did not bat an eye.

"They can be beautiful together." She flipped a few plastic-sleeved pages in the binder that rested on the table between them. "I can do a stunning sunset-themed bouquet, and I'm sure my supplier can get these for me on short notice."

She found the page she sought and pushed the binder toward Marla. Janice had to admit, the combination of orange chrysanthemums and yarrow with purple alstroemeria and a few calla lilies did make a beautiful bouquet.

"That's it." Marla tapped the picture. "What do you think?"

Byron cocked his head sideways and spent a moment examining the photo. "I think whatever my bride wants, my bride should have."

That had been his pat answer at both the bakery and the printer's. Janice had run into grooms before who paid little or no heed to wedding details. At least he'd come along. Some of them would rather leave all the decisions up to the bride.

Lucas had declined to accompany them this afternoon, though Janice half expected him to tag along. He'd headed for his room with LuAnn's copy of the journal, apparently intending to spend the entire afternoon reading.

"They are lovely," Janice admitted. "But the wedding is at ten o'clock in the morning. Not exactly sunset."

Marla's forehead wrinkled. "Does that matter?"

"Not a bit," Nancy assured her. "And I can do beautiful table centerpieces with lavender button mums and orange chrysanthemums."

"And baby's breath," Marla added. She grinned at Byron. "I've always wanted baby's breath at my wedding."

Byron covered her hand and squeezed. "Then you'll have it."

Janice halted the groan while it was barely a rumble in her throat.

"Excellent. Now let me go tally up the damage. I'll be right back."

Nancy disappeared into the back room. Marla and Byron clutched hands and gazed dreamily into each other's eyes, while Janice tried not to look like an intruder. That's what she felt like all afternoon, a useless appendage. She wasn't sure why she was even there, since Marla knew exactly what she wanted for her wedding, and apparently had the money to pay for it.

Janice's gaze strayed toward the front window. Though she may have little interest in what was going on in this shop, across the street lay one that drew her attention like cream draws a cat. Harry's Antique and Salvage Mall. As she watched, a car pulled up to the curb out front and a woman exited. Janice straightened in her chair. Why, that was Kate Campbell. She hadn't seen Kate in months. Surely it would be rude of her not to at least pop in and say hello.

Her recent conversation with Stuart replayed in her mind. True, she had no reason to shop at Harry's. But that didn't mean she couldn't peek in and greet an old friend, did it?

She stood, which drew Marla's and Byron's attention away from one another. "If I'm not needed here for a minute, I think I'll run across the street to Harry's. Do you mind?"

Marla turned a wide grin on Byron. "You've got to go to Harry's. It's an experience you don't want to miss. He has everything you can possibly imagine crammed into that shop."

Byron nodded. "We'll finish up here and then join you."

Janice retrieved her purse and draped her sweater across her arm as she left the store. If she could manage to get Harry off to one side, maybe he would open up to her since she was by herself this time.

The bells on the door jangled when she entered. A quick glance around the crowded front room revealed no one. Kate must have gone to the back. Janice headed that way and almost ran over Kenny, the high school kid who helped Harry part-time.

"Oh! Excuse me."

Kenny, who had been crouching on the floor before a shelving unit, stood. "Sorry, Mrs. Eastman. I didn't mean to startle you. Can I help you find something?"

Janice craned her neck for the back room. "No, not really. I'm going to look around. I thought I saw a friend come in."

"There's a lady in the back room."

"I'll run back and say hello."

She left Kenny and sauntered toward the rear of the shop, pausing occasionally to inspect an item, just in case anyone was watching. When she passed through the doorway leading to the second room, where Harry displayed some of the larger antiques, she spied Kate running a hand over a beautifully carved desk. Beside her stood Harry himself.

When Janice joined them, her nose twitched at the nearly overpowering aroma of Old Spice. Apparently Harry had bathed in the stuff that morning.

"That's a beautiful piece," she said.

"Yes, it is." Kate gave her a bright smile. "How are you, Janice? It's been ages, hasn't it?"

The two exchanged a hug, while Harry half-turned away, intent on rubbing at a spot on the desk's surface.

"And how are Corrie and Pamela?" Janice had taught Kate's daughters in Sunday school years ago.

"They're well. Corrie is still teaching at Marietta College, and Pamela has her hands full riding herd on the twins." Kate's smile widened, and she extracted a cell phone from her jacket pocket. "Would you like to see pictures?"

"Of course." Janice inspected several photos of identical five-year-olds with impish grins. "I'll bet they keep their mother busy."

"Oh yes." Kate re-pocketed the phone. "But she still manages to find time to spend with her mother. She comes over twice a week to, uh, help me."

Janice detected a note of strain in the comment. "Help? Or maybe meddle a bit?"

Though Harry had half turned away from them, his shoulders heaved with a silent laugh, and Kate's lips twisted into a wry smile.

"My girls have always been prone to meddle in my affairs. Especially after Glenn passed away. But they're just trying to help," she hurried to add.

"Of course they are." Janice knew exactly what Kate meant. Stacy had the same tendency. Perhaps it was a trait common to daughters. Or maybe young mothers.

The conversation died, and the silence that followed became awkward. Janice cast about for something to say. What she really wanted was to get Harry alone so she could question him.

"Well." Kate adjusted the purse strap on her shoulder. She patted the desk. "Let me think about this."

Harry jerked to attention. "Yes, definitely. You want me to hold it for you?"

Kate cocked her head sideways. "No, I don't think so. If you get an offer on it, go ahead and sell it." She smiled at Janice. "It was good to see you again. Pamela and I have been meaning to come by the inn for lunch, but with two rowdy boys in tow…" She shrugged.

"We love children," Janice assured her. "And I have a rowdy five-year-old grandson myself, as you know. Bring them in."

"Okay, I will." Her eyes flickered toward Harry. "Goodbye."

He mumbled something that sounded like, "See you around," and Kate left.

Finally alone.

Janice stepped around the table until she stood face-to-face with Harry. The smell of his aftershave almost burned her eyes at this close range. "Have you made any arrangements to start the cleanup in the church yet?"

He shook his head. "I'm waiting for Chief Mayfield to give the okay."

"When he does, I'd like to tag along."

He jerked a nod and then took a sideways step, eyeing his office. Janice also stepped sideways and blocked his escape.

"I've been thinking about what you said the other day. That you were out for a drive when you noticed the flames."

His expression became wary. "Yeah?"

Janice had not really planned how to approach this conversation. Best to just come to the point.

"Something is bothering me," she said. "If you were out for a drive, why weren't you in your car when you saw the man running away from the church?"

His shoulders stiffened. "Huh?"

Janice kept her tone light, conversational. "You said you had to unlock your car to get your cell phone out. But if you were driving, you would have already been in the car."

He lifted his work-roughened hand and raked his fingers through his thinning hair. "Uh, I took a walk?"

Janice didn't believe him. His entire manner, the way his eyes flickered everywhere but at her face, indicated that he wasn't telling the truth.

"It was a nice night for a stroll," she agreed. "But a bit unusual to drive all the way across town for a late-night walk."

Though his lips remained closed, his jaw worked for a second as though struggling to hold back a comment. Janice found herself rising up on her toes, anticipating the coming confession.

"Isn't this just the best place, honeybun?"

Janice whirled in time to see Marla and Byron enter from the front room.

Byron's head turned as he took in the mishmash of items crowded into the display space. "It sure is something."

"'Scuse me," Harry muttered as he shuffled away.

Janice watched him go, frustration tightening the muscles in her stomach. In another ninety seconds, she would have gotten what she was after. Information.

Janice waved goodbye to Marla and Byron when they dropped her off at the inn. She went inside, her mind full. She needed time to think, to sort out her thoughts. But there were too many of them rolling around in her head. Too many suspicions. Too many suspects.

Her stomach felt uneasy, even slightly queasy. She balled her fist and pressed it into her middle. Was she coming down with something? No, the problem was not physical. The problem was mental. Or maybe emotional. She didn't like being a suspicious person. Curious yes. But she had always liked people, had always thought the best of everyone.

Lord, what is wrong with me? Why can't I let the police do their jobs and find the arsonist?

But even as the prayer formed in her mind, she knew she would not stop pushing. Whoever had set that fire had come too close to something she cared about, deeply. Her church. Christ Fellowship had been part of her life for decades. She raised her children there. Served alongside her husband there. Those people were her family, even the irritating ones like Gloria. She couldn't stop now, couldn't let the matter drop until she knew the truth.

The piano in the parlor drew her attention. The piano at which she had spent so many hours they probably accrued to months and months of her life. It had been a gift from Pastor Ben and the church.

She hurried across the room and approached the piano as she would an old friend. With a sideways toss, she rid herself of her purse and jacket and then opened the lid on the bench. Music lay inside, neatly separated into two piles—sacred and secular. She flipped through the former until she found the piece she knew would calm her turbulent thoughts.

A few moments later, the beautiful melody filled every corner of the room while the words resonated in her soul.

When peace like a river attendeth my way,
When sorrows like sea billows roll;
Whatever my lot, thou hast taught me to say,
It is well, it is well with my soul.

Though she sat with her back to the main part of the room, in her peripheral vision she saw someone slip into one of the chairs over by the fireplace. Not Tess's copper curls nor LuAnn's billowy silver locks. Instead she identified their reticent guest, Pauline. Janice gave no sign that she had seen the woman and kept playing.

Though Satan should buffet, though trials should come,
Let this blest assurance control,
That Christ hath regarded my helpless estate,
And hath shed his own blood for my soul.

Janice did not need the sheet music. She'd played this song so many times she could picture the notes in her mind, and her fingers found the keys almost of their own accord.

It is well
With my soul,
It is well, it is well with my soul.

When the last strains of music faded into silence, Janice opened her eyes. Pauline was gone.

Janice was gathering her purse and coat when the front door opened and Chief Mayfield entered the inn. A flash of guilt shot through her. Had Harry told the chief she'd been around asking questions?

She pasted on a bright smile. "Hello."

He ducked his head while watching her with a pair of rather piercing eyes. "Mrs. Eastman. I wonder if I could have a word with you and your friends."

Impossible to guess the reason for this visit by looking at those impassive, stone-like features.

"Certainly. At least, I think so. I haven't seen LuAnn or Tess this afternoon. I've been running errands. Let me see where they are."

Glad for the excuse not to return that direct stare, she fished in her purse for her cell phone and sent a quick text.

Where are you? Police in the parlor to talk with us.

Almost immediately, she heard the ding of a text message being received, and LuAnn exited the office.

She smiled at the chief. "Tess went upstairs a little while ago. I think she may be taking a nap. Shall we call her?"

Janice's phone vibrated in her hand. An incoming text.

On my way down.

"No need. She'll be here any minute."

They invited the chief to have a seat, and he selected the chair nearest the fireplace, the one Pauline had occupied a few moments before, though he declined the offer of tea.

Janice cast about for something to say, chitchat to fill what threatened to become an awkward silence. "How's the investigation going?"

She almost winced. No doubt he would tell her that his investigation was none of her business.

Instead, a brief smile flashed onto his face. "We're making progress."

"I spoke with Harry Olson this afternoon, and he said you haven't quite finished whatever it is you need to do in the church belfry."

LuAnn gave her a sharp look but said nothing.

"That's right."

She realized her hands had tightened into fists and forced them to unclench.

"I only ask because I volunteered to help him clean the place up. Because of the bells, you know. We want them to ring. I mean, Marla does. At her wedding." She bit down on her lower lip. Goodness gracious goat, she was blathering again.

Tess's arrival saved her from further embarrassment. She slid onto the love seat next to LuAnn and turned an inquiring gaze on the chief.

"As I was just telling Mrs. Eastman, our investigation continues. We've made an interesting discovery, which is the reason for my visit."

Was the man actually going to share details of his investigation with them? Janice inched forward to the edge of her cushion until her feet rested flat on the floor.

"But before I continue, can you verify that all your guests were in their rooms Saturday evening around the time of the fire?"

Janice exchanged a wide-eyed look with Tess. Did he suspect one of their guests?

"Nooo," LuAnn said slowly. "I mean, I can't. I sat reading in our common room after supper until Brad called me to tell me about the fire."

Tess shook her head when the chief looked her way. "I was downstairs getting the last load of towels folded around seven, and then I went to my room and was writing a few emails when LuAnn rushed in and said Brad had called and the church was on fire."

When it was her turn, Janice told the chief that she was almost asleep when her two friends woke her and told her about the fire.

His pen scratched on the pad. "So you have no idea who was in the inn and who wasn't?"

All three women shook their heads.

He jotted a few more notes and then asked, "Would you happen to have a towel?"

Janice exchanged a glance with her friends. "A towel? Like a kitchen towel?" She was almost on her feet, intent on fetching one, but the chief shook his head.

"Not a kitchen towel. A bath towel. One like you use in your guest rooms."

Curiosity deepened on Tess's and LuAnn's faces.

"I'm sure we do," LuAnn said. "I'm afraid they're rather unremarkable, though. Just plain white bath towels."

The urge to give in to nervous chatter was almost overpowering, so Janice jumped in with an explanation. "We do that on purpose. That way we can put fresh linens in each room without having to do laundry every day. Unless, of course, we're full, and then we have to do laundry every day no matter what." She closed her eyes and snapped her mouth shut. She was still doing it.

LuAnn stood. "I can get one if you'd like to see them."

"Please."

She headed for the stairway to the basement, where they kept all the linens, soiled and clean.

When silence threatened again, Janice asked the question foremost in her mind. "What about the bells?" One of the chief's eyebrows twitched upward. "I mean, are they functional? Since we haven't been allowed up there, I'm curious about what shape they're in."

"I'm afraid they'll need some work before they can be rung again. The cast iron they're made of is fine, obviously. But the support structure was wooden, and directly above the central part of the fire. The main beam in the center of the bell gable took the brunt of the flames and cracked. Maybe it had been weakened with termite damage or something." He shook his head. "The last time I saw those bells, they were lying in a pile of ash. They can be re-hung, but someone will have to build a new support bracket."

"Oh dear," Tess said.

LuAnn returned and handed the chief a crisply folded bath towel. He stood and, with a flick of his wrists, shook it out.

Holding his arms up in front of him, he inspected the length and then rubbed the terry cloth between a finger and thumb.

"Are all your towels accounted for?"

What a telling question. Had someone found a towel? Was that the interesting discovery?

"As far as I know." LuAnn looked at Tess and then Janice. "The last time I cleaned the guest rooms I didn't notice anything missing. How about you two?"

"No," said Tess.

Janice shook her head. Whenever she cleaned the guest rooms, she always took enough clean towels to replace the soiled ones. If a towel had been missing, she certainly would've noticed it.

The chief heaved a sigh. "It was worth a try. And this is a pretty common type of towel. Just like the ones at the Lafayette. I guess it could have come from anywhere." He handed the article in question back to LuAnn.

"So you did find a towel?" Janice asked.

"We did," the chief said. "A dirty one. Filthy, in fact. Covered in soot."

"Soot, as in maybe ashes from a fire?"

"Exactly that kind of soot." He slapped his hands on his thighs and heaved himself out of the chair. "Thank you, ladies. It was a long shot, but one I had to follow up on."

That was it? He wasn't going to give them any more information than that?

Apparently not. He headed for the door, and Janice hurried after him, trying to come up with a question that would delay his departure and reveal something about their investigation.

"About those bells—" she began as he opened the door. She cringed. *Enough with the bells already.*

"Shouldn't be too much longer before my boys are finished up there. Then I'll give the church the go-ahead to start the cleanup and repair work."

Janice squeezed her eyes shut when he closed the door behind him. He'd give the church the go-ahead. In other words, the people in charge. Not her.

Well, that was as it should be. After all, she was only the former pastor's wife.

She turned to find both of her friends staring at her.

"Why did you go see Harry again today?" LuAnn asked.

"And without us," Tess said.

Goodness, this was what a bug pinned to a velvet board felt like. "I was right across the street at Tie the Knot with Marla and Byron, and I happened to look up and see Kate Campbell going inside. And I thought—" Janice snapped her mouth shut. These were her friends. No need to pretend around them. Her shoulders drooped. "Okay, I admit it. I went back to ask him what he was doing outside of his car when he told us he was out for a drive."

Tess pointed a finger at the chair Janice had just vacated. "Sit."

Her head drooping forward, Janice obeyed.

They returned to the love seat and both of them watched her closely. Janice shifted around on the cushion looking for a comfortable position. With them facing her like this, she felt as though she were the subject of an inquisition.

"I'm beginning to worry about you." LuAnn brushed a lock of hair away from her face. "You're obsessed with this fire."

Tess agreed. "I understand wanting to get to the bottom of things, really. Harry is definitely not telling us everything he knows. And I can even sort of understand your suspicions about Byron." LuAnn turned a surprised look on Tess, and she held up an outward-facing palm. "I love Marla dearly, but she can be a bit gullible."

"Exactly." Janice leaned forward, her elbows on her knees. "She's exactly the kind of woman who could be easily taken advantage of. And I can't stand by and watch that happen to a friend."

"Hold up, you two." A frown settled on LuAnn's face, looking out of place in unfamiliar territory. "I completely understand being concerned for a friend. But all you have to do is look at those two and know they're in love."

Janice did not agree. "True, lasting love does not happen overnight. People fall in and out of love all the time. That's why they shouldn't jump into marriage so quickly."

LuAnn dipped her head. "We're not talking about reckless teenagers with raging hormones. We're talking about two mature people who have been lonely their whole lives and have finally found someone with whom they want to spend the rest of their lives. Hasty marriages happen all the time, and sometimes they work out just fine."

"Sometimes they do," Janice said. "But look at the divorce rate these days. Divorce is at a crisis level. Homes are ripped apart and hearts broken, because people don't understand what a huge commitment marriage is." Goodness gracious goat! She sounded like she was standing on a soapbox. "I'm sorry. It's just that I feel protective toward Marla. She's part of the flock Lawrence and I shepherded. I can't stand by and watch her get hurt."

"I understand, I really do." LuAnn gave Janice one of the kind smiles that warmed her insides. "But what if you're wrong?"

Tess nodded. "Besides, what would be Byron's motive?"

Janice answered immediately. "William Still's Bible." Her friends both looked puzzled. "What if he knew about it? What if the only reason he came to Marietta was to find the Bible, and steal it, and sell it? Or maybe not sell it, but use it to prove his ancestry for...for...some reason." She ended lamely, as was evident by the skeptical looks on her friends' faces.

"That doesn't hold water," Tess said. "As far as we know, Marla doesn't even know about that Bible. She certainly hasn't gone looking for it, and she hasn't mentioned it at all."

True. "So maybe not the Bible. Maybe he doesn't know what he's looking for. My point is this: What if he is only stringing Marla along until he finds documentation that her ancestor rescued his ancestors?"

"I think you're grasping," LuAnn said. "If that were so, why set fire to the church? We took Marla's box out of the belfry, and she doesn't even know what was up there."

Janice interrupted. "She told us she thought she still had some boxes of family papers stored up in that belfry. And he was standing right here when she said it."

LuAnn acknowledged the comment with a nod. "But we took the box," she repeated. "So why would he set fire to the belfry? It doesn't make sense."

Tess looked thoughtful. "Well, he doesn't know we took a box. Besides, we only took one box. What if there were more? We didn't get all the way through the stuff stored up there."

Janice sent her a grateful smile. "That's right. He could have gone up there and found a second box with even more revealing information. Maybe even proving that William Still didn't lead his family to freedom after all." The idea solidified in her mind as she spoke, and words tumbled out. "As eager as both he and Lucas are to find documentation about his ancestors, if he found something to the contrary he would be very upset."

LuAnn scowled. "Upset enough to set a fire in the church?"

"Possibly," Janice said. "Or maybe…" An idea had been forming in the back of her mind, a possible motive. But she hadn't pulled it out and examined it, even in her own quiet time. She spoke slowly. "Or what if he set that fire for a completely different reason? What if he did it to delay the wedding?"

Both of her friends grew solemn.

"Go on," Tess said.

"What if Byron came down here with honorable intentions, but after he got here he developed cold feet?"

Tess picked up on her thought. "He wouldn't be the first groom to have icy toes. And especially when he's marrying a woman he's only seen in person once before."

But LuAnn was still not convinced. "I'm following you two up to a point. But if that were the case, why turn to arson? I think Byron is an honorable man. If he's had a change of heart, he would tell Marla outright."

A possible reason became crystal clear to Janice. "Maybe he hasn't changed his mind, but he's wavering. He set the fire to delay the wedding. He heard Marla say that all her life she has dreamed of having a wedding in that church with those bells ringing. If Harry hadn't seen the fire when he did, it could have spread to the whole church and been disastrous."

"It's too farfetched to think he would destroy the church just to get out of marrying Marla." Tess spoke slowly. "But a small fire, like in a stone belfry, could have caused enough damage to delay the wedding and give him more time to be certain."

Janice jabbed a finger in her direction. "Bingo."

They sat quietly for a moment, each lost in her own thoughts.

Finally LuAnn shook her head. "I'm sorry, but I don't believe it. Maybe I'm naive, but it feels like you two are grasping. I think Byron is completely transparent. That his feelings for Marla are genuine, and he's as eager for the wedding as she is."

As much as Janice respected her friend, she couldn't help but feel a bit frustrated. "But how do we know that? How can we prove it? What if he's a complete charlatan?"

Tess straightened on her cushion. "We can prove or disprove that one way or another. Let's call and verify his employment."

Janice wanted to slap her forehead. Why hadn't she thought of that?

"How would we do that?" LuAnn asked. "We don't know where he works."

"Of course we do. He works for Godfrey and Associates in Toronto."

Janice stared at Tess. "How do you know that?"

"Marla told us when she told us about the wedding. Don't you remember?" She included LuAnn in her glance. "We were all in the kitchen at the table having tea."

Though Janice did remember the conversation, details like the name of the accounting firm totally escaped her. She gave Tess an admiring glance. "You are so smart."

LuAnn glanced at her watch. "It's almost five o'clock. Is Toronto on the same time zone we are?"

"I think so." Tess pulled out her cell phone and began tapping the screen. A few seconds later she grinned. "Here it is. Now let's hope they're still open."

She held the phone to her ear while Janice and LuAnn watched and waited.

"Yes," she said in a bright and chipper voice. "I'd like to speak with one of your employees. Byron..." She looked toward LuAnn, her eyes frantic.

"Wickham," LuAnn whispered.

"Byron Wickham." Tess smiled, as though the person on the other end could see her. She waited a few seconds, and then a few seconds more. "Yes. Yes I'm sure." Her eyes grew round as the tops of Winnie's giant muffins. "I see. No, that's all right. Thank you." She lowered the cell phone to her lap and stared at the screen.

Janice couldn't breathe. "Well?"

Tess shook her head slowly. "There is no one by the name of Byron Wickham working there."

CHAPTER ELEVEN

I feel like a criminal," LuAnn whispered while Janice used the master key on the door to the Woodsmoke and Pine room.

In light of their discovery that Byron had lied to Marla about his employment, the girls had decided to double-check the towel inventory in his room. Tess had cleaned this room since their guests' arrival, and when pressed she could only say she was 98 percent sure no towels had been missing.

"Don't be ridiculous," Tess told LuAnn. "This is our inn, our property. We have every right to go in this room."

"Yes, but—"

Janice twisted the knob and threw open the door. With a furtive glance down the hallway, she led her friends inside. The faint scent of Byron's aftershave lingered in the air.

LuAnn hovered in the open doorway. "You two go check the bathroom. I'll keep watch."

Janice followed Tess around the foot of the tall king-size bed with an attractive plaid bedspread. They had assigned Marla's fiancé the room with the most masculine decor, and it was actually one of Janice's favorites.

Tess marched right into the bathroom and then stopped. "All towels present and accounted for."

Janice peered around her at the metal rack on the wall above the toilet. Two neatly folded towels, two hand towels, and two washcloths. She wasn't sure whether she felt disappointed or relieved. "I guess that proves he didn't set the fire."

"The only thing it proves," Tess said, "is he didn't steal a towel."

"But then—"

"You two hurry up." LuAnn's stage whisper interrupted the conversation.

They retreated and joined her in the hallway. Janice pulled the door closed, twisted the knob to make sure it was locked, and out of habit, set the flippy-thingy to indicate the room was clean.

Each room in the inn had a small metal rod attached to the doorframe, a holdover from the old days. When a maid finished cleaning the room, she flipped the rod around so the top rested against the closed door. When a guest opened the door, the lever dropped into the downward position. The girls had searched online and had even talked to other hotel proprietors, but the gadgets were so old no one knew what their proper name might be. So they became the flippy-thingies.

When Janice would have headed for the staircase, Tess jerked her head toward the door across the hallway, the Woodbine and Roses room. A soft moan escaped LuAnn's throat.

"What? They're best friends. If one of them is in on it, they both are."

Janice couldn't argue with that. LuAnn closed her eyes before agreeing with a single nod. They crept across the hallway, conscious that Pauline occupied the Lilac and Sage room right next door. Janice used the master key, and this time she led the way to the bathroom. She had cleaned this one herself and knew what they would find, but if Tess needed verification, so be it.

This towel rack held exactly the same number of linens as the one across the hall. No one said a word as they scurried from the room.

They had not yet reached the staircase when a ding from the inn's front door alerted them to someone's arrival. The rumble of male voices drifted up the staircase.

Eyes round as oranges, LuAnn hissed, "It's them."

Panic gripped Janice's stomach. What would their guests say if they caught them sneaking around their hallway?

"Quick." Tess nearly ran down the stairs. Instead of going all the way to the main floor, she stopped on the second and gestured for Janice to unlock the door to the Honeymoon Suite.

Though Janice knew they had every right to be anywhere in the entire inn, her fingers trembled as she unlocked the door. Her friends piled into the room after her. The door shut with a soft *click*, and the three of them huddled together, their ears pressed to the wood.

"What are we doing?" LuAnn whispered. "We should have marched downstairs like we own the place. Because we do."

"Too late now," Janice said. "They're coming this way."

They followed the men's progress by the sound of their voices. Not until they'd heard two doors being shut on the floor above them did they relax.

LuAnn collapsed against the wall. "That was close."

"Too close." Janice dried her damp palms on her slacks.

"Don't be silly." Tess eyed them both. "We haven't done anything wrong. We haven't lied, but those two have. At least, Byron lied, and since he and Lucas are such good friends, I think it's safe to assume he knows what Byron is up to. So, what are we going to do about it?"

"We have to tell Marla." Janice closed her eyes, dreading the confrontation.

LuAnn looked hesitant. "I'm not sure we should." Janice goggled at her, and LuAnn held up a hand. "I mean not right away. The news will break her heart."

Tess folded her arms over her chest. "Better to break her heart now than stand by and let her be hurt by a charlatan."

"Obviously we will have to tell her what we've discovered. But I think we should approach the situation with caution. There could be a reasonable explanation."

Janice could hardly believe her ears. "What possible explanation could there be for a bald-faced lie?"

LuAnn's features settled into a stubborn expression. "Maybe we called the wrong accounting firm."

Janice opened her mouth to argue, but LuAnn went on before she could voice an objection.

"Maybe Marla got it wrong. I've never heard Byron mention the name of his employer, have either of you?"

Janice had to think about it a minute, but finally she shook her head.

"Me neither," Tess admitted. "But if so, then Byron will explain. No harm done."

"I don't agree. A lot of harm will be done. I know both of you have more experience with marriage than I do. But I know something about relationships. A seed of doubt, once planted, can grow like a weed and choke out everything else in the garden."

Though she hated to admit it, Janice saw the wisdom in LuAnn's analogy. Hadn't she and Lawrence counseled enough couples whose marriage was in crisis because one partner did not trust the other?

"We have to tell her sometime. She has a right to know."

"Should we confront him ourselves?" Tess asked.

A shiver rippled across Janice's shoulders. If there was one thing she hated worse than dishonesty, it was confrontation. She would go to almost any length to avoid it.

LuAnn looked doubtful. "I'm not sure *confront* is the right word. But maybe a few questions would be in order."

"I vote for the questions," Janice said.

"But before we do anything, there is something else we need to do." Janice and Tess both looked at LuAnn. "We need to pray about this."

Janice heaved a soft sigh, the rightness of LuAnn's words loosening several tense knots in her stomach. Prayer was exactly what they needed.

Without another word, the three friends left the Honeymoon Suite. Janice pulled the door shut behind them and set the flippy-thingy.

They headed for the stairs, and Janice glanced at the doors to the other two rooms on the second floor. She came to an abrupt halt, and Tess ran into her from behind.

"Look at that." She pointed toward the door on the Lily and Lace room. "The flippy-thingy is flipped."

LuAnn led the way, and the three of them examined the lever, which hung downward.

"That makes no sense," Tess said. "I cleaned that room last week, and I am positive I flipped the thing. I always do."

"Has anyone else gone in there?" Janice asked. "I know I haven't."

The others shook their heads.

"Maybe we'd better have a look inside." LuAnn gestured for Janice, who still held the master key clutched in one damp hand.

Janice turned the key in the lock and opened the door. If Woodsmoke and Pine was the most masculine room the inn had to offer, Lily and Lace was arguably the most feminine. Janice glanced at the framed watercolor hanging on the wall above the four-poster bed, its hand-tatted antique mat a work of art in itself. Pale green and cream-colored silk pillows lay scattered on the bed in what looked like a careless arrangement, but in truth was carefully orchestrated to achieve an artistically casual feeling. A close examination of the pillows revealed them to be in perfect order.

Tess poked her head into the bathroom. "Everything looks fine in here. No towels missing."

LuAnn moved toward the north-facing window and then came to an abrupt halt. "Look here."

She pointed to a dirty scuff mark on the carpet. Janice knelt and brushed it with a gentle finger. "It's dirt. And not dirt that's been dropped there, either. It looks like mud that has dried to the nap of the carpet. Like from someone's shoe."

"I guarantee that was not here when I cleaned this room," Tess said.

LuAnn sidestepped the muddy smudge and opened the closet door. "There's more in here."

The girls crowded into the doorway. Suspicion stirred in Janice's mind. "Is the trap door locked?"

One of the tasks Robin had performed for them was to install a latch on the inside of the trapdoors that accessed the ladder. It wouldn't be safe to leave those doors open to guests, but neither did they want to place an ugly padlock in two of their beautiful rooms. Robin's solution was to screw in a simple hook-and-eye-type latch on the inside of each door, accessible only from the ladder side.

"Let's find out." LuAnn knelt to grasp the thin strip of leather that served as a handle for the trap door. In their attempt to maintain the authenticity of the historical aspects of the inn, they had left the leather intact.

When LuAnn pulled, the trap door opened.

Tess gasped. "Someone has unlocked it from the inside."

Janice eyed the muddy trail. "And since there's no mud in the basement, whoever it was must have used the tunnel."

LuAnn closed the trap door. "I wonder if this is the only latch that has been unhooked."

The ceiling above them creaked. All three tilted their heads to look upward. Heavy footsteps, a man's footsteps, trod across the sturdy floor of the room above them. Woodsmoke and Pine, which was occupied by Marla's dishonest fiancé.

Another shiver rippled through Janice. The secret ladder continued upward through the closet in the room occupied by Byron. But it did not stop there. Directly above that was her own closet.

Their cozy common room didn't seem so comfortable at the moment. Not with the threat of a trip through the secret tunnel looming ahead of her.

Janice avoided meeting her friends' gazes. "I think we should wait until morning. It's too dark to see anything tonight."

Upon leaving Lily and Lace, the three had gone straight upstairs to Janice's closet. Thank the Lord, the latch on the inside of the topmost trap door was still in place. Tug though she might, Janice had reassured herself that the trap door had not been opened. At least not from her side. But she determined that first thing in the morning, she would contact Robin to put a lock on her side of the door. Historical integrity aside, she would have no peace of mind until she knew no one could climb into her apartment while she slept.

After checking the security of the closet, they'd gathered in their common room for prayer. Ultra-conscious of Marla's tender feelings, no one felt any peace about confronting Byron yet. They'd decided instead to trace the source of the muddy tracks.

"It's always dark in the tunnel," LuAnn pointed out. "We'll take flashlights."

Seated in her overstuffed chair, Tess leaned over to tie the laces on the tennis shoes she had retrieved from her apartment. "We have to check to see if the door is still locked. I, for one, won't be able to sleep a wink without making sure nobody can get into the inn through the tunnel."

Though the simple latches on the inside of the trapdoors provided sufficient safety inside the inn, they had decided to padlock the door on the river side of the entrance to the tunnel. They kept the key on a nail just inside the tunnel on the inn side. In retrospect, perhaps not the safest place to store the key, but at the time they'd thought only of keeping intruders out, not keeping their guests in.

"Shouldn't we call Chief Mayfield?" Janice looked from Tess to LuAnn.

LuAnn shook her head. "I'm not sure we should involve the police at this point. As far as we know, no crime has been committed."

"As far as we know," Janice repeated ominously.

Her shoelace tied into a neat bow, Tess straightened. "I know what you're thinking, but there's absolutely no evidence linking mud in Lily and Lace with the fire at the church." When Janice would have argued, Tess held up her hand. "Yes, we have some questions about the integrity of one of our guests. But we've prayed about Byron, and I believe the Lord will nudge us in the right direction when the time is right."

Janice shut her mouth. How could she voice an argument to waiting for God's direction?

LuAnn leaned forward and covered one of Janice's hands. "I know what's bothering you, and you don't have to go in the tunnel. Tess and I will go."

Despite herself, Janice relaxed. She had been in the tunnel, and she found it fascinating—from a distance. But there were most definitely mice living in there. And spiders. And, on one occasion, at least, skeletons. And who knew what else?

She managed a smile. "Are you sure?"

LuAnn patted her hand before straightening. "Of course I am. You don't even have to go in the basement if you don't want to."

They agreed on a plan. LuAnn and Tess would check the lock in the tunnel while Janice started supper. Together they trooped down the stairs. Janice helped her friends gather flashlights and check the batteries, and when they headed for the basement, she began pulling the ingredients for spaghetti from the pantry.

"Hello?"

She poked her head out of the pantry to see Lucas in the kitchen, holding LuAnn's copy of the journal.

"I was going to return this to LuAnn." He glanced around the room. "Is she here?"

"Yes, she's—" *No need to explain.* "—busy for a minute. But she'll be here shortly if you want to wait."

He hesitated. "Could I just leave it with you?"

"Certainly."

He set the journal on the table and turned to leave. As he did, Janice realized this was a golden opportunity to get some information about Byron. Curiosity, or a nudge from the Lord?

She said the first thing that came to mind. "Do you have plans for supper?"

At least that halted his retreat. "Byron just left to pick up Marla for dinner. I plan to walk down to Front Street and grab something in a bit."

Holding the box of spaghetti aloft, she said, "You're welcome to join us if you like."

"Thanks, but I'm not much of a pasta person."

"I can scrounge up something else." She picked up a red onion and deposited it on the counter, then headed for the freezer. A string of chatter might delay his departure. "We have the ingredients for a salad in the fridge, and I can whip up a big one for you. But it's a shame you don't like spaghetti. The sauce is kind of famous here locally. A friend of ours makes it, and we freeze quarts of the stuff to keep on hand."

"I'm sure it's very good."

After removing a container of sauce from the freezer, she opened the industrial-sized refrigerator. "Have you and Byron been friends long?" she asked in the same conversational tone.

To her relief, he answered. "We met in college."

"Did you take classes together?" Random pieces of conversation whirled in her mind. But how to get around to the burning question of Byron's employer?

"A few, but we first met at the student center. He saw me sitting alone and introduced himself." One side of his mouth curved upward at the memory. "As you've probably noticed I'm kind of quiet, whereas Byron can talk to anyone."

"He is a very personable man," she agreed.

The half-smile faded. "Byron is a great guy. The best. He invited me to play basketball with some of the guys the next day." He shrugged. "We became friends from that moment."

She sliced into a plump, ripe tomato. "A writer and an accountant. It's a good thing you had basketball in common since your career paths must have taken you in opposite directions." Good. She congratulated herself on turning the conversation to their jobs.

"Not as opposite as you might think."

"Oh?"

He still stood by the table, his hands resting on the top of one of the high-backed chairs. Should she invite him to take a seat? No. That might scare him away. Though working at the kitchen counter, she stood with her body half-angled toward him.

"I write a column on business and finance, remember? And Byron is a financial whiz. He's better at interpreting the economic impact of market trends than I am. I doubt I could do my job half so well without him."

The tomato chopped, she swept it into a bowl full of lettuce and started on a green pepper. "Is that why you were so eager to help him trace his family history? Out of gratitude?"

"At first," he answered slowly. "But then I guess the researcher in me took over. My family's past isn't noteworthy, but the Wickhams have a fascinating history. Once I got on the trail, it was hard to stop. And Byron works long hours, so he doesn't have as much time to devote to research as I do."

Finally, an opening. She kept her gaze fixed on her hands as they sliced the pepper. "Where does he work again? I think Marla mentioned it, but names fly right out of my head."

She held her breath waiting for the answer.

"Godfrey and Associates. It's one of the top accounting firms in Toronto."

Stacy's childish voice echoed in her head from decades ago. *Liar, liar, pants on fire.*

Certain she could not keep her face impassive, Janice shifted her weight to turn her back on the man. Either Lucas was in on Byron's lie, or he was being hoodwinked just like Marla. Either way, she wasn't about to question him alone. Thank goodness, the sound of footsteps on the stairs saved her from making a reply. LuAnn and Tess entered the kitchen and stopped short when they caught sight of Lucas.

"Oh. Hello." Tess smiled at him.

He ducked his head and then looked at LuAnn. "Thank you for letting me read the journal. It was fascinating."

"You're welcome." She laid a protective hand on the pile of papers. "At times it feels like Prudence is our own personal tour guide into history."

In her peripheral vision, Janice saw his head move as his gaze swept toward the ceiling. "You're fortunate to live in a place that played such an important part in the Underground Railroad. Think of how many people escaped to freedom through here."

"We do," Tess told him. "It's one reason we bought the inn."

LuAnn continued. "We view our work here as a ministry. We offer our guests a comfortable place to stay, and we're available to talk to them or even pray with them if they want. Prudence helped people escape to physical freedom." Her tone warmed. "We like to think we're available to help people find spiritual freedom."

Lucas cleared his throat, an awkward-sounding noise, and a faint blush colored his cheeks. "Uh, that's...nice. If you'll excuse me, I'm going to grab a jacket and go out for a while."

Janice waited until his footsteps fell away before whirling toward her friends.

"Whatever Byron is up to, Lucas is either in on it or he's being suckered too. He just told me Byron works for Godfrey and Associates."

LuAnn glanced at the empty door through which he had gone. "Don't jump to conclusions."

"Did you see how uncomfortable he looked when you mentioned our ministry?" Tess said.

"We definitely need to pray for him. Regardless, whatever he and Byron have in mind, we still don't have any reason to believe it's associated with the fire."

Janice wasn't sure, but she was unable to find a solid connection between Byron's dishonesty and an illegal act of arson. At least, not a connection she could articulate to the police without sounding like a suspicious meddler.

She set the knife on the cutting board. "What did you two find in the tunnel?"

"Nothing *inside* the tunnel," LuAnn said. "The key is hanging on the nail exactly where we left it. The padlock is still there, still locked tight."

"Nothing *inside*, you said?"

Tess cast a furtive glance over her shoulder before answering. "It's hard to tell with just a flashlight, but we think we found something on the river side of the door."

LuAnn nodded, eyes wide. "Footprints. In the mud."

The importance of the discovery slammed into Janice like a fist in the stomach. "We have to call Chief Mayfield right now."

LuAnn and Tess exchanged a glance.

"We talked about that down in the tunnel," LuAnn told her, "and we think we should wait until tomorrow."

"Are you crazy?" Janice held a hand before her and ticked off a finger. "Muddy footprints outside the tunnel." She ticked another finger. "Mud in one of our guest rooms where no one should have been." A third. "And an unlocked trap door in that room. Which just so happens to be right below the room of a man we know to be dishonest. What part of all this says 'wait' to you two? Because it's all screaming 'call the police' at me."

"I understand what you're saying—"

Tess cut LuAnn off. "LuAnn thinks that's all circumstantial, and if we call Chief Mayfield, he'll explain everything away and make us look like idiots."

LuAnn's mouth tightened into a line. "Not exactly the words I used, but Tess is right. There wasn't just one set of footprints outside the gate, there were many. Plenty of people in this town are aware of that tunnel. And we didn't see any mud inside the tunnel, so we can't be sure that whoever's prints are outside actually came in. And besides, the gate is still locked and the key is exactly where we hung it."

Janice set the salad bowl in the center of the table with a little more force than necessary. "The key being in place doesn't prove a thing, except that it's possible for someone inside the inn to use it to unlock the gate and then put it back where he found it."

"But why would he? The fire was set and the arsonist was seen running away long before we locked the front door that night. If Byron set the fire, he would have no reason to use the tunnel. We don't lock the front door until eleven o'clock."

"Besides," Tess put in rather glumly as though she hated to admit it, "he didn't know about the tunnel until a couple of days later when I gave him the tour."

Everything they said made sense, but all the pieces still didn't add up in Janice's mind. "What about the mud on the carpet?"

"If we found mud on the carpet in Byron's room then we would have a stronger reason to suspect him. But Tess has cleaned that room every day and seen no sign of mud." LuAnn glanced at Tess for confirmation, and she nodded.

"There's more," Tess said. "The most recent footprints–the ones covering up the others–were small. Not man-size."

Janice digested that. "You mean, like child-size?"

"Possibly. Or." Tess's gaze swept upward, toward the ceiling. "Or woman-size."

"There aren't many women who'd hang out down—" Janice gasped. "Do you mean Pauline?"

Tess shrugged. "It's too dark to really see much right now."

LuAnn came around the table and grasped Janice's hand in one of hers, and Tess's in the other. "Girls, we do have a mystery on our hands, I don't deny that. Someone unlatched the trap door in the Lily and Lace room. Maybe it was one of our workers. It could have been Thorn or Robin, if they went in there to check on a maintenance issue.

But neither one of them would have left mud on the carpet. Janice opened her mouth to say so, but Tess squeezed her hand to stop her.

"Or maybe it was Larry."

Janice's mouth snapped shut. Her grandson was an expert at disappearing and getting into things he shouldn't. The thought of him climbing that ladder up two or more floors halted the breath in her chest, but she had to admit it was entirely possible for the little rascal, who had run off on more than one occasion.

"All I'm saying is let's not jump into anything tonight." LuAnn squeezed their hands. "If we get the police out here after dark it may upset our guests, and it will definitely make us look foolish if the chief determines those footprints on the outside of the door aren't suspicious."

Tess gave a slow nod. "I'm okay waiting until tomorrow. We can sleep on it, and all of us pray about it. But in the morning, in the light of day, if anything still looks suspicious we'll call then, right?"

"Absolutely," LuAnn agreed.

That sounded like a reasonable compromise. Janice nodded. "Agreed."

Perhaps due to several restless nights in a row, Janice fell into a deep sleep almost as soon as she pulled the covers over her. When she awoke several hours later, she had not shifted an inch on the mattress.

What was that sound? Her half-conscious mind struggled to emerge from the grip of a dream. Her room was dark, with only the glow of the alarm clock on her nightstand to break the blackness. Struggling to focus, she peered at the window. Normally moonlight filtered through. Had she drawn the curtains?

Her foggy brain finally identified the sound. Rain striking her window. A lot of it, judging by the roar that filled her room. The wind must be blowing from the south and pelting water against her window.

She sat straight up in bed, sleep deserting her in an instant. If driving rain was striking her window, that meant it was also being blown against the entrance to the tunnel three floors below.

Washing all the footprints away.

CHAPTER TWELVE

J anice awoke to a glorious sunny day. The night's rainstorm had swept away remnants of dirt and dust from the roads and sidewalks surrounding the inn, leaving them wet but sparkling clean.

The rain had also obliterated any sign of footprints outside the tunnel gate. LuAnn confirmed that fact at first light.

Wednesdays were Janice's turn to help Winnie with breakfast. She whispered a prayer of thanks, since she did not trust herself to serve Byron and Lucas with the necessary hospitality. Instead, she bustled around the kitchen, assembling the various flavored syrups to be delivered with tall stacks of Winnie's flapjacks. The odor of vanilla and pancake batter created a homey atmosphere that helped to soothe her troubled thoughts.

Tess entered the kitchen, the cheerful floral print apron she favored when serving breakfast to their guests tied around her trim waist. "There's someone out there to see you, Janice."

"Me?" She rinsed her hands of the sticky syrup. "Who is it?"

"I can't remember her name. She attends Christ Fellowship, but she's fairly new. She's waiting by the fireplace."

Janice dried her hands on a paper towel and tossed it into the garbage on the way out of the room.

Only two of the tables in the café were occupied. She forced herself not to look toward Byron and Lucas seated by the front window but cast a broad smile toward Pauline, who sat alone at the table farthest away from the men. A quick smile, devoid of any real feeling, flashed onto her face and then faded almost as soon as it arrived. She looked especially sad today. Janice made a mental note to stop by her table on the way back to the kitchen, and then headed for the reception area where a young woman was seated at a chair near the fireplace.

At her approach, the woman rose. Correction. She was little more than a girl, probably in her early twenties. She did look familiar, though Janice could not place her name. One of the newer attendees who'd begun attending Christ Fellowship after Pastor Ben's arrival.

"Hello." Janice extended a hand and smiled into an anxious-looking face. "You'll have to forgive me. I'm sure we've met, but I can't remember your name."

"Erin Peterson." She grasped Janice's hand with soft fingers and released it immediately. "Actually, I'm not sure we've ever officially met. But I know who you are, Mrs. Eastman."

"Please call me Janice."

She gestured toward the seat in which Erin had been sitting and started to settle on the love seat nearby.

The young woman's eyes flickered beyond Janice to the café. "Would you mind if we sit over there?"

She pointed toward the chairs in the area they referred to as the parlor, the ones surrounding the piano. Janice saw the advantage of the area immediately. Though this entire lobby area was open, the parlor was tucked into a corner, out of sight of the café. There they could speak in relative privacy.

Interesting.

"Of course."

When they had settled in the parlor, Erin stared at the floor between them. A struggle appeared on her face. "I-I'm really not sure how to begin."

Janice had been in enough counseling situations to recognize the signs. This girl was experiencing problems of some sort, and they were causing her a great deal of anxiety. A glance at her left hand revealed a largish diamond and a wedding ring. She looked very much like a young woman Janice had counseled a decade or so ago, who was having marital problems.

She put on her most soothing pastor's-wife smile. "Why don't you start by telling me about your husband. How long you've known each other, and how long you've been married."

Questions appeared in Erin's eyes. "Okay. Jarrod and I dated the last two years of college. We've been married about eighteen months." Her mouth snapped shut.

She was going to have to be guided a bit, until she became comfortable talking.

Janice gave an encouraging nod and asked a question that provided an opening. "And are things going well between you?"

"Well—" A struggle appeared on Erin's face. Then it cleared, and she leaned forward. "Mrs. Eastman...Janice. I'm afraid you've misunderstood. I'm not here to talk about my marriage."

Oh dear. Janice folded her hands and rested them in her lap. "I see."

"I mean, you're right. Jarrod and I are going through a hard time right now, but Pastor Ben and Paige are helping us. Pastor Ben has taken Jarrod under his wing, and I can't even tell you how wonderful Paige has been to me."

Janice leaned slowly back until she rested against the chair's rear cushion. How embarrassing. And how arrogant of her to assume that this young woman was coming to her for counseling. Of course she would seek out her pastor's wife.

"I'm so glad." She forced the words out. "They are a lovely and wise couple."

Erin nodded her agreement. "That's kind of what I came to talk to you about. See, there are some rumors circulating among the young couples group at church."

Young couples group? Did they have a young couples group? Janice wasn't even aware of it.

Erin continued. "I guess some of the older people in the church are saying that Pastor Ben might have set that fire last week. But here's the thing. He didn't. I know he didn't because Jarrod and I were at their house when the fire was set."

Janice couldn't look away from the earnestness in the young woman's gaze. "Did you tell the police?" A nod. "Well, that should settle the matter. Pastor Ben has an alibi. You and your husband."

Relief washed through Janice, so strong that she was glad she was sitting or she may have wilted to the ground. Relief, tinged with guilt. Though she'd nearly talked herself out of it, she really had suspected Pastor Ben of setting the fire. She'd done him a great disservice.

"That's the thing." Erin stared down at her hands, which twisted in her lap. "We don't want anyone to know we're in counseling. It's a personal thing, and we'd prefer not to have it spread around the church or even our small group."

"If you've told the police, then that's all that's required."

But Erin shook her head. "All those old—" Her mouth snapped shut and she looked slightly embarrassed. "I mean, the elderly ladies in the church are still talking about it. I heard someone last night at our small group meeting say that Pastor Ben is being investigated as a possible arsonist." Her hands balled into fists. "He's not, Janice. That's why I'm here. I want you to put a stop to the gossip."

Janice jerked upright. "I detest gossip. If I did suspect Pastor Ben of setting that fire, I wouldn't mention it to anyone." Well, except to her closest friends, who wouldn't spread it any further.

The young woman looked horrified. "Please don't think I'm accusing you. I'm not. Really. I just thought you could use your influence with your friends at church."

Realization spread through Janice's mind like a thick puddle of slime. This young woman had come to her to stop the spread of gossip among the older women of the church. Erin assumed that Janice held a position of authority among the gossipers. Heat crept slowly up her neck and into her face until her cheeks flamed.

Erin leaned forward and extended a hand toward Janice. "I've offended you. I'm sorry. That wasn't my intention."

With an effort, Janice swallowed around a gigantic lump that had somehow lodged in her throat. "No, it's all right. I'm not offended." She managed what she hoped was a sincere smile. "In fact, I'm flattered that you trusted me with your confidence. I'm afraid you might have overestimated my influence, but I'll do whatever I can to stop the gossip."

Erin studied her for a moment before nodding. "Thank you." She bit her lower lip. "And you won't say anything about Jarrod and me being counseled, will you?"

"You have my word."

When she had seen Erin to the door, she stood beneath the inn's front awning and watched her car rumble down the brick-paved street. Pastor Ben's request when last they spoke returned to her. She had promised to pray for the church, and she had not done it. Now she had even more reason to pray.

How had she become known as part of the anti-Pastor Ben group? And not only part of it, but apparently considered influential among those who disapproved of their new pastor? She didn't! She'd grown to love the young couple and supported everything they were doing at Christ Fellowship. How could she make that clearer?

A dividing line had been drawn, a line between the old and the new. Between the former pastor and the current one. No wonder Pastor Ben had asked her to pray.

A disturbing idea fell into focus. What should her role at Christ Fellowship be? Should she back out of all activities? Become one of those Sunday-only churchgoers? The only alternative that came to mind was one she couldn't even think about—leaving the church completely.

Janice parked her car at the curb across the street from the church. She gazed at the building through tear-filled eyes. The many-peaked roof, the beautiful stone rotunda with the arched windows and stained glass. Leaning across the steering wheel, she looked upward to the five-story bell tower. From this angle, she could see no signs of smoke damage. How many years had she and Lawrence called this place home?

She nearly leaped out of her skin when someone rapped on the window beside her. Heart pounding, she looked up to find Paige standing beside the car.

"You scared me half to death," she said.

"Sorry." The young woman's voice sounded muffled.

Janice pressed the button to lower the window.

"I didn't mean to startle you. I just wanted to say hi." Though she was too polite to ask, questions lay heavy on Paige's face.

"I was sitting here admiring the building." Janice managed a trembling smile, but to her horror, tears once again blurred her vision.

"Oh, Mrs. Eastman." Paige reached through the open window to place a hand on Janice's shoulder. "What's wrong? What can I do to help?"

Sniffling, Janice pulled her purse onto her lap and rummaged inside for a tissue. "Nothing. I'm on my way to talk to your husband."

"Ben isn't there. He's out doing hospital visits." The young woman hesitated. "Will I do instead?"

Janice drew in a shuddering breath. She would much rather speak with Pastor Ben. On the other hand, perhaps the former pastor's wife should confide in the current pastor's wife.

"Do you have a few minutes to talk?"

"Sure. I was only taking a walk to get a little fresh air. Do you want to come back to the house with me?"

Back to the parsonage that was hers and Lawrence's home? Janice had not been inside since she moved out. In her current emotionally charged mood she wasn't sure she could handle stepping into that house.

She shook her head. "Maybe we could sit in the sanctuary."

When Paige agreed, Janice closed her window and locked the car. Together they mounted the old stone stairs. The doors were locked. Janice rummaged in her purse for her keys, but before she located them, Paige pulled her own set from her jacket pocket.

"I've got it."

Janice stood back while Paige unlocked the door. How fitting. And how symbolic. It was time for her to step back and let the next generation take up the work.

Once inside the beautiful sanctuary, Janice followed Paige down the center aisle to the front pew. They settled beside one another, and Paige awarded her a smile.

"Do you remember telling me I would get accustomed to sitting here by myself on Sunday mornings?"

Janice certainly did. She lowered her gaze briefly to Paige's thickening waist. "You won't have to sit here alone for long."

Paige covered her stomach with her hands, and her smile brightened like the sun coming out from behind a cloud. "I can hardly wait." Then she sobered. "Now please tell me what's happened to upset you. I want to help if I can."

Now that the time had come to say the words, Janice found herself struggling with them. All day she'd prayed as she worked, and though she had found no joy in her decision, she was determined to see it through.

"I have a question for you, and I want you to be completely honest with me." She drew in a deep breath. "Do you think I should leave Christ Fellowship and look for another church?"

The alarm that erupted on Paige's face could not be faked. "But...but...you can't. This is your home. What would we do without you?"

At the word *home*, tears once again stung Janice's eyes. "You would do just fine."

"No we wouldn't," Paige insisted. "You're one of the pillars in this church family. People look up to you. They respect you."

"That's the point, dear." Janice spoke in a gentle tone. "Without me hovering around, reminding people of the old ways of doing things, they'll be far more open to the changes you and Pastor Ben introduce. I haven't purposefully opposed anything you've done. In fact, I've openly supported most things." She gestured toward the projection screens on each side of the altar. "But recently I've been made aware that some people consider me..." She cast about for the right description. "As the leader of the opposition. Or something along that line."

The fact that Paige did not immediately deny the statement told Janice a lot. The young woman stared down at her hands for a long moment.

"That's not the only reason." Janice struggled to put words to the thoughts she'd battled most of the day. "For most of my life my ministry was right here." She lifted her head and looked around the beautiful sanctuary. At the cross hanging above the platform that she and the other women of the church had worked so hard to raise money to purchase. At the altar rail where she had knelt to pray for her church family. She glanced toward the small stand Pastor Ben used, which stood in the exact place of the pulpit, where Lawrence had preached countless sermons while she sat right here on this front pew and prayed silently for him. Then her gaze settled once again on the young woman beside her. "But God has given me a new ministry at Wayfarers Inn. How can I embrace that new ministry while I'm still holding on to the old one?"

Paige grew very still, and her eyelids fluttered shut. At first, Janice thought she might be fighting tears, until she realized her lips were moving. Paige was praying.

She lifted her head and looked into Janice's face. "I understand what you're saying. And I have to respect your desire to do the work God has given you to do at this point in your life." A struggle appeared on the lovely young features. "But God has given me a ministry too. Right here." She splayed her hands to indicate the church. "And to be honest, I don't feel equal to the task." Janice opened her mouth to disagree, but Paige held up a hand to stop her. "Maybe it's wrong of me, but I depend on you to help me. To be honest, I think of you as a sort of mentor."

"You know I'm happy to give you advice anytime you want."

"I do." Emotions played across Paige's face. "I have an idea. What if we made that mentor relationship official?"

Something stirred deep in Janice's chest. "Go on."

"What if we let it be known that you are officially mentoring me in my ministry as a pastor's wife? I think if people know that I'm relying on you for advice and direction, they'll view me differently. Maybe even with a little more respect for my position as Ben's wife." She rushed on, the words coming more rapidly. "But I don't mean this would be just for appearances. I would truly like you to become my mentor." She reached out and grabbed Janice's hands in both of hers. "Maybe we could meet for coffee once a week. We could pray together. And talk about..." She shrugged. "Stuff."

The idea bloomed behind Janice's breastbone like a daffodil opening its arms to the sun in springtime. What a beautiful solution. She would have given anything for a mentor when she was Paige's age. Experience and godly wisdom were invaluable to a young pastor's wife. And Janice could stay here, with her church family, while still serving.

Is this You, Lord? Is this Your idea?

Janice closed her eyes and reveled in the rightness of this solution.

Then she grinned at her young protégé. "I accept. I would love to meet with you every week to pray and talk about *stuff.*"

CHAPTER THIRTEEN

J anice's heart, as she left the church, was far lighter. She descended the stairs, her hand resting on the railing with a touch so light as to almost be a caress. She loved this church.

Thank You, Lord, for making a way for me to stay.

At the bottom of the steps, Paige hugged her. "Are you sure you wouldn't like to come back to the parsonage? I can put on coffee or tea or something."

Janice shook her head. "Thank you, but I should probably head home."

As the words left her mouth, she felt reluctant to follow through on them. Her eyes strayed up Schimmel Street, where at the top of the brick road lay the main entryway to Mound Cemetery. When the kids were little, they would sometimes take a picnic lunch to the top of the mound in the center of the gated graveyard. Some might find it odd to picnic in a cemetery, but Janice had always found the place peaceful.

"On the other hand, maybe I'll take a walk before I head back. I have some praying to do."

Paige bid her farewell and continued down the street toward Janice's old house.

Correction. Toward Ben and Paige's house. It's not mine anymore. And that's okay.

Janice went in the opposite direction, up the wide street to the end, where ornate steel gates guarded the entry to the historic cemetery. The main gates were kept closed to prevent vehicles from entering, but smaller gates on each side were open for foot traffic. Janice slipped inside and paused, as she always did, to close her eyes and let the peace of the place wash over her.

Ahead of her, a brick walkway carved a path through the center of the cemetery, where the prehistoric mound rose high above the surrounding grave markers. She bypassed the sign describing the historical significance of the mound. When the kids were little they'd stop to read it every time, about how mounds were constructed between 800 B.C. and 700 A.D. by the Hopewell Indians, and how soldiers of the American Revolution received land grants for military service that they used to secure this ancient burial place and transform it into a cemetery. Janice had long since memorized the epitaph. She climbed the steep stone stairway that led to the top of the mound. Stacy and Stuart used to race each other while Janice followed at a more sedate rate and prayed no one would fall. Today she made use of the handrail to half-pull herself up the thirty-foot incline.

The top of the mound had been flattened and concrete paving stones placed there decades ago. Benches had been installed on multiple sides, and Janice went to one of them, where she collapsed to catch her breath. A time capsule marker rested in the center of the mound with instructions to be opened on July 4, 2076. Janice had been in attendance for the burial of that capsule. She wouldn't be around for its opening. But her grandson would.

Her even breathing restored, Janice leaned against the back of the bench and closed her eyes. How many times had she climbed up here to think and to pray? It comforted her to know that this mound had been erected before Christ's birth. Awe-filled chills raced down her arms.

Her ears picked up a sound coming from below. She stood and walked to the edge of the paving stones, scanning the cemetery until she caught sight of the source of the noise. A man down below was walking among the gravestones, his feet kicking through the thick layer of brittle leaves that covered the grass.

Wait a minute. She blinked to refocus. Why, that was Lucas down there.

She cupped her hands around her mouth to shout to him. But then she changed her mind. One of the benefits of being thirty feet above ground level was solitude. Unless someone below lifted his or her gaze in this direction, a person could go completely unnoticed. She returned to her bench, from where she could see him wandering through the northwest section of the cemetery. That was the location of the oldest graves and included the final resting place of many black people who had settled in Marietta. Was he looking for Byron's ancestors? But no, Byron's ancestors had escaped to freedom.

She watched for nearly ten minutes as he methodically covered every inch of ground in that section of the cemetery. Janice and her friends had conducted similar searches many times when Prudence's journal made mention of a package that "expired."

Lucas stopped before an old grave marker. He knelt before it and stayed still for a long time, staring at the words engraved on the stone. Had he found the one he was looking for?

He stood abruptly, so quickly that he had to step back to keep his balance. Then he turned away from the marker and headed for the exit at something just short of a run.

How peculiar.

Janice waited until Lucas's car disappeared down Fifth Street, leaving her alone in the cemetery. Curiosity proved to be more than she could stand. She descended the uneven stone stairs and hurried across the leaf-strewn grass, her gaze fixed on the gravestone that had commanded Lucas's attention.

It was definitely one of the older ones but not necessarily the oldest in the cemetery. This stone marked the grave of someone named Lucian Tankard who'd been born in 1806 and died in 1857. That was it. No other details. An inspection of the surrounding stones revealed no other Tankards in the area. This man had not been buried with family. And he definitely wasn't a Wickham. So, what was Lucas's interest in this grave?

Janice slipped her cell phone out of her pocket and snapped a picture of the gravestone.

Back in her car, she turned left and executed a U-turn to go south on Fourth Street. As she did so, she carefully avoided a car parked at the curb. The rear window displayed one of those funny little pictures of a stick figure family—a father, a mother, two boys, and a dog. The boys were the same height, and Janice realized the car was parked in front of Kate Campbell's house. Pamela, the mother of twins, must be visiting her mother today. How nice.

When her front bumper cleared the car, she stepped on the gas. A thought flashed inside her brain like someone had just plugged in a neon sign. She slammed on her brakes. Twisting in the driver seat she looked over her shoulder at Christ Fellowship.

And a puzzle piece snapped into place.

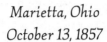

Marietta, Ohio
October 13, 1857

The bell above the front door of the Riverfront House jangled, heralding the entry of a pair of men. Prudence, whose duties for the day included transporting guests' luggage to their rooms, scurried from the laundry to the front room in time to see Mr. Bickerton emerge from the den. She hovered in a corner, waiting for an indication of which rooms these men would occupy.

"Greetings, friends." Bickerton's voice filled the room all the way up to the pressed tin ceiling two stories above. "A pair of weary travelers, I see."

Prudence kept her head bowed but risked a quick glance at the newcomers' garb. Travel clothing, their breeches creased from long hours in the saddle, and their coats wrinkled from excessive use since the last pressing.

The taller of the two stepped forward and swept his hat from his head. "You're an astute observer, sir." His accent held the twang of a not-quite-southern drawl. "We've spent the better part of this day in the saddle and only just ferried across the river from Virginia. Might you have rooms available for a few days?"

"A few days?" Bickerton strode across the room and took up a stance behind the ornately carved bar that he had commissioned and recently installed. "Then you plan to enjoy a stay in our fair town?"

"Perhaps *enjoy* is too strong a word," the man replied, his tone every bit as pleasant as Bickerton's. "We are seekers, here to follow up on information we've recently received concerning some missing property."

Prudence drew in a silent breath and held it until it burned in her lungs.

Mr. Bickerton's cheerful tone did not alter in the slightest. "Property? Pardon my assumption, but seeing that we are located at the convergence of two major rivers, one of course does encounter a common goal amongst one's guests. You seek a fugitive slave, then?"

"An astute observation. We've reason to believe a runaway Negro I purchased two years ago is seeking shelter in this town. Or soon will." The man removed his gloves, one finger at a time, and then slapped them against his thigh. "It is our intention to intercept his flight and return him to his lawful home."

Prudence stood as still as she could manage. Her knees threatened to buckle, and she flexed them barely an inch lest they cave under the pressure and dump her to the floor.

"I see." With a smooth movement, Mr. Bickerton opened the leather cover of the ledger where he always recorded the names of the guests who rented rooms at the Riverfront House. "Would you require one room or two?"

The newcomers exchanged a glance. Though Prudence kept her head down, she watched their movements from the corner of her eye.

"Two, most definitely." The gentleman reached for a wallet that hung at his side. "Though I will assume financial responsibility for both."

"Excellent." Mr. Bickerton uncorked an inkwell and dabbed a quill into it. "Under what names shall I register the rooms?"

The one who had remained silent thus far took a step toward the desk. "My name is Lucian Tankard."

At the sound of his gravelly voice, memories surged forward from the darkest of Prudence's nightmares. She clutched at the wall behind her to keep from sinking to the ground.

"It was him," Prudence told Jason while she clutched Ezra Junior to her chest. "The slave tracker who took my family. The one who grabbed me in the night and pulled me into the dark woods."

She stood in the doorway of their home, pleading with her husband as she held tightly to the child.

Jason leaned heavily on the makeshift crutch he had fashioned for himself. "Has thee lost thy mind?" He pointed at the little boy. "Think of him, Wife. Thee will be the death of us all."

Tears threatened to choke her. "What would thee have me do? The baby began to cry, and his voice filtered through the floor. They noticed, Jason. They heard."

Jason searched her face with a piercing stare. "And what did Mr. Bickerton say?"

Ezra Junior began to whimper, his frightened gaze fixed on Jason, who displayed his sternest countenance. Prudence hugged the boy close to her body. "He told the tale of a maid with a sick child, but I saw their doubt." She squeezed her eyes shut, willing her mind to banish the sight of those two faces. One cleanly shaven and wearing a polite smile. The second rough, scowling, and oh so familiar. Lucian Tankard, the very slave tracker who had captured her family and forced her into slavery. Though age had ravaged his features, Prudence would never forget that foul countenance. "I could not leave him, Jason. They would have searched and discovered the rooms. Discovered Becca. I had no choice." With her eyes, she begged him to forgive her.

Jason held her gaze for a long moment, during which the baby's whimpers increased in volume and he struggled in her arms.

"He's hungry," she whispered.

At that moment, she saw acceptance dawn in her husband's eyes. Acceptance…and forgiveness.

"Then we must feed him," Jason said in his gentlest voice.

Prudence released the breath that had been trapped in her lungs.

CHAPTER FOURTEEN

Janice barged through the door of Harry's Antique and Salvage Mall. Kenny turned a surprised look her way.

"Where's Harry?" she asked.

The kid pointed toward the back room and opened his mouth to say something, but Janice didn't wait to hear. Instead, she zigzagged her way through the crowded front room. When she did not immediately spy Harry, she marched to the rear office and barged in.

Seated behind a battered metal desk, Harry looked up from his paperwork, his sparse gray eyebrows arched high on his forehead. "Janice, is something wrong?"

"Why didn't you tell me?"

"Tell you what?"

She could hardly keep the grin off her face. "That you and Kate Campbell are seeing each other."

He reared back in the desk chair as though slapped, his face instantly devoid of color. "How did you…" His lips snapped shut. He left his chair and pulled the office door closed and then pointed at the only other seat in the cramped room, a scarred and not-too-sturdy-looking wooden chair. Janice sat.

Instead of returning to his seat, Harry leaned against the corner of the desk and watched her, alarm plain on his face. "What makes you think Kate and I are stepping out together?"

Her grin deepened at the old-fashioned term. "When I saw you two together the other day, it was obvious to anyone with eyes that you're attracted to her." True, Janice had not consciously noticed the attraction at the time, but in retrospect it was crystal clear. "You were obviously uncomfortable when I walked into the room. And it seemed both of you were waiting for me to leave. But mostly it was your cologne."

Those expressive eyebrows crashed together. "My cologne?"

She giggled. "Next time don't bathe in it. Just use a splash. Less is more, as they say." She became serious. "But honestly, it didn't occur to me until just a little while ago when I drove by Kate's house. I realized that is the perfect vantage point from which to see someone running down the alley beside Christ Fellowship."

His head dropped forward until his chin rested against his chest. "Ain't nobody supposed to know, and now the whole town's gonna find out."

Janice tried not to feel offended. "You can trust me to keep your secret. If you ask me not to tell anyone, I won't." She nibbled on her lower lip a second. "Except LuAnn and Tess, I mean."

He stabbed a finger in her direction. "See? In a couple of days there'll probably be an article in the paper."

"Of course there won't. No one will find out from us, you have my word." Then she tilted her head and watched him. "But why in the world would you keep it secret? Kate is a widow. You aren't married. There's nothing wrong with the two of you enjoying each other's company."

"On account of her kids." Now he looked glum, his shoulders drooping. "Kate's afraid they'll pitch a fit."

Now the reason made sense. From what Kate said the other day, her girls, and especially Pamela, had taken an almost parental role over her life.

"Would that be a bad thing?"

"That's what I said." He shrugged. "Kate isn't ready to put up with the hassle. I ain't gonna push her until she is."

Though that wasn't the way Janice would have handled the situation, the decision was not hers to make. "So, you were at Kate's house the night of the fire and that's why you were able to see the man running away."

"We'd gone over to Parkersburg to get a bite to eat and see a movie."

Janice started to ask why they'd driven all the way to West Virginia for dinner, but then she realized. They'd been hiding from Kate's daughters.

"I walked her up to the front door." His face flushed red, and Janice hid a grin. Apparently, they'd enjoyed a good-night kiss. He cleared his throat. "I was coming back to my car and that's when I saw him. And then I saw the fire." He looked her straight in the eye. "And that's why my cell phone was locked in my car. I just punched the lock button like I always do."

Janice lowered her gaze to avoid the accusation in his. "I'm sorry. I didn't mean to imply..." Actually, she *had* meant to imply that he'd either started the fire or had some other unsavory reason for being in the area. "I'm sorry," she repeated.

"That's okay. To be honest, it's kind of a relief that somebody knows about me and Kate. Maybe now she'll get the courage to tell those girls of hers."

Janice gathered her purse and stood. "Tell Kate any time she wants to talk, I'm available. Sometimes all a girl needs is a friendly ear to get the words flowing."

The sun was well on its way toward setting behind the western horizon when Janice returned to Wayfarers Inn. She found her friends in the kitchen. Tonight was Tess's turn to cook dinner, and as Janice entered the room, she slid a tray of chicken into one of Big Red's ovens.

"You two are not going to believe this," Janice blurted. Then she stopped. That sounded an awful lot like gossip. *Sorry, Lord.*

Her friends looked at her. "Well?"

She took a breath, letting the words form in her mind before she spit them out. "I have proof that Harry did not set the fire." There. She'd presented the information in a positive, ungossipy manner.

Seated at the table with a pile of mail before her, LuAnn sliced open an envelope. "I thought you'd gotten over your suspicions of Harry."

"I did, but now I have proof. And I know why his cell phone was locked inside his car. He wasn't really out for a drive like he told us."

"Then where was he?"

"He was on a date with Kate Campbell."

LuAnn and Tess both stopped what they were doing to gape at her. Janice tried not to enjoy delivering the news too much, but the more she thought about it, the more a relationship between Kate and Harry tickled her.

When she'd explained all the information she had gotten from Harry, she told them about her visit to Mound Cemetery and seeing Lucas there.

Tess took the dish in which the chicken had been marinating to the sink. "Maybe while he was researching the Wickhams he ran across somebody else's name." She shrugged. "He was probably following up on that."

LuAnn tapped her mouth with the letter opener, her gaze distant. "Or maybe he was following up on something he found in the journal."

Since she had not yet taken her copy back upstairs, she retrieved it from the office. The girls huddled around the table while she turned pages.

"The entry about Byron's great-great-great-grandmother's arrival was in October 1857." LuAnn flipped to that page. "Right there."

She turned the page. The next entry was more than a week later, from October 13th.

My nightmare has returned. He checked into the hotel this afternoon, just before the evening meal. Thank the Lord I saw him first and hid in the kitchen. He is older, but the face is one I will never forget no matter how age changes it. He may not recognize me, since I am now grown. But I will take no chances. Nor will I risk the precious package below. Jason will be unhappy, but he is a good man. He will see the necessity.

"Her nightmare is a man?" Janice looked up from the familiar script.

Tess brushed her finger across the page. "Apparently some-one from her past returned, someone she hoped would not recognize her."

"Might it have been the slave tracker who caught her and her parents and took them into slavery?"

The story was a heartbreaking one that they had discov-ered by piecing together snatches of tales told by Brad's aunts, who were descendants of the original owners of the Riverfront House, along with facts extracted from hours of research. Pru-dence had been born Melungeon, one of a common blend of races in this area of Ohio. Her parents were escaped slaves who settled in Marietta. Though Prudence had been born free, when a slave tracker captured and returned her parents to their plantation owner, he took little Prudence as well. Only the Lord knew what horrors the poor child had been through before she finally escaped and returned to Ohio. She was adopted by a Quaker couple, who passed her off as white. She never saw her parents again.

Janice had read the journal many times, and though Prudence made occasional references to the time of her enslavement, which she referred to as her nightmare, Janice had never seen a mention of the slave tracker's name.

LuAnn turned the page, and they read the next entry.

October 19, 1857

Tending for our young guest has been pure pleasure. Even Jason loves him like a son. And how could he not, since the little one follows him around the farm like a puppy? My heart will break when we say goodbye, but that day is upon us. The reunion takes place tonight, and by tomorrow this special package will be on its way, the good Lord willing.

"She must have taken the little one home with her to keep him safe," Tess said.

"*The reunion takes place tonight,*" LuAnn read in a thoughtful voice. "Do you remember what Byron told us? That according to family legend, William Still arranged for his great-great-great-grandparents to escape separately and then meet on the road to continue their journey."

Janice drew in a quick breath. "The reunion."

"It could be," LuAnn said. "I wonder if Prudence's 'nightmare' was still in Marietta at that point."

Tess rested a hand on her collarbone. "How terrifying for them all."

Janice pointed at the journal. "What happened next?"

LuAnn turned the page to reveal a brief and totally unsatisfying entry from the next day.

Shipment transferred. The nightmare is over.

Janice dropped into a chair. "Really? That's all we get?"

LuAnn paged through the next several entries. "I'm afraid so."

Tess continued to stare at the page. "I wonder what she means by 'the nightmare is over.' If she is referring to the man who enslaved her, did he leave and go back where he came from?"

"Or did he die?" LuAnn asked.

Janice stiffened. If someone had died in Marietta, they would have been buried here. Back in those days bodies weren't shipped home as they were today. She jumped up and ran around the table to her purse, which she had hung on the doorknob when she came in.

"Is something wrong?" Tess asked.

"I have a hunch." Janice fished out her cell phone and pulled up the picture she'd taken at the cemetery. "We need a computer."

They trooped into the office, where LuAnn fired up the computer they used for registrations and accounting. Janice tapped her foot while waiting for the monitor to come to life. When it did, she snatched the mouse and brought up an internet browser.

"What are you looking for?" LuAnn asked.

"This."

She set her cell phone beside the keyboard and typed "Lucian Tankard 1857" in the search bar. Several entries were displayed on the screen. At the top was an article labeled African-American History. She clicked on it and scanned the screen while LuAnn and Tess gathered close on each side so they could read as well.

In October 1857, a 22-year-old slave known as Ezra escaped from his owner, Stephen G. Bolling, and made his way from Bolling's Mason County, Kentucky, plantation to Marietta, Ohio. Marietta was known as a station along the Underground Railroad as well as a center of abolitionist support. Bolling hired renowned slave tracker Lucian Tankard to track Ezra and return the slave to Kentucky. Tankard suffered an accident and perished before accomplishing the task for which he had been hired.

Janice pointed at the screen. "That's it. Tankard was the slave tracker who was sent to capture Byron's great-great-great-grandfather. But he died."

"That's not all he was," LuAnn said. "Tankard was Prudence's nightmare. The one who captured her and her parents."

Tess clapped her hands. "Well done, girls. We've solved the mystery. Of course, Lucas solved it first because he's been researching Byron's family. He must have read the journal and put two and two together just like we did."

Something else stirred in Janice's memory. Something she'd seen lately. She squeezed her eyes shut trying to pinpoint a stray piece of information she'd—

"That's it!" She left her astonished friends with their jaws dangling as she dashed up the stairs to her apartment. By the time she got to the fourth floor her breath came in painful heaves, but she ignored that and ran into her apartment. Taking William Still's Bible from her nightstand, she flipped pages until she came to the verse she wanted. Triumphant, she returned downstairs.

"I was right." She entered the office holding the Bible in front of her. "Take a look at this." She set the book on the desk and pointed at Romans 6:23.

LuAnn read the verse aloud. "'For the wages of sin is death; but the gift of God is eternal life through Jesus Christ our Lord.'"

"Look at the note in the margin." Janice tapped the cryptic notation. "'10/20/1857 L.T.'"

Tess gasped. "Lucian Tankard."

"The date matches the journal," Janice said. "The verse is about death, and we just read that he met an untimely end in Marietta. I think William Still was present when Tankard died."

"It's possible," LuAnn admitted. "Especially since Lucas's research uncovered the fact that William Still was in Marietta at the same time as Byron's ancestors."

"That Lucas is a pretty good researcher to have dug up Tankard's grave." Tess's lips twitched. "So to speak."

"You know what this means." LuAnn turned a serious stare on Janice. "You have to give them this Bible."

Normally Janice considered herself an easygoing person, but on occasion she had been known to display a stubborn streak. She did so now.

"Not yet." Janice snatched up the Bible. "Not until Byron comes clean with Marla."

She half-expected her friends to argue, but neither voiced an objection. Janice returned to her apartment—this time by way of the elevator—and tucked the Bible back into the safety of her nightstand drawer.

When she returned downstairs, she found the office door closed and the kitchen empty. Tess's voice sounded in the distance, and she traced it down the stairs to the basement.

"What are you two doing down here?" She peered closely around the floor before she stepped off the bottom step. No mice in evidence.

"Folding." LuAnn smoothed the wrinkles out of a hand towel on the laundry table. "Come help us so we can get the laundry finished before dinner."

Janice picked up the corners of a bed sheet, which Tess held at the other end. They'd developed a technique in the months since the inn opened, and between the three of them, they quickly folded all the clean linens. Janice picked up a neat stack of top sheets and carried it to the cabinet they used as a linen closet. Tess set the fitted sheets beside them, and they returned to the table for the rest.

LuAnn set the folded white bath towels in the cabinet. Then she ran a finger down the edge of the stack, a puzzled expression on her face.

"What's wrong?" Janice asked.

She looked up, clearly disturbed. "I thought the towel stack looked short, so I counted. We have a towel missing."

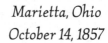

Marietta, Ohio
October 14, 1857

"Patience, thee must learn manners. Ezra is our guest." Prudence could not stop a giggle from invading her scold, thereby lessening the impact.

Ezra Junior raced across the grass on chubby legs after the goose, his giggles floating high into the crisp autumn air. The indignant goose squawked her displeasure as she ran ahead of him while maintaining a safe distance from her pursuer. Either the plantation on which he had been born included geese, or this little one displayed unusual courage for a child not yet two years of age. When Patience extended her slender neck, her head topped his by several inches, but Ezra found her much more fascinating than the chickens. Probably because the hens scattered at the first sight of him, while Patience hovered anxiously, a careful eye fixed on her owner.

Jason sat on the porch with his leg propped on a stool, watching the antics with the occasional chuckle of his own. Prudence's heart warmed to see him enjoying their guest, as she had known he would.

A bright orange leaf blew across the grass, distracting the child. He stopped his pursuit of the goose and turned instead to follow the tumbling leaf. Momentarily forgotten,

Patience hurried to Prudence's side, honking her displeasure at being subjected to such an undignified chase. Ezra caught up with the leaf, and Prudence watched with an indulgent smile as he picked it up and held it in one chubby hand for a close inspection. Such an inquisitive little boy. No wonder he cried in the close confines of the hidden rooms beneath the Riverfront House, where his mother now remained in hiding alone.

If Prudence could have brought Becca here with her child, she would have. But Jason would no doubt have insisted that they return. And rightly so. If pressed, they could pass this child off as a nephew or cousin. Though his skin was as brown as a chestnut and Prudence's light enough to pass for a white woman if necessary, skin color varied greatly among Melungeon families. Ezra could easily be the child of Prudence's sister.

But not so Becca, not with the scar that branded her as a fugitive slave.

"No, no!" Prudence raced for the child as he shoved the leaf in his mouth. She knelt before him and removed the slimy object. "Thee must not eat the leaves. Only look at them."

"No, no," Ezra repeated, watching her with solemn round eyes.

Her heart warmed at the sound of his childish voice. They were the first words she had heard him speak. She snatched him up into her arms for a hug and then settled him on her hip. How natural it felt, to carry a child thusly.

As she turned to return to the house, her gaze snagged on something in the gnarled oak tree. A scrap of fabric tied to a spindly branch. Her heart thudded.

"I will go," Jason said in a low voice, his gaze fixed on the smoldering remains of the note in the fireplace.

Prudence held her tongue. They both knew he could not attend the requested meeting in her place. Though the identities of the conductors were closely guarded, her coworkers in the Cause knew that the contact for the Riverfront House was a woman. And they certainly couldn't both go and take little Ezra. Someone must stay here with him.

On the woven rug at their feet, Ezra Junior played with the wooden toys Jason had carved for him. He kept up a stream of quiet but contented baby babble.

Jason lifted his gaze to hers, and she read the knowledge in them. He knew the truth as well.

"It will be a short errand," she said. "A few hours at most. I will be fine."

"But in town where anyone might see thee."

"Anyone might see me when I do the shopping. Or when I am at work at the hotel." She spoke in a soft voice and carefully filtered any trace of fear from her tone.

"That is different, which thee knows well. Thee is expected in those places."

His words sent a chill racing through her veins. It was true she rarely had reason to shop at the dry goods store in town. Why had the meeting been set up in broad daylight in such a public place? But she could not question the conductor who had left the note. She could only attend the meeting or fail to appear at the appointed time.

"Thee knows I must go. As the note suggested, I will shop for a new milk bucket, since ours has begun to leak."

His chest heaved as he grunted in acknowledgment of the made-up errand. "And what of him?"

She knew what he was asking. What if she failed to return? What would Jason do with the child of a runaway slave?

Her gaze rested on the boy, and she deliberately misinterpreted the question. "Thee two will be fine here for the length of such a short errand. And besides, thee has Patience to help." She glanced toward the corner, where the goose sat in her straw-filled bed with a wary eye fixed on their young visitor.

Jason chuckled, and Prudence stood to retrieve her cloak and bonnet.

Sullivan's Dry Goods lay a block inland from the Ohio River amid a growing number of stores on Front Street. Her pace quick from nerves, Prudence arrived early. She sauntered down the street, peering into shop windows and attempting to look as though she were intent on no particular errand, while keeping a sharp eye toward Sullivan's. People came and went, both men and women, more white than black. Though Ohio was a free state, its proximity to Virginia tended to make even free black people nervous. She recognized most of those she encountered, and exchanged a quiet greeting or even a few casual words with some.

At exactly the appointed time, a well-dressed pair of strangers exited the front door of the Mansion House, a hotel situated on the corner where Front Street ended at the river. The two men, both black, turned left and sauntered down Front Street, the taller of the two talking as they walked. They both wore loose frock coats with wide lapels, white dress shirts, and fancy waistcoats. A heavily starched cravat had been tied high beneath the shorter man's chin.

Prudence paused in front of the milliner's shop and pretended to inspect a bonnet in the window display. Without seeming to do so, she traced the strangers' path down the street and into the dry goods store.

This must be her meeting.

Her mouth dry, she gathered her skirts and crossed the dusty street. She paused only a moment to glance in Sullivan's front window before entering the store.

The clerk behind the counter glanced up and nodded a greeting. A quick scan around the store's interior revealed a few shoppers. The two men who had just arrived had made their way to the back corner. Following the instructions in the note, she strode boldly to the counter.

"How may I assist you?" the clerk asked.

"Does thee have a milk pail?" She spoke in a voice loud enough to be overheard by anyone in the store. "Mine loses half the milk between the barn and the house."

He came out from behind the counter and led her toward the rear of the store, where he pointed out a display of pails in varying sizes. She now stood within a few feet of the two well-dressed strangers.

After she had allowed the clerk to assist her in her selection, she thanked him and hooked the handle of the pail in the crook of her arm as she would her gathering basket. When she turned to inspect a row of scrub brushes, the clerk returned to the front counter, leaving her and the strangers alone in that section of the store.

"Pardon my intrusion, madame."

Prudence's heart rose into her throat as she faced the tall man with a polite expression. She looked up into liquid dark eyes. He wore his hair short and parted on one side in the modern style she had seen adopted by many of the guests at the Riverfront House. "Yes?"

"My business associate and I are traveling through town on our way home to Pennsylvania. I intend to take a gift of fabric to my wife, but I find myself uncertain of the best choice." He gestured toward the back wall, which held dozens of bolts of fabric in a rainbow of hues. "May I impose upon you long enough to give your opinion?"

From the corner of her eye, Prudence saw a woman shopping near the front of the store glance their way.

"I am happy to assist thee," she replied.

One eyebrow arched at her use of the Quaker term, but he made no comment. Carrying her milk bucket, she strode to the back wall and stood beside him to inspect the display.

"My apologies for the unusual request." Now he spoke in a voice low enough that only she and his silent companion could hear. "We planned for a smooth convergence of shipments, but complications have arisen. We received news that a patter roller has arrived in town."

The code made Prudence wince. A patter roller was a slave tracker. So this man knew of Tankard's arrival.

She fingered a green gingham print. "Thee is correct."

"Am I correct in understanding that the dry goods are no longer being stored at the station?"

News did carry along the railroad, but in this instance, the message was incorrect. "The dry goods are safe and sound at the station." The effort of maintaining a pleasant tone was starting to wear. She rubbed a tight knot in the back of her neck. "But the small package that arrived at the same time had to be moved."

The second man jumped as though stung. "My boy? Somethin' gone and happened to my boy?"

His frantic whisper sent an answering chill zipping down Prudence's spine. This man's speech bore no resemblance to the polished eloquence of his companion. Prudence risked a glance into his face for the first time, and recognized the features instantly. The wide nose. The slightly protruding ears. He stared back at her with Ezra Junior's eyes.

The taller man placed a restraining hand on Ezra's arm, and the fugitive slave's throat convulsed as he gulped and cast a panicked glance around the store.

"The package is safe." She deepened her smile as she tested the strength of a bolt of linen. "And exceedingly pleasant."

Ezra's chest deflated as he blew out a pent-up breath.

The other man pulled the bolt of linen from the rack and ran a hand down the length. "The train schedule has been changed. It leaves the station tonight."

Tonight? With Tankard prowling around the Riverfront House?

Prudence shook her head and took the bolt of cloth from his hands. She returned it to the stand and instead picked up the green-and-white-checked gingham. "This one is a much safer choice for thee."

When she handed it to him, she tapped four fingers on the surface and poured meaning into the gaze she fixed on his face. Four days would hopefully be long enough for Tankard and Mr. Bolling to satisfy themselves that Ezra was not in Marietta.

Unless this man, obviously a conductor himself, insisted on parading him openly around town.

"But thee must keep it well wrapped up as thee travels, lest the colors are damaged from exposure." She flicked her eyes toward Ezra and then back at the conductor's face.

A sad smile curved the generous mouth. He glanced around the store while pulling a sheet of folded paper from his waistcoat pocket. Holding it at waist level, he unfolded it for her to read. "I fear this change of schedule cannot be avoided."

Prudence read the paper at a glance.

$200 REWARD

Ran away from the subscriber, living in Mason County in the state of Kentucky, a male Negro slave named Ezra. A strong man about 22 years of age, very dark colored, back covered in whip scars. Heard to be traveling toward Ohio. I will pay $200 if delivered to me in residence in Mason Co. Kentucky at the mouth of Bull Creek. $100 if I travel to pick him up.

S. BOLLING

Prudence had seen many such reward notices, and they all sickened her. She couldn't help glancing toward Ezra's fine white shirt and waistcoat that hid the scars he had received from a whip. More easily hidden than his wife's scar, but she knew they had been inflicted with much cruel torment.

The conductor refolded the notice and secreted it in his pocket. "Can the package and the dry goods be ready on schedule?"

She would have to take Ezra Junior back to the hotel. Though the risk of discovery was great, especially with the object of her nightmares prowling the building above their very heads, she could not risk holding the reunion at her house. About that, Jason was right.

Swallowing hard, she nodded. Then she pressed the bolt of gingham into his hands and spoke in a calm tone that amazed even her. "But heed my words, and keep the fabric wrapped. Else, I fear thee will not be happy with the results."

CHAPTER FIFTEEN

B efore we jump to conclusions let's all count the towels." Tess headed toward the cabinet, Janice on her heels, where they took turns counting.

"I come up with one missing," Janice said when she had finished.

"That's what I got too." Tess looked at LuAnn, who nodded.

"Now we *have* to call the police." Janice folded her arms across her chest and faced her friends. "The arsonist is one of our guests. We have proof. And my money's on Byron, based on the fact that we know he's dishonest."

Tess appeared ready to be convinced, but not LuAnn.

"We haven't proven anything."

Janice stared her down. "He had access to the tunnel, access to the ladder, and access to our towels. Harry saw a black man running away from the church. And we know Byron is a liar. What more proof do you need?"

"There was no towel missing from his room," LuAnn reminded her. "Or any of our guest rooms."

Tess waved a hand at the linen cabinet. "I think it's pretty obvious that he took the towel from here. Then he went out through the tunnel and unlocked the padlock with the key we have hanging there. And when he came back he left footprints in the mud, and instead of going up the stairs where he might have been seen, he climbed the ladder."

"Then why would he go into Lily and Lace?" Tess asked. "The ladder goes up to his room."

Janice thought quickly. "He lost count of the floors? He was probably frantic after having run away from the fire."

"Unlikely. And don't forget those footprints we saw were small." LuAnn cast an apologetic glance toward Janice. "I still believe the prints were Larry's."

A frown creased Tess's forehead. "Or they could have been Pauline's. I thought they looked too big for a child but not big enough for a man. She's tall enough that Harry might have mistaken her."

"You can't possibly think Pauline set that fire in our church," Janice argued. "First off, she's a woman, unlike the man seen running from the church. And second, why would she? What possible reason could she have?"

"I'm not suggesting that at all." LuAnn backed up and leaned against one of the washing machines. "There's no reason to believe the person whose footprints were outside the tunnel is the same person who set the fire."

"Except a missing towel," Tess pointed out. "The chief found a towel like ours covered in soot from the fire."

Everything was so confusing. Janice grabbed a handful of her hair and tugged, trying to force her brain to make sense of all these disjointed facts. The Bible. The footprint. The towel. The soot.

She jerked her head up. "What if the soot wasn't from the church?"

"Of course it was—" Tess began.

Janice didn't wait for her to finish. She practically ran to the center of the basement, where the ancient wood-burning furnace used to stand. She'd noticed the pile of ash earlier, remnants of the last fire burned before the furnace was moved. Now she pored over every inch. Then she turned a triumphant grin on her friends, who had followed her. "Voilà."

Tess and LuAnn joined her. An indentation in the ash pile might have been a handprint. "What if whoever took our towel also helped himself to ashes before he left?"

"You mean to darken his skin?" Tess's eyes grew round. "Byron wouldn't have to darken his skin."

Janice could hardly believe she was about to say this. "Lucas would."

LuAnn shook her head. "But why? To try to pass himself off as a black man in case he was spotted?"

Tess stuck a finger in the ashes. When she pulled her hand back, her fingertip was almost black. "Or to pass himself off as Byron."

LuAnn repeated her question. "But why? I've never been convinced that Byron would break into the church in order to search for Marla's papers. Or to delay the wedding, either. It makes even less sense for Lucas to do it for either of those reasons."

"Lucas is extremely interested in Byron's family history." But even as the words left Janice's lips, she had a hard time believing

Lucas capable of culpability to that extent. When they discussed his friendship with Byron, he had been sincere in his admiration for Marla's fiancé. Janice would've spotted insincerity.

"If we call the police now, all of this will come out." LuAnn looked from Tess to Janice and held her gaze. "We'll have to lay it all out to the chief, and then he will question Byron and Lucas and Marla and Pauline. Are we prepared to put our guests and our friend through that, based on footprints that are no longer visible and a bunch of old ashes?"

"Don't forget Byron's lie about his job," Tess added.

LuAnn conceded the point with a nod. "There is that. No doubt the chief will be very interested in getting to the bottom of this whole thing."

An understatement, to be sure. Everything they had dug up might be circumstantial, but Chief Mayfield would pounce on it like a cat on a mouse. And what happened to a mouse when a cat got it? Janice shuddered. She had no fondness for mice but wouldn't wish a violent end on one.

"Maybe we should talk to Marla first," she suggested. "Before we call the police, and I do think we should, we owe it to our friend to prepare her. But hopefully tomorrow we can arrange a private conversation with Marla when Byron isn't around."

"That's a good plan," Tess said. "Be sure to pray for the right words to use."

"Definitely," LuAnn agreed.

Janice's jaw went slack. "Me? You know how I hate confrontations. Either of you would do a better job than me."

LuAnn's expression softened. "You're the most gentle-hearted of the three of us, dear. And you have the most experience handling brokenhearted women from your years as a pastor's wife."

"Besides," Tess added, "Marla didn't ask either of us to plan her wedding. She asked you."

With a sinking feeling, Janice realized they were right. "But you'll both be there, right? For moral support?"

"Of course we will," LuAnn assured her. "For Marla, and for you."

At least she wouldn't have to do it alone. And if she did anything stupid, like burst into tears or faint or anything, one of her friends would take over.

Janice heaved a sigh and nodded.

They were finishing up the supper dishes when the bell on the front door sounded.

Janice folded the damp dish towel and hung it on the hook where they kept it. "I'll see who it is."

In the front room, she found Pauline shutting the door behind her. Janice couldn't stop herself. She glanced down at the woman's shoes. Sensible black pumps, and very small for someone so tall. A print left by shoes this size could easily be mistaken for a child's, especially in dim lighting.

She smiled a cheerful greeting. "Welcome back."

Then she caught sight of Pauline's face, and compassion squeezed her heart. Recent tears had left streaks on her cheeks, and the skin beneath her eyes was puffy and red. Her nose looked raw, as though it had recently been blown a dozen times using rough tissues. "My dear, what is wrong?"

Pauline's jaw trembled, and then her features scrunched as a new wave of tears arrived.

Janice hurried forward to put a comforting arm around the sobbing woman, and guided her, unresisting, to the parlor. Pauline perched on the edge of a chair, her purse resting on her lap. She clutched the strap with both hands while tears flowed freely down her face.

Janice retrieved a box of tissues from a table and set them within reach. Then she settled in the closest chair and waited for the storm to pass.

Three tissues later, the sobs receded into shuddering breaths.

"I hate losing control like this." Pauline plucked a fresh tissue from the box and held it first to one eye and then the other, sniffling. "I'm sorry."

"Don't be," Janice told her. "My late husband pastored a large church, so I'm quite comfortable with emotional women."

The comment produced a silent laugh. "I'm sure you are. But I'm not accustomed to being one of them." She smoothed the tissue out on her knee with an absent gesture. "Your late husband, you said?"

Janice nodded. "Lawrence passed away about two years ago." Grief filled her, but she pushed it aside. Time enough for that later, when she was alone.

Pauline's mouth trembled. "My Mark has only been gone three months."

Janice shut her eyes for a moment of shared sympathy. No wonder the woman always looked sad. "I'm so sorry."

Pauline continued to smooth the tissue. "It was unexpected. A heart attack. He never had any symptoms. One day he was there, and the next—"

She might have been talking about Lawrence. "I know exactly what you're going through. I had no warning either." Those early months after the funeral were like raw wounds in Janice's memory. How lost she had felt. How bereft. If it had not been for Stacy and Stuart, and for little Larry, she didn't know how she would have made it. "Do you have children?"

Pauline shook her head. "We were never able to."

So now, she was alone. Tears prickled behind Janice's eyes as she realized the reason for Pauline's stay at the inn. "Is this your first trip without your husband?"

More tears rolled down her cheeks as she nodded. "I couldn't stay home. Everywhere I look, Mark is there."

For the first time, Janice realized how fortunate she'd been. Because they lived in a church-owned parsonage, she had not been forced to deal with living there without Lawrence. Oh, Christ Fellowship had given her plenty of time to find a new place. But she'd moved from the parsonage into the apartment above Stacy's garage as soon as she could. There she wasn't surrounded by as many constant reminders.

"You came here because you and Mark have never been here."

Pauline nodded. "I figured if I could go somewhere brand-new, I could explore places by myself and maybe make some new memories." The tears came faster, and her voice rose to a squeak in an effort to hold back sobs. "But Mark is still here with me." She put her hand to her head and then to her heart. "Everywhere I go."

Explore? The word triggered a thought. "And have you? Explored, I mean." Janice kept her tone soft. "Around the inn, and maybe...inside it?"

Guilt flashed onto Pauline's face. "I found the key to the door at the end of the tunnel. It was kind of exciting, to be honest. But I promise I locked it every time I used it."

"And the ladder too?"

She nodded. "I know I shouldn't have gone into that room up on the second floor. But there were people down here and I didn't want to see anyone. I just wanted to be alone. So, I climbed up the ladder instead of taking the stairs." She bit her lower lip. "I'm sorry. I didn't disturb anything, and I did lock the door behind me."

Janice leaned slowly against the seat back. Several mysteries solved. The small footprints. The unlatched trap door. And the flippy-thingy.

"You didn't happen to borrow one of the towels from the linen closet downstairs, did you?"

219

Surprise dawned on the woman's face. "No. Is one missing?"

Janice studied her face for any sign that she might not be telling the truth but found none. "Oh, it will turn up." She brushed the topic aside. At the moment, the grieving woman before her needed comfort. "What made you choose Marietta?"

Pauline looked down at her hands. "You'll think I'm silly."

"I won't. I promise," Janice said. "Besides, no one could be sillier than me."

"Well." She twisted the Kleenex. "I was searching the internet for bed-and-breakfasts, and when I came across your website about the inn and the soup café, I knew this was the place." Her shoulders heaved with a silent laugh. "My mom's name was Mary, and Mark's mother was Etta, and they used to compete to see who could serve us the best soup."

A sense of *rightness* stole over Janice. This woman's presence here was no accident.

"Do you believe in God, Pauline?"

"I used to. But lately I have so many questions. Where was God while Mark was dying? Couldn't He have given us some kind of warning?" Her eyes squeezed shut and the anguish returned to her voice. "Doesn't He know how lonely I am?"

"Of course He does." Janice leaned forward and reached for her hand. "I asked the same questions when I lost Lawrence. I don't think there are any easy answers, but one thing I do know for sure. Our Savior understands sorrow. He's even called the Man of Sorrows. And because He loves us, He wants to heal our hurts and give us peace."

Red-rimmed eyes bored into hers. "I wish I could believe that."

Janice squeezed her hand. "You can. It won't be easy, and it may not happen quickly, but if you let Him, God can heal you and give you a joy you can't imagine at this moment."

"Has He done that for you?"

A smile spread Janice's lips wide. "Yes, He has. And I don't believe you coming here was an accident. I think God sent you so you could see what He's done in my life and know He wants to do the same for you. Would it be all right if I pray for you?"

Pauline swallowed several times before nodding and bowing her head.

As Janice prayed aloud, a sense of renewed purpose settled over her. This was the ministry to which she and her friends had been called. She could hardly wait to tell them that God had sent a hurting soul to find comfort at Wayfarers Inn.

Janice awoke Thursday morning with one thought in the forefront of her mind. Today they would tell Marla what they'd discovered about Byron and Lucas. Whether either of them, or maybe both of them, were responsible for the fire in the church was almost beside the point. Marla deserved to know the truth about the man she was supposed to marry in two days.

The idea of what was sure to be an emotional conversation left her feeling queasy. She slipped out of bed and fell to her knees.

God, You are the Lord of truth. Please let the truth come out today.

A half hour later, she followed the scent of cinnamon down the stairs and entered the kitchen to find LuAnn and Tess already seated at the table. Winnie pulled a muffin tin from Big Red and set it on a cooling rack on the counter.

"Good morning," LuAnn greeted Janice. "I hope you had a better night than I did."

Refreshed from her morning prayers, Janice smiled as she poured coffee into a mug. "I can't say for sure. I slept right through it."

Tess gave her a droll look over the rim of her mug. "At least one of us got a good night's sleep. It's going to be a busy day."

The reminder sobered Janice. "I suppose it is." She glanced toward Winnie, who was humming to herself as she tested the top of a muffin with an expert finger. "I don't look forward to our conversation with Marla."

"You don't know the half of it." LuAnn slid a paper across the table. "Read this."

Her frown alerted Janice to the seriousness of what she was about to read, but nothing could prepare her for the vicious essay on the computer printout. With increasing distaste and anger, she read an inflammatory discourse written by someone with hateful opinions that turned her stomach.

She shoved the paper away, disgusted. "Where did you get that?"

"I found it on the internet last night." Tess looked as sick as Janice felt. "You had already gone to bed but I showed it to LuAnn."

"No wonder you two didn't sleep well." Janice shuddered.

LuAnn was watching her closely. "Did you see the signature line?"

Janice shook her head. "I didn't read past the first few sentences. I don't want to put garbage like that in my mind."

LuAnn slid the paper over and pointed at a place toward the bottom. "Look at that."

With reluctance, Janice did. When she read the author's name, her hands turned clammy. *Robert Newsome.* "Newsome. Isn't that Lucas's last name?"

Tess nodded. "After our discussion last night I decided to do some poking around on the internet. I read a couple of Lucas's articles, which were actually pretty good. And then I found that." The look she gave the paper was full of loathing. "Robert Newsome is Lucas's father."

"Lucas's father is a writer too?" Winnie approached the table. "That young man must come by it naturally. Here you are, ladies. Hot from the oven."

Tess snatched up the paper and folded it as Winnie set a plate of muffins in the center. Judging by her cheerful countenance, Winnie had not read the article. A good thing too. Janice would have wept to think their beloved African-American friend would be subjected to such trash.

Prejudice was not something Janice witnessed on a regular basis, which was one thing she loved about Marietta. Because of its extensive history and the significant role the town played in helping slaves to freedom during the Underground Railroad era, people of all races lived side-by-side here. The color of one's skin was rarely noticed, much less remarked upon.

Winnie started to turn away, and then halted and snapped her fingers. "I almost forgot to tell you. Byron and Lucas stuck their heads in here this morning right after I got to work. They were just leaving, heading up to Columbus to get Byron's family from the airport. Wanted to tell me not to fix their breakfast." She smiled. "That was right thoughtful of them."

Janice's stomach churned. "Yes," she said. "Very thoughtful."

CHAPTER SIXTEEN

C an someone give me a hand back here?"
Janice looked up to see Robin entering through the back door. The pretty young woman always brought a smile to Janice's face. She left the dishwasher half emptied and hurried over to hold the door while Robin scooted a large box through.

"We were lucky," the young woman said. "These are the last two rollaway beds in all of Marietta." She disappeared for a moment and returned with a second identical box. "Where do you want them?"

The three friends had discussed the room assignments for Byron's family. Unfortunately, Marla had passed along only sketchy information. All of the rooms would be in use for the next two days except the honeymoon suite. The night of their wedding, Byron and Marla would stay there.

At least, that was the plan so far. Janice was fairly sure the wedding would be canceled after their discussion with Marla today.

"Put them up in Sunshine and Daisies, please. Byron's brother has twin fourteen-year-olds who will have to sleep in their parents' room until after the wedding. Would you like some help?"

Robin shook her head. "Thanks, but they're really not heavy, just bulky. I'll take them up on the elevator."

Janice glanced at the clock as she returned to her task. Almost three. Marla would be here soon, and then Janice would deliver the blow that would break her heart. Tears stung her eyes as she set a stack of clean soup bowls in the cabinet.

Tess entered the kitchen holding a damp rag with which she had cleaned the tables in the café. "Any word from them yet?"

"I haven't heard anything." Janice began taking spoons from the dishwasher one at a time and polishing them with a soft dry cloth. The machine sometimes left spots, and they didn't want to serve their guests with spotty silverware. "The last time Marla called she said their flights had been rerouted due to weather but they were expected to land in Columbus at two o'clock."

Tess glanced at her watch. "They ought to be here in half an hour or so. When is Marla coming?"

The bell above the front door sounded a split-second before a voice shouted from the front. "Yoo-hoo? Where is everybody?"

Janice's stomach muscles squeezed tight. "There she is now." She closed her eyes and whispered a prayer. "*Oh Lord, guard her feelings.*"

"Amen." Tess looked almost as sick as Janice felt. "We're in the kitchen, Marla. Come join us."

Marla bustled into the room. She wore a grin that could have lit up a football stadium at midnight. "I just got a text from my honeybun. They'll be here in an hour. Is everything ready?"

"LuAnn is upstairs giving the rooms a final inspection," Tess told her.

"The inspection is finished." LuAnn entered the kitchen. "As soon as Robin gets the rollaway beds set up in Sunshine and Daisies, everything will be ready to go." She pulled Marla into a hug. "How are you, dear?"

"I am fabuloso! I'm getting married in two days to the best-looking man in the whole USA." Her features scrunched. "Uh, and Canada."

Janice felt sick. "Would you like some tea or a soda or something while we wait?"

"How about some water?" Marla patted her pudgy midsection. "I'm going to have to start watching my weight, now that I'll have a husband to keep happy." She waggled her eyebrows.

LuAnn turned quickly away but not before Janice saw tears sparkling in her eyes.

The three friends had planned how they would approach this discussion. Though she dreaded having to do it, Janice would take the lead. LuAnn and Tess would be available for moral support—for Marla and for her.

Janice approached the table. "Sit down, please. There's something I need to discuss with you."

Marla peered closely at her face. "Must be bad news. You look a little green around the gills."

"It's a serious matter."

Marla slid into the chair at the head of the table, and Janice selected the one to her right. LuAnn set a glass of ice water in front of her and then sat opposite Janice while Tess hovered behind her.

Marla's gaze slid from face to face. "Goodness, y'all are starting to scare me. What's wrong? Isn't the cake going to be ready in time?"

"I'm afraid it's a little more serious than that." Janice reached over to cover Marla's hands with one of her own. "We've discovered something we need to tell you. It's about Byron."

Questions appeared on Marla's face, but her smile dimmed only a fraction. "That man is a talker, isn't he? Why, given half a chance he'd talk the ears right off a rabbit. That's one of the things I love about him. I couldn't live with a man who just sat around saying nothing all the time."

"Yes, well, this isn't something he told us. It's something we discovered on our own." Janice cleared her throat. "You see, we did some checking into Byron's employment."

For a moment, Marla didn't react. Then her eyes narrowed slightly. "Why would you do that?"

"Because we care about you, dear," LuAnn said.

Still standing, Tess clutched the chair back. "We wanted to make sure our friend is going to be well cared for."

Marla looked from them to Janice. "Are you going to sit there and tell me you called his boss and asked how much money he makes? Because I can already tell you that. Byron and I have had this conversation." A stubborn expression crept over her face. "And I got to tell you girls, that's really none of your business."

"You are absolutely right," Janice hurried to say. "What Byron makes is none of our business. But..." She squeezed the woman's hand, prepared to deliver the blow. "But what we discovered is that he doesn't have a job at all."

LuAnn leaned forward. "At least not at Godfrey and Associates."

Marla snatched her hand from beneath Janice's. "That can't be true. He's a senior accounting analyst up there."

"We called Godfrey and Associates. The receptionist told us no one by the name of Byron Wickham worked there." Janice held Marla's gaze, and saw the moment doubt crept in.

She shook her head slowly. "I don't understand. Why would she say that? Byron has worked there for over ten years."

"How do you know?" Tess asked.

"Because he told me so."

The pain in Marla's voice stabbed at Janice's heart. "Have you ever seen proof? A paycheck stub or a business card or something?"

Marla stared at the place mat on the table in front of her. As Janice watched, a tear slipped over the rim of first one eye, and then the other. Finally, she shook her head.

"Why would he do that? I'm not rich. I have my house, but it's nothing special. I do have some savings but just barely enough to see me through."

Janice glanced up at Tess. Should they voice their suspicions that Byron was searching for documentation regarding his ancestors? As though Tess read her mind, she shook her head. Janice saw the wisdom in that. They'd already said enough. Leave it up to Marla to discover the reason behind Byron's deception.

She used her most compassionate tone. "I am so sorry, Marla."

Marla sniffled, and Tess dashed to the counter to grab a box of tissues.

Marla took one and blew her nose. "It's okay. I guess it takes a true friend to break a girl's heart this way."

Her choice of words shoved the guilty knife deeper into Janice's chest. "I want you to know that I will do whatever I can to help you get through this. If you want me to make the calls to cancel the flowers and the cake—"

Marla's head snapped up. "What do you mean cancel the cake? You can't have a wedding without cake."

Stunned, Janice could think of no reply.

LuAnn tucked a lock of hair behind her ear. "Surely you aren't planning to still marry him after he lied to you?"

"Oh, you can bet I'm going to get to the bottom of the lie." She snatched another couple of tissues from the box. "We're gonna clear that up first thing. You can't go into a marriage with that kind of thing hanging between you."

Janice could hardly believe her ears. "But, Marla, you can't marry a man who's deceived you like this. How can you be sure he won't do it again?"

Marla's expression softened. "I appreciate you looking out for me and all. I really do. But you've forgotten one thing. I love him. And I think he loves me. If he lied about where he works, maybe it's because he doesn't have a job. Or maybe he's got a lousy job and he's embarrassed by it. But that won't make me stop loving him."

So many arguments came to mind that Janice had a hard time deciding which one to voice first. From the stunned look on LuAnn's face and the way Tess's jaw dangled, they felt the same. With her eyes, she silently begged one of her friends to say something.

A second later, the opportunity was gone. The bell above the front door dinged, and Marla leapt to her feet.

"They're here. Now, y'all just come with me and we'll get to the bottom of this right away."

She marched from the room, leaving Janice, Tess, and LuAnn no choice but to follow.

The reception area was quickly filling with people and luggage. Janice caught sight of Byron and worked hard to stop a scowl from appearing on her face. Marla marched across the floor and planted herself in front of him, hands on her hips.

"Now look here—" She stopped when another man walked through the front door.

Janice did a double take. It was Byron with his arms full of luggage, followed by Lucas.

It took only a second for him to spot Marla, who looked absolutely as confused as Janice felt. He threw back his head and roared with laughter.

"Gotcha, didn't we?" He set the suitcases down and crossed the floor to sweep Marla into a hug. "You thought that was me, didn't you?"

Her mouth gaping, she nodded, which caused every person in the room to laugh.

An elderly black woman with thin gray hair came to Byron's side and smacked him on the arm with surprising strength. "Are you gonna stand there and tell me you never mentioned having a twin brother?"

"A twin?" Marla asked.

Rubbing his arm, Byron grinned at Marla. "Sugarplum, I'd like you to meet my mama." A tall, distinguished-looking man entered the door pulling a rolling suitcase behind him. "And over there is my father." Byron slipped an arm around Marla's waist and pulled her close. "Mama and Dad, I'd like to introduce you to your new daughter, Marla Still. Soon to be Marla Still Wickham."

Janice, Tess, and LuAnn stood off to one side watching as a speechless Marla was pulled around the room and introductions were made. Two women who looked around the same age as Mr. and Mrs. Wickham, Aunt Cordelia and Aunt Lizzie. Next came Byron's twin nieces Holly and Daisy, fourteen-year-old beauties who resembled their mother, Louise.

"And last but not least," Byron said, "this fine-looking fellow is my brother Myron."

"Myron," Marla repeated. "Your brother."

Myron took her hand and pressed a kiss on it as though she were a princess. "It's a pleasure to finally meet you. Byron has spoken of nothing else since he got back from Marietta a month ago."

"Has he now?" Marla stepped away from Byron's side and once again planted her hands on her hips.

He assumed the expression of a shamefaced seven-year-old. "Now, Sugarplum, I know I should have told you about my brother. But I couldn't wait to see the look on your face when you met him."

"It seems there's something else you haven't told me."

Here it comes. Janice desperately wanted to loop arms with her friends for support. Her knees felt wobbly.

Byron looked confused. "What else do I need to tell you? You know everything there is to know about me."

"That so?" She cocked her head sideways while holding his gaze. "How about you tell me where you work?"

He glanced at his brother, his eyes full of questions. Everyone in the room focused on the two of them. "I already told you, Sugarplum. I work at an accounting firm called Godfrey and Associates."

"Not according to my friends, you don't." Marla took one hand off her hip and pointed directly at Janice. Every eye in the room turned toward her. "They called up there to check on you and found out Godfrey and Associates never heard of you. Now how about you come clean right now?"

"There's some mistake." Byron shook his head and turned an imploring look on Janice. "You must have misunderstood."

Her mouth completely dry, Janice swallowed a few times before she could manage to speak. "Is there more than one Godfrey and Associates in Toronto?"

Tess shoved her with an elbow. "Of course not."

The door opened again, and a couple entered. The man was Caucasian and short, just a few inches taller than Janice herself. He held the door for a woman with fiery red hair beneath a butter-yellow hat.

Byron practically leaped across the room toward the couple. "Here's somebody who can clear this up right now."

Marla drew herself up to her full height and looked down her nose at the little man. "And who might you be?"

He peered up at her, his expression puzzled. "My name is Charles Godfrey, and this is my wife, Ruby."

"Godfrey?" Janice managed to choke out.

"As in Godfrey and Associates?" Tess asked.

The little man's face lit. "That's right. I suppose it's too much to hope that you've heard of my firm's reputation way down here in the states. Instead I suppose Byron here has told you about us."

Marla, whose mouth had been gaping open, snapped it shut. "You're Mr. Godfrey. Byron's boss?"

"That's right. And you must be Marla." He came toward her with both hands extended. "I can't tell you how happy I am to make your acquaintance. I have known Byron for more than ten years, since he came to work for me, and I've always known it would take a special woman to capture his attention. I can see I was right."

"Wait a minute." Tess marched forward until she stood beside Marla. Janice and LuAnn hurried after her. "I called Godfrey and Associates in Toronto myself. The receptionist told me there was no Byron Wickham working there."

The little man's brow furrowed. "When was that?"

"Tuesday," Janice answered.

"It was late in the day," LuAnn said. "We were afraid the office might even be closed."

Mr. Godfrey's wife rolled her eyes. "I told you not to hire her. She's an airhead."

Mr. Godfrey addressed Marla. "I think I see what happened. We hired a new receptionist. She started on Tuesday, and I had to let her go on Wednesday. She..." He cleared his throat. "She wasn't a good fit."

"She had feathers for brains," Mrs. Godfrey put in.

Her husband winced but didn't correct the observation. "I don't know why she would have said Byron doesn't work there, though she didn't meet him, since he was already on vacation when she was hired, and we're setting him up as a remote employee so he can move down here. But his name is right there in the company directory." He cast an anxious look back and forth between the couple. "I'm so sorry if this has caused a problem between you two."

If she could get away with it, Janice would have slunk away and stayed in her room until all these people were gone. Instead, she took a fortifying breath and approached Marla. "I am so sorry. This is all my fault." She turned to include Byron in her apology. "I'm sorry I was suspicious of you. I hope you can forgive me."

Kindness peeked out of his dark brown eyes. "You were just looking out for your friend. Of course I forgive you."

A second later, she was shoved out of the way as Marla threw her arms around her fiancé. "I should have trusted you no matter what. I'm sorry, honeybun."

While the two embraced, Byron's mother came close and put a hand on each of their shoulders. "Honey, I want you to remember those words. They've saved my marriage more times than I can count, and they'll save yours too."

Wise advice. Her face still burning, Janice watched as the Wickhams pressed in to enclose the couple in the center of a family group hug.

Tess nudged her with an elbow. She glanced up and then followed Tess's gaze. With a backward glance at the Wickhams, Lucas crept up the stairs alone.

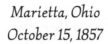

Marietta, Ohio
October 15, 1857

"Thee will stay only long enough to take the child?"

Darkness had long since covered their farm. Prudence glanced at the heavy curtains over the kitchen window, assuring herself that they were drawn closely so that the light from their single candle could not be seen from outside. Though she would prefer a cheery bright print, these dark curtains had served them well over the years.

She cut a generous wedge of cheese from the wheel. "I must hand them over to the next conductor. Thee knows this, Jason."

"And the other conductor? The one who displays so little caution as to parade his package down a busy street in broad daylight?" A scowl lay heavy on Jason's face. "What part is he to play in this?"

The question had occupied Prudence's thoughts for the past few hours, when she should have been sleeping. The truth was she did not know what the well-dressed conductor intended. But she was certain he did not know the route in this area. Prudence was one of the few who knew the location of the transfer point where she would hand off her charge. The next conductor would guide them through the heavily wooded area north of Marietta toward Lower Salem.

From there she didn't know the trail that Becca, Ezra, and their son would travel on the Freedom Train. It was best that she not know.

She wrapped the cheese in waxed cloth and set it in the dark-colored bag in the center of the table. "Does thee truly think him reckless?" Since she could not speak to the well-dressed conductor's role in the upcoming transfer, she turned the conversation. "To be sure, 'tis a bold move to disguise a man as free and travel openly, but perhaps not as foolhardy as it may appear. I mistook Ezra for a free man. Why would others not do the same?"

Jason was not convinced. "The man from Kentucky would recognize him at first glance. And no one is safe with the slave tracker in town."

Her hands trembled at the words. No one. Not even her. Though she had been born free, that had not stopped Tankard from capturing her along with her parents. And because she had not been born into slavery, she had no papers proclaiming her freedom. Could she be taken captive again?

"Perhaps, but how could they have known Mr. Bolling would travel all the way to Ohio? It is not normally done."

Jason stopped her in the act of heading for the pantry with a hand on her arm. "Nothing about the Cause is normal."

She held his gaze for a long moment, and then gave a single nod of agreement. Every move they made was fraught with danger. Every encounter held the threat of discovery. Of capture and punishment.

But every success meant another human being was one step closer to freedom.

Gently, she removed his hand from her arm and kissed his fingers. "The time is late. I must hurry."

She kept to the woods that grew along the riverbank, shielded by the dark cloak that she had secured around herself and Ezra Junior. Long before she arrived at the hotel, her muscles began to ache with the child's weight. She shifted him from one arm to the other and resettled his head on the opposite shoulder. He sighed and made a soft cooing sound but thankfully did not waken.

The moon rode high in the sky this night, a slender crescent that nonetheless cast enough white light on the earth to be dangerous. Prudence hovered just inside the cover of the trees where they grew closest to the tunnel's entrance and scanned the area. Her senses on high alert, she strained to detect any unusual noise. The sound of the river gently lapping against the shore provided a constant background to the soft rustle of wind and the leaves above her head. No light shown in the windows of the hotel tonight, thank the Lord. Still, she waited at least a hundred breaths past the time when she thought she was safe before stepping into the open.

Her feet making absolutely no sound on the moist grass, she held her breath and scurried toward the trio of bushes. Not until she was safely inside the tunnel did she exhale. The skiff lay propped against the dank brick wall, exactly where she'd left it. Clutching Ezra Junior in a tight embrace, she tiptoed into the darkness.

At the place where the tunnel ended inside the hotel, she located the first room and, after the softest of knocks, opened the door and slipped inside. The candlelight dazzled her eyes, and she blinked hard to clear them.

Becca huddled on the cot, her back pressed into the opposite corner of the small room, her eyes huge in the dainty face. Then she recognized Prudence and unfolded her frail body. Off the cot in a flash, she crossed the room in two long strides, her arms outstretched.

"You brung him back," she whispered. "They told me you would, but I was afraid."

Prudence stopped her before she took the baby. "We mustn't wake him. Thee is moving on tonight, and thee will be safer with him asleep."

Becca shrank. "I can't go without Ezra. I wouldn't know what to do."

"Ezra is here. Thee will meet him soon." Though the instructions for this meeting were sketchy, Prudence and Jason had outlined a plan. Prudence would take Becca and Ezra Junior through the woods to the regular meeting place. And pray that word had reached the other conductor to deliver Ezra to the same place.

She laid the sleeping child on the cot and then un-slung the bag that she had packed from her shoulder. "Quickly now. I brought thee traveling clothes and some food for the trip."

She removed the dress. It was one of her own, altered yesterday morning to accommodate Becca's more slender frame. Though no match for the finery with which Ezra's conductor had dressed him, this garment was far more suitable than the rags in which Becca had arrived.

Becca reached a tentative hand out to finger the fabric. Tears swam in her eyes. "I ain't never had nothing so fine."

Prudence smiled. "Thee can't show up in the Promised Land wearing a tattered skirt." At the girl's startled look, she chuckled quietly. "The Promised Land. It's what we call freedom. Now hurry."

She had just settled the dress on Becca's narrow hips when a knock sounded on the door. Alarm zipped up her spine. She grabbed the girl and thrust her backward and then took up a stance in front of her.

Without a sound the door swung inward on well-oiled hinges. In walked the last person she expected to see.

"Mr. Bickerton?"

"It's good to see you, Prudence. We've missed you upstairs the past few days." He looked from her to Becca crouching behind her. "And it's good to meet you, my dear. I have someone here I think you want to see."

He stepped aside to reveal Ezra standing in the doorway. With one look, Becca threw herself forward and into her husband's arms, sobbing. Ezra engulfed her in a hug, though Prudence feared the strength of his embrace might squeeze the breath from her frail body.

He looked up and spied the sleeping child. "Is that my boy?" The awe in his tone raised goose bumps along Prudence's arms.

When Becca tugged him forward to the cot, the well-dressed conductor from the dry goods store stepped into the room. Prudence backed up until she pressed against the rear wall. There was barely enough space to hold them all.

Watching the tender scene, a wide smile lit the man's face. "*What therefore God hath joined together, let not man put asunder,*" he quoted, then turned that smile on Prudence. "Hello again."

Mr. Bickerton gestured to him. "Prudence, I understand you met Mr. Still this afternoon."

She almost corrected him. Workers in the Cause never identify themselves. But then the name registered. Her lips parted and she drew in a quick breath. "Mr. William Still?"

Could it be? Was the man before her truly William Still? An outspoken antislavery activist, Mr. Still hailed from Pennsylvania and was chairman of the vigilance committee of the Pennsylvania Antislavery Society. Though forthright in his beliefs, only those who served the Cause knew of his tireless work to support the Freedom Train and his passion to assist refugees in their escape from slavery. Prudence found herself unable to speak.

Mr. Still stepped forward, his hand extended. "Mrs. Willard, it's a pleasure to finally meet you. I've long known of your work here, though not your name. And how is your husband?"

Prudence found her hands engulfed in his warm grip and managed to stammer, "He's...He's well, sir."

His expression sobered. "When news reached me of his injury, I prayed for him. I continue to do so whenever the Lord brings him to mind. Please tell him so." He rubbed his hands together and glanced around the room. "Now. Where is this tunnel I've heard about?"

"Right here." Mr. Bickerton put both hands on the stool and pulled it back, revealing the brick-lined passageway.

"Impressive." Mr. Still turned to Prudence. "And you've used this to assist how many souls on the Freedom Train?"

She drew a breath to answer, but before she could speak, another figure stepped into view. At the site of his grizzled features, a small scream escaped Prudence's throat. Her knees trembled, and her nightmares threatened to crash in on her. Lucian Tankard. In his hand, he held a pistol pointed in their direction.

His nostrils curled in a smirk. "Looks like I'll be needing a bigger money pouch after tonight. I've struck gold."

"Mr. Tankard." With one step, Mr. Bickerton positioned himself between Prudence and Tankard. "Hotel guests are not permitted in this area of the building. How did you come to be here?"

A cold smile on Tankard's face sent a ripple of fear through Prudence. "I've been keeping my eyes open. I knew something wasn't right with this place, so I watched." He sidestepped so he could see both Mr. Still and Ezra. "I saw these two sneaking around in the dark, and watched you let them in the back. Nice arrangement you've got here, hidden stairs and all. Maybe you ought to put a lock on them, though." His sharp eyes fixed on Ezra, who stood with his arms wrapped protectively around Becca. "There's somebody upstairs who wants to see you real bad." He looked at Becca and his lids narrowed as he studied her. "I remember you. Stephen Duncan, right? Long way from home, aren't you girl?"

Becca pressed her face hard again into Ezra's shirt.

"Look here, Tankard. We can discuss this." From her position, Prudence could not see Mr. Bickerton's face, but never had she heard such dislike in his tone.

The gun's barrel didn't waver. It remained pointed at Mr. Bickerton's chest.

"Oh, we've got a lot to discuss, that's for sure." Tankard made a show of inspecting the room and then stabbed a finger toward the tunnel. "That must have taken a lot of work. And everybody thinking what a fine, upstanding man Howard Bickerton is." His shoulders heaved in a silent and humorless laugh. "Won't they be surprised to find out you're nothing but a lawbreaking thief?"

Mr. Bickerton's back stiffened. "I beg your pardon?"

"You heard me. Hiding other people's property is the same as stealing it yourself." He inclined his head to indicate Ezra and Becca. "And it's against the law. To think, I get to be the one to put a stop to your illegal activities. It'll be a pleasure to see you sitting in a jail cell." For the first time, his gaze fixed on Prudence. "You and all the people who help you."

An icy feeling trailed across the back of Prudence's neck. She did not breathe until those intense eyes had moved away from her.

"But you." He jerked a nod toward Mr. Still, an unpleasant grin stretching his lips wide. "Hoo-wee, I struck pay dirt tonight. There's a lot of people going to look up to me for putting you out of action."

Prudence risked a sideways glance at Mr. Still's face. He wore no expression whatsoever. If the man felt any fear at all, he had mastered the art of hiding it. If she weren't completely gripped by terror, she would have felt admiration for him.

Becca's soft sobs seemed to echo off the walls. Prudence glanced at the sleeping bundle on the cot. *Lord, keep him asleep. Calm that baby's fears. Keep him safe.* She tried to portray the same calm countenance that Mr. Still maintained, but her heart struggled against the weight of terror.

"It occurs to me that we have an opportunity before us." Mr. Bickerton spoke in a coldly polite tone. "We are reasonable men, you and I. Perhaps we might reach an agreement to our mutual benefit."

She swallowed a disgusted grunt. How could anyone refer to the vile man standing before them as reasonable?

"What kind of agreement?" Tankard held the upper hand, and the deepening smirk proved he knew it.

"As it happens, I am a man of some means. And it appears that you have aspirations of being the same."

"Like I said, after tonight I'm going to be rich."

Mr. Bickerton lowered his voice. "I can make you richer."

For the first time, the barrel of the pistol wavered. "What do you have in mind?"

"Five hundred dollars in cash."

The number reeled in Prudence's brain, rendering her knees even weaker. She wavered, and Mr. Still put a supportive hand under her arm to keep her from falling. Five hundred dollars was a fortune she could not even begin to imagine.

Tankard cocked his head. "In return for what?"

The answer came with no hesitation. "You go upstairs right now. Return to your room. Go to bed. In the morning, take your money and leave. Never say a word about what happened here tonight, and we won't either."

Prudence leaned against the support of Mr. Still's hand. If he accepted, they might escape tonight with their lives, but that would mean an end to their work for the Cause. The corrupt man before her could not be trusted to keep the existence of the tunnel and the hidden rooms secret. Beyond that, she and Jason would have to leave Marietta. Sell the farm and move north. She could never stay here as long as that man knew where she lived.

"You'd expect me to let him go free, I suppose."

The gun barrel shifted then, toward Mr. Still. Had he not been holding her arm, Prudence would not have known that his muscles tensed when the weapon pointed at him.

"That would be the bargain, yes." Mr. Bickerton might have been bartering for catfish to serve his guests for dinner, so calm was his manner.

Tankard pursed his lips and sucked in his cheeks, clearly considering the offer. "Goes against my grain to let this one go." He gestured toward Mr. Still again with the pistol. "But he won't get too far."

Bickerton spoke quickly. "Part of our bargain would be time. I need your word that you will curtail your, uh, activities for a week."

Tankard scowled. "Three days. That's all you get. A man's gotta make a living after all." His eyes moved in their sockets and settled on Ezra. "But I get these three."

Prudence's legs trembled, and the volume of Becca's sobs increased.

"I must not have made myself clear," Mr. Bickerton said. "These people are guests of my hotel. They will be traveling north as planned."

"That man there is worth a hundred dollars, cash money. I haven't heard the bounty on the girl and the kid yet, but I know Stephen Duncan to be a generous man. I'm figuring at least another fifty for the pair. I'm not walking away from a hundred fifty dollars."

A rumbling roar filled the room. The sound so startled Prudence that her knees gave out and she dropped into a crouch, hugging her legs. Movement drew her gaze and she looked up in time to see Ezra cover the short distance between him and Tankard, his head lowered like a charging bull. His skull connected with the slave catcher's stomach at the same time he swept a hand upward. The pistol bounced off the wall and crashed to the floor. With a string of curses, Tankard flew backward, propelled by the force of Ezra's body slamming into his. A sickening thud reached her ears at the same moment the curses stopped.

Mr. Still and Mr. Bickerton rushed forward. Becca threw herself toward Prudence, who wrapped her arms around the sobbing girl. A small wedge of light spilled into the tunnel from the candle, and Prudence saw Ezra stand and then stagger on his feet. All she could see of Tankard were his boots, which lay unmoving in the doorway.

Mr. Still's whisper reached her, barely discernible above Becca's cries.

"He's dead."

CHAPTER SEVENTEEN

I feel like an intruder." Janice caught a glimpse of the crowd of family members and friends gathered in Marla's backyard while LuAnn parked on a side street and shut off the engine. Strings of lights crisscrossed the lawn and combined with the Indian summer weather to give the setting a perfect party atmosphere.

"I know what you mean." In the front passenger seat, Tess unsnapped her seat belt. "Especially after we almost wrecked the wedding."

LuAnn pulled the keys from the ignition. "The Wickhams are a gracious group of people. I love the way they not only forgave us for interfering but insisted on including us in their first evening together."

"It's a lovely evening, but I do wish they had let us host this gathering at the inn." Janice eyed the tidy little house, with white painted brick columns, wood siding, and steeply pitched roof, its yard not much bigger than a postage stamp. She pulled in a deep breath. "Even outside, we're going to be packed together like pickles in a jar."

"Let's not stay too late," LuAnn suggested.

"Agreed. We'll stay just long enough to be polite," Tess said.

"And to give them our gift." Janice got out of the car and then leaned back in to retrieve the box from the seat.

As they walked around the side of the house into the backyard, Marla was stepping through the screen door from the kitchen onto the porch, her arms loaded down with a tub of soft drink cans on ice. "Welcome! Y'all just make yourself comfortable. You might have to fight over a place to sit, though." She laughed and nodded toward a cluster of lawn chairs nestled under the trees, where various Wickham family members sat. "I got to tell you girls, these people are a hoot." She lowered her voice only slightly. "Aunt Cordelia and Aunt Lizzie are a couple of old maids with vinegar for tongues, especially when they're talking about each other behind their backs. But oh! Don't they love each other. And they all love the Lord. Even Holly and Daisy, Byron's nieces. Why, they're active in their church youth group and next summer they're gonna be counselors at church camp for the younger kids." Her grin widened even more. "I've found myself the best family in the world."

"We are so happy for you," LuAnn said as she helped Marla set the tub of soft drinks on the patio table. The two gave each other a quick hug while Tess arranged the items on the table to make room for more food.

Marla eyed the box in Janice's hands. "What's this? Did you bring us a wedding present?"

Janice chuckled. "Sort of. We'll show you in a bit."

Janice placed the box beneath the picnic table for safekeeping and joined the party in progress amid a good deal of laughter and joking. Not only that, but she heard more than one person exclaim, "Praise the Lord!" It was apparent that Mr. and Mrs. Godfrey felt right at home with the Wickhams, indicating they celebrated together often.

The only person who seemed out of place was Lucas, who sat in a folding chair near the screen door to the kitchen and only spoke when someone spoke directly to him. Janice glanced his way often. What was he thinking as he watched this happy family interact with one another and with their white friends? Did he share his father's views? If so, she had certainly never glimpsed evidence of them. What an enigma he was. An openly bigoted father and an African-American best friend. Or, was that African-Canadian?

The conversation turned to Byron's first trip to Marietta, when he came to follow up on Lucas's research about his family's escape to freedom. "I came here hoping to find evidence of my ancestors." He gazed at Marla with an adoring smile. "And instead I met the love of my life."

Mrs. Wickham cast a grin around the room. "Isn't that just like our God? He had a plan all along."

"I think that's our cue," LuAnn whispered to Janice.

"Since we're on the subject." Janice stood from the lawn chair she had commandeered under a buckeye tree. "We have something we'd like to give the bride and groom."

"In fact, it's really a gift for the entire family," Tess said.

Janice retrieved the box from under the picnic table. She stood in front of Marla and Byron. "While we were trying to clean out the church belfry, we came across something that belongs to you." She set the box on Marla's lap.

"That's my writing." Marla looked at Byron. "I told you I thought I had stuff stored up in that church attic."

Janice unfolded the flaps and pulled out the Bible, which rested on top. When people caught sight of it, a hush fell over the gathering.

She held the precious book in one hand and rubbed the old leather cover with the other. "I've intended to give this to you ever since we found it. But I hesitated because..."

Byron spoke in a soft voice. "Because you wanted to make sure your friend wasn't making a mistake."

She managed a sheepish smile. "Marla, this Bible belonged to your great-great-great-grandfather, William Still." A collective gasp rose from the crowd. "But it's even more than that. We didn't realize until yesterday that this Bible connects your family to Byron's."

No one made a sound as Janice opened to the book of Mark. She found the verse she sought and read it aloud. "'What therefore God hath joined together, let not man put asunder.'"

"Praise be to God," whispered Mrs. Wickham.

"Mr. Still circled that verse and wrote a pair of initials beside it." Janice handed the Bible to Byron. "Would you like to read what he wrote in the margin?"

"'E.B. 10/19/1857.'" He looked up, his eyes full of questions.

Janice took something else from the box. "This is a copy of the page from Prudence Willard's journal dated October 19, 1857."

She handed the sheet, encased in a plastic sleeve, to Marla, who squinted at the old-fashioned script. Then she sucked in a breath and read aloud. "'The reunion takes place tonight, and by tomorrow this special package will be on its way, the good Lord willing.'" She turned shining eyes on her fiancé. "'The reunion.' Do you know what that means?"

Tears glimmered on his lashes. "E stands for Ezra and B stands for Becca. They came to Marietta to be reunited before they escaped to Canada." He placed a reverent hand on the open Bible. "This is the proof I was looking for. Sugarplum, your ancestor really did guide my ancestors to freedom."

"Praise be," Mr. Wickham whispered.

"I knew I should have gotten up there to that church attic long before now." Marla sniffled. "And there's way more stuff piled downstairs in my basement. Boxes like this here one, just full of papers that my daddy said were family documents passed down to him. I'm just betting some of those belonged to William Still. Only God knows what we'll find down there."

"Well, this calls for some sort of special celebration, don't you think?" Mr. Godfrey asked.

"I think that's what we're having," his wife said with a grin.

"What we aren't having is a prayer," Mrs. Wickham said. "Jack, you want to do the honors?"

They all bowed their heads while Byron's father led them in a heartfelt prayer, not only for the evidence that had been uncovered but for the freedom that every person in that gathering enjoyed because of Christ's sacrifice. By the time he said amen, Janice's were not the only wet eyes.

"Let's have us a toast." Marla jumped to her feet. "We have diet soda, unsweetened iced tea, or water."

She recruited the teenagers to help her fill red plastic cups with ice and beverages while she went inside to get a pitcher of iced tea. The rest of the family gathered around Byron, who had camped himself in a chair under the trees and was paging through the historic Bible. Aunt Cordelia and Aunt Lizzie scooted the box between their chairs and began going through the other contents.

Janice sidled up to LuAnn. "Is it time for us to leave?"

Tess nodded, but LuAnn said, "We should at least wait until after the toast."

"I'll give Marla a hand." Janice headed for the kitchen. She still felt horrible for having planted a seed of doubt in Marla's mind two days before her wedding. Though she had apologized, she felt like perhaps she should grovel a lot more between now and Saturday, if only to ease her own guilty conscience.

Janice found Marla rummaging in the refrigerator of the tiny kitchen when she stepped inside.

"Here we are." She turned around to display a plastic pitcher filled with tea.

"What can I do to help?" Janice asked.

Marla pointed toward the pantry. "There are sugar and sweetener packets in there. Would you grab them for me?"

Janice turned in that direction and then halted. She drew in a breath through her nose. "Do you smell smoke?"

Marla dipped her head. "I do, a little. Where's it coming from?"

Janice glanced around the small room. The back door still stood slightly ajar. "Could one of your neighbors be burning trash outside?"

Marla pulled the door open, sniffed, and shook her head. "It's not coming from outside."

"Where does this go?" Janice twisted the knob on a door beside the refrigerator. When she pulled the door open, smoke billowed into the kitchen.

"The basement!" Marla shouted. "My basement is on fire."

"Fire!" Marla yelled out into the yard, her hands flapping in the air.

"Out of the house, Marla! Go!" Janice commanded, slamming the basement door shut. Iced tea sloshed from the pitcher in Marla's hand as Janice followed her out the door.

Everyone in the yard stood, frozen, for a brief second, before they began to scurry about in total confusion. Then Byron took charge of the crowd. "Everyone gather in the front yard! Now!" He clutched the Bible in one hand as he ran to Marla's side and held her tight with the other while they ran. LuAnn spoke into her cell phone, telling someone on the other end to send the fire department. Presumably she had called 911. Once they'd gathered on a sidewalk by the street, Janice started to perform a head count, and then realized she couldn't remember how many Wickhams were present. She sought out Byron's mother.

"Is everyone here and accounted for? We need to make sure no one is in the house."

Mrs. Wickham's finger danced in the air as she counted. "Eight, nine, ten. That's how many plane tickets we had. Byron and Marla make twelve."

"LuAnn, Tess, and I make fifteen." Janice started to say everyone was there, but then she stopped. "Where's Lucas?"

They both scanned the group.

"Lucas?" Mrs. Wickham shouted. "Where are you?"

Byron jerked upright. "Luke?" Panic choked his normal baritone voice into a tenor. "Do you think he went inside to try and put out the fire?"

Everyone began shouting. Their discovery of the terrible blog post fresh in her mind, Janice exchanged a glance with LuAnn. Would he stoop so low as to set fire to Marla's house? She could hardly believe it of him. But if not, then where was he? The last time she'd noticed him, he'd been in a chair right by the back door.

Sirens sounded in the distance, their volume increasing as the fire trucks drew closer. Thank the Lord, help was near.

Byron thrust William Still's Bible into Marla's hands and sprinted for the house.

"Byron," screamed Marla and Mrs. Wickham in unison.

Myron dashed after his brother and entered the front door on his heels. A thin stream of smoke trickled outside through the open doorway. No flames that Janice could see, which was a blessing. The teenagers began to cry, and their mother gathered them into a hug.

The fire trucks arrived, and as firefighters leapt from inside, three police cars screeched to a halt beside them. Blue and red lights flashed off Marla's white house. Chief Mayfield exited one of the cars and began shouting orders at his deputies. Janice spotted Kevin Franklin jumping to the ground from the second fire truck.

"My fiancé's in there," Marla shrieked at him.

Kevin wasted no time. He darted toward the house, two firefighters behind him.

A few moments later Kevin returned with Byron and Myron in tow. The teenagers tackled their father, sobbing with relief, while Marla threw herself at Byron. For a moment, Janice thought he might lose his balance but he recovered and held her tight.

Kevin held both hands high in the air and addressed the crowd. "Folks, we're gonna need all of you to move across the street. You'll be safer over there."

Everyone obeyed except Byron. "My friend's still in there."

"We'll find him. Now please, sir, wait over there."

Tess and LuAnn appeared beside Janice and grabbed her hands. The three crossed the road to join the others. The vantage point was not good, since the fire trucks stood between them and the house, but at least they were safe. Janice whispered a prayer for Lucas, wherever he was.

Their group began to swell as neighbors left their houses and came to find out what was going on. Word spread in whispers through the group that someone was still inside and may be trapped.

"I could be very wrong," Tess said in a low voice, "but I don't think he's in there."

"Neither do I," LuAnn said.

Janice didn't know what to think. After she had so badly misjudged Byron, she didn't trust her instincts.

They stood there long enough for the night's chill to seep into their bones. Janice huddled in a close knot with her friends, drawing and offering what little warmth they could muster. Finally, Kevin stepped between the two fire trucks, scanned the crowd on the sidewalk, and headed toward Marla.

"Good news. We contained the fire to the basement. There was a lot of stuff piled down there, but it looks like most of the damage was to boxes full of papers and books. Unfortunately, most of those are a complete loss."

Byron stepped toward the fire chief. "What about my friend?"

Kevin shook his head. "We searched the house from top to bottom. There's nobody in there."

Janice tightened her arms around Tess's and LuAnn's waists.

"I don't understand," Byron said slowly. "He was right there with us."

A deep voice behind them spoke up. "Is this the guy you're looking for?"

Janice and her friends turned to see Chief Mayfield leading Lucas toward them with a firm grip on his upper arm.

Byron rushed forward. "Thank the Lord." He pulled Lucas into a quick hug and then released him but continued to thump him on the back. "I thought you were dead, buddy. I went in after you, but I couldn't find you and they made me leave."

Disbelief dawned on Lucas's face. "You went looking for me?" He jerked his head in the direction of the house. "In there?"

"Of course I did. But you weren't there." His head tilted sideways. "Where were you?"

Lucas's head dropped forward, his gaze fixed on the concrete between them.

The answer came from Chief Mayfield. "We caught him half a block down that way." With his free hand, he jerked his thumb behind him. "Arsonists never run far. They like to stick around and watch their handiwork."

Janice was not the only one who gasped.

Marla pushed her way forward. "You set my house on fire?"

Before Lucas had a chance to answer, Janice blurted out a question of her own. "Did you set the church on fire too?"

Though Chief Mayfield sent a withering glance in her direction, Lucas's shoulders drooped further. His nod was barely discernible.

"But why?" Byron asked. Janice's heart twisted at the pain in his tone. "You're my best friend. Why would you light a fire in my fiancée's house?"

"The answer is obvious." Marla stepped closer to Byron. "He was trying to stop our wedding. Maybe he's jealous."

"No!" Lucas's head snapped up. "It's not like that, really. You're my friend, and I want you to stay my friend. But when you find out—"

Chief Mayfield interrupted him. "You better think real hard before you say another word, son. You might want to contact an attorney."

Clearly miserable, Lucas shook his head. "I don't need an attorney. I'll tell you whatever you want to know. I set the fires." His gaze locked onto Janice's, and her breath caught in her throat. "Both of them. But not to stop the wedding. I was trying to"—he gulped—"get rid of the evidence."

The answer became clear in an instant, like the tumblers of a lock clicking into place in Janice's mind. "Lucian Tankard."

She might as well have struck him. Lucas winced.

"Who is Lucian Tankard?" Byron asked.

At a glance from the chief, one of his deputies pulled out his phone and began tapping with his thumbs. Taking notes, no doubt.

LuAnn answered. "Lucian Tankard was a slave tracker. He came to Marietta in 1857 looking for an escaped slave." She looked at Byron. "Unless I'm mistaken, that escaped slave was your ancestor."

"You're not mistaken." Lucas spoke in such a low voice that Janice had to strain to understand. "Tankard was hired to catch and return Ezra to Kentucky. He tracked him to Marietta, where Becca and the baby were being hidden." His glance flickered upward, toward Janice, Tess, and LuAnn. "They were in hiding at the Riverfront House."

Janice interrupted only to explain the connection to those who were unaware. "That was the name of Wayfarers Inn back then. The Riverfront House."

Byron's father, standing with the rest of the family behind them, spoke up. "But he didn't succeed. Ezra and Becca escaped to Canada."

At Lucas's nod, Byron looked even more confused. "Then what were you trying to cover up?"

Janice knew the answer before Lucas's tortured whisper came.

"Lucius Tankard was my great-great-great-grandfather." Marla sucked in a breath that sounded like a hiss, and Lucas's head jerked upward. "You see? Here you are marrying the descendent of a man who set people free. And here I am, the descendent of someone who tracked them down, captured them, and took them back to slavery. But there's more. I've heard the story from my father. Tankard was well-known for branding runaways." He cast a pleading look toward Byron. "Runaways like your ancestor."

Mrs. Wickham spoke in a tortured tone. "Was he the one who branded Becca?"

Tears flooded Lucas's eyes. "I don't know for sure." He squeezed them shut. "But I think so. That's why I couldn't risk you finding out who I am. Where I come from." He peered into Byron's face. "Ever since you came back from Marietta in September I've been putting the pieces together from my family's records." He looked at Marla. "That first day we met, you said you had stuff stored in the church, family records." His glance fell on Janice and her friends next. "And you were cleaning that stuff out of there. You might have found something to implicate Tankard. And once his name came up somebody would have traced his family line all the way down to me. So while Byron and Marla were at dinner that night, I pretended to be working on an article in my room."

When he paused, Tess took up the story. "You went down into the basement and covered your skin with ashes from that old furnace. And you took a towel from the laundry." Chief Mayfield perked up at the mention of a towel. "And then snuck out through the tunnel."

Lucas shook his head. "That's not how it happened. Yes, I got the ashes from a pile on the floor in the basement of the inn and I took the towel from the cabinet down there."

"You blackened your face?" Byron sounded hurt. "Were you trying to make it look like I set the fire?"

"No!" Lucas answered. "White skin reflects the moon-light. I was just trying to disguise myself. And I didn't even know about the tunnel then. I was just checking out the inn quietly, looking for a way to get in and out without that bell ringing. I didn't see anything down in the basement so I went out the kitchen back door and left it unlocked until I returned."

"We've got to do something about that," LuAnn muttered under her breath.

"When I got to the church and saw all that junk, I knew I'd never find anything. And the place is made out of stone. It wasn't going to burn down. Somebody would spot it before then. So I lit a candle with my cigarette lighter, and I set it on the floor thinking it would catch and spread after I was long gone. But the next thing I knew those old beanbags were in flames, and I panicked. I ran." He averted his eyes. "Same as tonight. When Marla said her basement had family papers stored down there, I slipped away and went down to check them out." He shook his head. "But there was so much stuff down there. Boxes and boxes of it."

"But why? Our ancestors lived more than a hundred sixty years ago." Byron scrubbed a hand across his mouth. "What made you think I would care?"

Lucas's tears flowed more freely now. "Because of my family. My father." A sob heaved in his chest. "He's a racist, Byron. Didn't you ever wonder why I never introduced you to him?" He wiped away the tears and looked at the group of people behind Byron. "You're all great people. You love each other. You accepted me the first time you ever met me. My father would not do the same." He sobbed again and went on in a tear-strained voice. "I'm ashamed to even tell you what he would say if he met you."

Janice scanned the faces of Byron's family. Instead of the anger she expected to find, she saw nothing but compassion.

Chief Mayfield still had a grip on Lucas's arm, but Byron left Marla's side to step forward and place one large hand on his other shoulder. "Do you think I didn't know that?"

Lucas's face jerked upward.

"I've known who your father is—what your father is—almost as long as I've known you."

"We all have," Mrs. Wickham said.

"Hard not to," Mr. Wickham added, "with him blasting his opinion all over the internet every time a body turns around."

Byron gave Lucas's shoulder a shake. "But you are not like your father, any more than you are like that slave catcher. You're my friend. And I forgive you."

Disbelief dawned on Lucas's face. "How can you do that? I've never understood how you can say those words so easily."

Byron spoke slowly, enunciating every word. "I can forgive you, because Jesus Christ forgave me."

In the moment of silence that followed, Janice had to clench her teeth from shouting *hallelujah*. She had just seen a true demonstration of God's love at work, and her heart longed to celebrate.

Chief Mayfield broke the moment. "You're going to have to continue this conversation another time. Visiting hours down at the jail are Monday through Friday, 8:30 to 4:15." He led Lucas to his cruiser.

"I'll come tomorrow," Byron called after them.

Byron's mother and father came to his side.

"I am proud of you, son," Mr. Wickham said.

As the three embraced, Marla approached Janice. "I think I'll suggest that he take Pastor Ben with him when he visits. If any man ever needed to know the Lord, it's that one." She jerked her head toward the police cruiser.

"That's a very good idea." Janice looked closer at Marla. "Forgive me for saying so, but you don't seem nearly as upset as I would be if someone had just tried to burn my house down."

She didn't. In fact, sparkles danced in her eyes and dimples carved each round cheek.

Marla shrugged. "My house didn't burn down. Nobody got hurt." The grin broke free. "And I'm getting married in *two days!*"

CHAPTER EIGHTEEN

Janice had long ago lost count of the number of brides she had helped get ready in this room. Located on the second floor of the church tower, the room was perfect for sequestering the bridal party while guests found their seats in the sanctuary below.

Holly and Daisy were pictures of elegance in their matching lilac dresses, with wispy hems fluttering just below the knees.

Janice adjusted the bow around Daisy's waist. "I don't know how you managed to come up with such beautiful bridesmaid dresses so quickly," she told their mother, "but you are to be congratulated."

Louise flicked a tiny speck of dust from Holly's puffy sleeve. "My cousin got married this summer, and the girls were in the wedding. Thank goodness they haven't grown much in the past few months."

Marla called from the other side of the room. "They look great. But my face is a disaster. I need help!"

Janice hurried over to the bride, who was seated at a dressing table, moaning at her reflection in the mirror.

"You face is not—" Janice covered her mouth when she caught sight of Marla. "Well perhaps you have overdone the makeup just a bit, dear."

"I look like I'm going to a clown convention," she moaned.

Behind them, the girls giggled.

"When Byron sees me walking down that aisle, I want him to think I'm beautiful, not to run in the opposite direction."

Janice snatched up a package of makeup-remover cloths and extracted one. "Here. Wipe it off. We'll start over."

"There's no time. I don't want to be late for my own wedding."

Janice had dealt with far more hysterical brides than Marla. She knew exactly the right tone to adopt. "There's always time. You are the bride. Today is your special day. Everyone else can wait."

A wide grin spread across Marla's face. "I am, aren't I?"

Janice nodded. "Now scrub."

Someone tapped on the door and it opened a crack. Paige peeked inside. "Can I come in?"

Marla twisted on the bench. "Can you do makeup?"

When Paige caught sight of her half-cleaned face, her eyes widened. "Actually, yes I can."

"Then get in here, girl. I need you."

Janice hid a grin as Paige scurried across the room to help the bride. This was exactly the kind of task that would spread throughout the church and leave a good impression on the congregation.

The clown-like makeup removed, Paige went to work on Marla's face. "I actually came up here to give you a surprise."

"A wedding present?" Marla asked.

"Sort of." Paige glanced at Janice with a grin. "Ben has worked something of a minor miracle and gotten those bells in working order."

Marla whirled around on the bench, her hands clasped before her mouth and her eyes sparkling. "Do you mean those bells are gonna ring today?"

Page couldn't stop smiling as she nodded.

Marla threw her hands up in the air. "Thank the Lord for Pastor Ben."

Janice couldn't agree more.

When Paige applied a final brushstroke to Marla's cheek, she straightened and stood back. "What do you think?"

The teenagers applauded and Janice nodded her approval. "Lovely. Now let's get that dress on."

The wedding gown had been another minor miracle. Marla was set to wear her Sunday best, a smart-looking cream skirt and jacket with a silky pale pink blouse. But Harry had called late Friday to say he'd found a dress that looked to be about Marla's size on a salvage job down in Huntington, West Virginia. Marla had fallen in love with it, though Janice privately thought the all-over beading and lace design and the wide scalloped hemline a bit elaborate for a mature bride. But this wasn't her wedding. The dress had only needed to be let out a bit, and though the waist still hugged Marla a tad more snugly then strictly appropriate, she did look lovely.

Paige, Louise, the girls, and Janice stood back while Marla twirled in front of a full-length mirror and clapped with delight when the skirt swirled elegantly. Stars danced in her eyes.

"All right y'all. Let's go get me hitched!"

Thirty minutes later, the hitching was done. Janice, Tess, and LuAnn stood on the sidewalk outside the church along with around forty other guests awaiting the appearance of Mr. and Mrs. Byron Wickham.

"That was a lovely service," Tess said.

LuAnn agreed. "Pastor Ben did a beautiful job, didn't you think, Janice?"

The service had been a difficult one for Janice, which surprised her. This was the first wedding she had attended at Christ Fellowship since Lawrence's death. How odd to sit in the pews and watch another man officiate the ceremony. A single tear still clung to one of Janice's eyelashes. She brushed it away. "I thought it was absolutely beautiful."

LuAnn put an arm around Janice's shoulders and hugged her. Her friends knew without her having to say a word.

Holly appeared in the open doorway at the top of the old stone stairs. "Here they come!"

And then the bride and groom emerged from the church. On cue, the bells in Christ Fellowship's belfry began to ring. As their glorious song filled the air, Marla's face broke into a smile so bright she rivaled the sun in the clear blue October sky. Byron grabbed her hand and lifted it to his lips, his eyes full of love. Then the two descended the stairs amid a shower of birdseed.

When their car had disappeared up the brick street and turned the corner in front of Mound Cemetery, Janice faced LuAnn and Tess. "Well, that's done. Now we can get busy on our next project. Harvest Celebration dinner is in one week."

Tess groaned. "I can't believe we committed to hosting a big community dinner after all we've been through."

Janice chuckled. "We just pulled off a wedding in eight days. I think we can handle a simple dinner."

"You know what they say." LuAnn looped one arm through Janice's and the other through Tess's and pulled them toward the car. "There's no rest for the weary."

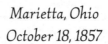

Marietta, Ohio
October 18, 1857

Prudence hurried through the woods, her feet rustling the leaves that covered the ground. What a pleasure to walk beneath a canopy of golden, orange, and deep-red leaves without fear of making a telltale noise. The sun had descended low enough that the still-thick foliage cast deep shadows, and she pulled her cloak together at her neck against the chill. Winter would be upon them soon enough, and she would not be surprised to see snowflakes falling within a few weeks. But for now, she inhaled the rich, earthy scent of autumn.

When she came within sight of her house, she spied Jason seated in his chair on the front porch and picked up her pace. She burst out of the cover of the trees and into the waning sunlight at a run. Patience rounded the corner of the house then, as though alerted to her presence by some unknown sense shared by beloved pets everywhere. She raced across the grass, honking a welcome.

Alerted by the commotion, Jason looked up. The smile that lit his face resonated in Prudence's heart. Skipping up the porch steps, she threw her arms around him, nearly knocking him from the chair.

Laughing, he returned her embrace. "Thee is happy today. The news is good, then?"

She nodded. "The burial was today. There was talk of nothing else among the hotel staff, or the guests either."

In the two days since she had ushered Ezra, Becca, and their precious little one into the woods and released them to the conductor who would guide them on the next step of their journey, tension had kept her stomach in knots. Would the truth be discovered? Would lawmen burst through the doors of the hotel at any moment to take her and Mr. Bickerton captive?

But that was all in the past.

She left Jason's embrace and settled in the chair next to him. "Mr. Bickerton attended, though to my understanding he was one of only a few."

Her employer had not spoken a private word to Prudence since the harrowing moment when he instructed her to leave through the secret tunnel with her charges and then go home by a different route. She had hurried to obey, leaving him and Mr. Still to make arrangements for the slave tracker's body and a story to cover the manner of his death. In the two days since, the Riverfront House had been filled with inquisitive people, both official and unofficial, asking questions. An article in the newspaper, which Prudence had read over the shoulder of the cook in the kitchen, reported the details.

Mr. Lucian Tankard, recently of Georgia, suffered an unfortunate accident while staying as a guest at the Riverfront House. Mr. Tankard was reported to have imbibed a sufficient quantity of brandy to render him unsteady on his feet. While engaged in conversation with Mr. Bickerton in his private office, Mr. Tankard fell and struck his head against the stone hearth. The article concluded with a quote from Mr. Bickerton.

"We regret that such an unfortunate accident occurred on the property of the Riverfront House. We hold our guests in the highest esteem, and naturally this incident has been quite disturbing to me, my family, and the entire staff."

Prudence detailed as much as she could remember of the article to Jason, who listened attentively.

"And what of Tankard's traveling companion?"

Bolling, the wealthy plantation owner. "He attended the burial with Mr. Bickerton, and then left to return to Kentucky."

Thankfully, Prudence had not encountered the man before his departure.

They fell into a companionable silence while the sun sank lower. The hens, apparently determined to make the most of the waning light, wandered around the yard, pecking at the grass. One strayed too close to the porch, and Patience was quick to defend what she considered to be her territory, running at the poor creature with her wings flapping. Prudence laughed, as always amused by the haughty goose's antics. Then she sobered.

Ever alert to her moods, Jason watched her closely. "What is troubling thee?"

She plucked at a loose thread on the hem of her cloak. "It is wrong to rejoice in a man's death," she said slowly. "And yet his death means that others will be delivered from their suffering."

"Does thee rejoice? Truly?"

Trust Jason to ask the question that caused her to pause and consider. *Do I, Lord?* The answer became clear in her mind, and she exhaled a relieved sigh. "No, I do not rejoice. Though it would be untruthful to say I am not relieved that a threat that has caused me much turmoil has passed."

He reached out to take her hand. "No life lost is a cause for rejoicing. Instead, we must pray for a lost soul, and trust that our God is not only the Lord of justice but of mercy."

Satisfied to leave the matter in the Almighty's capable hands, Prudence settled more comfortably in her chair. Then her gaze snagged on something in the distance. She straightened. Was that a scrap of fabric hanging in the oak tree?

Jason followed her gaze, and then nodded. "I saw it earlier. There is another message."

"Already?"

"The prophet spoke truly when he penned the words of Lamentations." He lowered his voice to quote the verse. "'Our necks are under persecution: we labour, and have no rest.'"

Prudence closed her eyes. One day perhaps their service to the Cause would come to an end. But for now, how could she rest when others suffered under the yoke of slavery?

CHAPTER NINETEEN

Janice stood behind the antique bar they used as a reception desk and admired their handiwork. The first floor of Wayfarers Inn had been transformed. Fall leaves of rich brown and deep orange had been artfully arranged with pumpkins and pine cones to bring autumn indoors. White candles flickered everywhere—she made a mental note to keep an eye on Larry. The small round tables had been removed from the café to make room for three long tables where their guests could eat family-style. Beneath the rust-colored tablecloths and hand-stitched runners, the tables were really constructed of long planks balanced on sawhorses that Thorn had scrounged from somewhere, but the effect after the table decorations had been added was stunning. Tess had fussed a bit about removing the café furniture, but how could one host a community dinner with guests scattered individually all over the place?

"Mother, how does this look?"

Janice turned to find Stacy putting the finishing touches on a beautiful arrangement of pine cones, ribbons, and white pumpkins on a table near the fireplace.

"It's lovely. I knew you would put exactly the right touches on that piece."

Beaming, Stacy glanced toward the long tables. "I have to admit, the inn looks lovely. And everyone is so excited, it's almost as good as Thanksgiving."

Janice put an arm around her daughter's waist and hugged. "I'm glad you agree."

Stacy leveled a stern eye on her. "But don't overdo it, okay?"

"I won't," Janice promised, and turned away to hide an eye roll.

LuAnn exited the kitchen carrying a basket full of silverware and napkins. Brad followed with a stack of plates, which he began distributing around the center table. LuAnn worked alongside him arranging the cutlery. He said something in a voice too low to be overheard, and LuAnn laughed.

"So, are those two an item yet?" Stacy whispered.

"They won't discuss it." Janice grinned. "But Tess and I are hopeful."

A thud sounded on the other side of the wall, which made them both turn.

"Did that sound like a football hitting the building?"

Stacy heaved an exaggerated sigh. "That's exactly what it sounded like. I'd better go check on Larry and Uncle Stuart before they tear the place down."

Janice went to lend a hand in the kitchen and found a cheerful bustle of activity that warmed her heart. At the counter Winnie was putting the finishing touches on a cream pie, her knife creating artful swirls in the fluffy white stuff.

Tess lifted the lid on a giant simmering pot on the stove and reared her head back to escape a billow of steam before poking at the contents with a fork.

"The broccoli is ready for the cheese sauce," she announced.

At the table, Robin sat before a mound of celery sticks, patiently spreading pimento cheese into the center of each one and then arranging them on long platters. The back door opened, and Paige entered carrying two gigantic reusable canvas bags.

"Happy harvest," she called in her cheerful voice. She was answered with a chorus of return greetings.

Janice hurried over to take one of the heavy bags. "What do you have in here? It feels like bricks."

"Olives and pickled asparagus." She wrinkled her nose. "I can't stand the slimy stuff, but Ben loves it."

"Where is Pastor Ben?" Winnie whisked a finished pie off the counter and put it into one of the big refrigerators before beginning another.

"I left him outside playing football with Stuart and the other guys."

Robin looked up, her fingers covered in pimento cheese. "Stuart is here?"

Janice suppressed a smile at the sudden enthusiasm in the young woman's expression. Now if only Stuart would return Robin's interest.

Paige nodded as she pulled cans and jars from her bags and set them on the table. "There's about a half-dozen or so guys. I think they're trying to scrounge up enough players for a game." She accepted a can opener from Janice. "Has anyone heard from the newlyweds?"

Marla and Byron had stayed in the Honeymoon Suite on the second floor for their wedding night, and then left early the next morning to drive to Florida.

"I've gotten one picture text." Janice slipped her phone out of her apron pocket and pulled up the picture before passing it to Paige.

The young woman giggled. "I love the mouse ears with the bridal veil."

Tess stood on tiptoe to grab a colander from the top storage rack. "Byron's mother called yesterday to try to weasel Winnie's gumbo recipe out of her."

Winnie's grin stretched from ear to ear. "I told her I wasn't going to share my secret with anyone else. One Wickham knowing it is enough."

A soft cough sounded from the doorway. Janice turned to find Pauline hovering there, her hands clasped tightly before her.

"Hello, and happy harvest," Janice greeted her in a cheerful voice.

Pauline managed a small smile. "I wondered if you could use some help in here."

"We sure can." Janice pulled her gently into the room. "Many hands make light work, as they say."

"Ugh." Her nose scrunched, Paige held a newly opened jar of asparagus at arm's length while her other hand pressed against her belly. Her skin had taken on a greenish tint that resembled the loathsome vegetables. "I cannot handle the smell. Either someone else is going to have to deal with these, or Ben will just have to do without."

Janice smiled at Pauline. "Sounds like you're just in time. I'll get a dish."

"We pulled it off." Standing beside Janice, Tess wore a satisfied smile as she scanned the happy faces of their dinner guests.

The final head count was forty-seven, including more than a dozen children. Janice and her friends had selected chairs at the end of the table nearest the kitchen, in case they needed to replenish dishes.

Janice nodded. "It looks like we even managed to heal a few rifts in the process."

At the opposite end of their table Kate Campbell sat between a beaming Harry and her oldest daughter, Corrie. When they arrived, Kate confided that Corrie had been thrilled to discover her mother's secret relationship, while Pamela reacted exactly as Kate feared. But she was confident the bridge would soon be mended. Probably the next time Pamela needed a babysitter. At the moment, Corrie was engaged in a conversation with Pauline, who looked more relaxed than Janice had yet seen her.

Perhaps even more satisfying was the conversation taking place at the center table, where Gloria Bellamy and Becky

Eberly sat with Paige and Pastor Ben, their expressions animated as they talked.

"Larry sure is attached to his Uncle Stuart, isn't he?" Tess whispered.

Janice glanced to her left, where Larry sat between Stacy and Stuart. The little boy commanded his uncle's full attention as he pantomimed throwing a football and chattered about running the winning touchdown. On the other side of Stuart, Robin sat quietly, though every so often she glanced his way. Unfortunately, Stuart's attention was riveted on his nephew and he seemed completely unaware of Robin's presence.

On Tess's right, LuAnn leaned forward to catch Janice's eye. "I asked Pastor Ben to say the blessing. I hope that's okay."

"Of course." Janice smiled at Brad, who had not left LuAnn's side since he arrived this morning. That was a relationship that would have to develop on its own. Janice and Tess had been told in no certain uncertain terms that their meddling would not be appreciated.

At the head of the center table, Pastor Ben picked up his iced-tea glass and attempted to get everyone's attention by tapping it with his table knife. Since the glass was full, the soft *clank* failed to rise over the happy chatter in the room. Instead, he cupped his hands around his mouth and shouted.

"Could I get everybody to quiet down for a minute?" He pointed at his tea glass and laughed. "That works better in the movies." A chuckle swept through the hungry crowd. "I've been given the honor of asking the Lord's blessing on this food. If you don't mind, could we all hold hands?"

Some good-natured shuffling occurred as the people at the ends of the tables reached backward to grab the hands of those seated behind them, but finally everyone in the room grasped the hands of those closest to them. On Janice's left, Stacy's hand felt soft and precious in hers. She squeezed and received a smile in return.

Then she squeezed Tess's hand on her right. Beyond her, LuAnn smiled at Janice.

"God is so good," she whispered.

The three friends bowed their heads, their hearts full of gratitude for God's bountiful harvest in their lives.

Dear Reader,

It can be tricky to write a novel set in a real town. Authors want to be as accurate as possible, but we also enjoy the creative prerogative of dreaming up fictional characters, settings, and incidents. Before I began writing *A Flame in the Night* my husband and I took a trip to Marietta, Ohio, so I could absorb the atmosphere of that delightful city. We climbed to the top of the mound at the center of Mound Cemetery. We shopped and had dinner on Front Street, and walked beside the river on Ohio Street. Naturally we visited the Levee House, on which Wayfarers Inn is loosely based. We were fortunate to be some of the last visitors, since as of press time the restaurant has closed. We found a gorgeous church at the corner of Scammel and Fourth Streets, and I used that building as the model for Christ Fellowship. I hope I've accurately portrayed the charm of Marietta.

Writing a book with a historical setting is even trickier, especially when the story features real people like William Still. To research that aspect of this story, I visited the Washington County Historical Society and pored over documents from the mid- to late-1800s describing Marietta's fascinating role in the Underground Railroad. The story of Ezra and Becca is based on factual accounts of fugitive slaves I read about there. Though those two characters are products of my imagination, their stories were all too real for many people of that era. I'm sure I'm not the first to shed tears over the tragic circumstances suffered by countless enslaved people during that terrible time in our nation's history. Nor am I the only one who rejoices in the freedom that was bought through the sacrifices of so many faithful workers, like the fictional Prudence and the real-life William Still. It is my hope that this book will help keep the memories of those sacrifices alive.

Sincerely,
Virginia Smith

ABOUT THE AUTHOR

Virginia Smith is the best-selling author of more than thirty novels, an illustrated children's book, and over fifty articles and short stories. An avid reader with eclectic tastes in fiction, Ginny writes in a variety of styles, from lighthearted relationship stories to breath-snatching suspense. Her books have received many awards, including two Holt Medallion Awards of Merit. She and her husband enjoy exploring the extremes of nature, from scuba diving in the warm waters of the Caribbean to motorcycling in the Utah mountains and the curvy roads of her native Kentucky. Learn more about Ginny and her books at VirginiaSmith.org.

ABOUT WILLIAM STILL

Prominent abolitionist William Still (1821—1902) was born to former slaves. His father purchased his own freedom. His mother escaped with four of her children, was captured and returned to slavery. She subsequently escaped a second time with only her two daughters, leaving behind two sons who were then sold to a plantation owner in Lexington, Kentucky. Though Still was free from birth, he was passionate in his determination to assist runaway slaves to freedom. He was a member of the Pennsylvania Society for Promoting the Abolition of Slavery, and was chairman of the Vigilance Committee of Philadelphia.

Over the course of his abolitionist work, Still helped hundreds of slaves escape to freedom and earned the title Father of the Underground Railroad. Only Harriet Tubman helped free more slaves than Still.

Though he received little formal education, Still placed a high value on literacy. He kept detailed notes about the condition and struggles of the runaways he assisted. When slavery was finally abolished he assembled those notes into a book entitled *The Underground Railroad,* which was unique in its focus on the activities and experiences of escaped slaves rather than on those who helped them. You can download it for free here: http://www.gutenberg.org/ebooks/15263.

While gathering material for his book, Still interviewed countless former slaves. During perhaps the most moving interview he conducted, Still realized he sat across the desk from his own brother, Peter, one of the two boys his mother had been forced to leave behind when she fled.

Something Delicious from our Wayfarers Inn Friends

Winnie's Creole Gumbo

Ingredients:

1 tablespoon vegetable
  shortening
1 tablespoon flour
1 large onion, sliced
1 chicken, cut up in small
  pieces
2 cups plus 2 quarts boiling
  water, divided
10 allspice berries, ground
  (or 10 tsp ground allspice)

8 whole cloves
Red and black pepper,
  parsley, and thyme to taste
1 quart canned oysters, liquid
  reserved
1 tablespoon ground filé
  (sassafras leaves, dried and
  pulverized; or purchase
  through retail outlets)

Melt shortening in a deep pot. When hot, whisk in flour and stir until brown. Add onions and fry until soft and translucent. Skim off onions and set aside. Fry chicken until browned, turning frequently. When chicken is brown, return onions to pot and add 2 cups boiling water. Reduce temperature to a slow simmer. Add 2 quarts boiling water and the liquid from the oysters. Stir in allspice, cloves, peppers, parsley, and thyme. Simmer gently, covered, for two hours. Add oysters during the last fifteen minutes. Right before serving, stir in the filé. Serve over rice cooked dry.

Read on for a sneak peek of another exciting book
in the Secrets of Wayfarers Inn series!

NEVER THE TWAIN
SHALL MEET
by Beth Adams & Ellen E. Kennedy

Tess Wallace sipped a cup of strong dark coffee and held
her breath as Jack Willard jumped down the last three
stairs. The three- year-old was adorable, with his dark hair and
big blue eyes, but he had more energy than he knew what to do
with. The boy landed with a thud, hooted his excitement, and
then ran into the café, where Winnie was just writing out the
menu on the large chalkboard. Well, hopefully, none of their
other guests had been trying to sleep in this morning. Sharon,
the boy's mother, was halfway down the stairs, tiny Sadie tucked
into a sling against her chest.

"I'm so sorry," Sharon said, nodding toward the boy, who
was scrambling onto a chair in the café. There were dark half-
moons under her eyes. The baby must have kept her up last
night. Tess's own children were grown and her daughter, Lizzie,
had children of her own, but Tess still shuddered when she
thought about the overwhelming exhaustion of those first few
months. "I told him to go down quietly, but..."

"He's three," Tess said. "I have three grandchildren his age, so I totally understand."

"Three of them?" Sharon's eyes widened. Tess could just make out the infant's downy head poking out the top of the sling.

"Triplets." Tess smiled. "Two boys and a girl."

"Oh wow." Sharon laughed and shook her head. "Oh wow."

"They're a huge blessing, but they're quite a handful." Tess thought for a moment about their sweet faces, with their big brown eyes and sandy-colored hair. Sweet Liam and Henry and Harper. She missed those little imps. "Anyway, I understand about the futility of trying to convince a three-year-old to walk anywhere when he could just as easily run."

"Thank you for understanding. I just hope the other guests aren't too put out."

"You're kind to worry. But for now, just enjoy your breakfast. You look like you could use it."

"Thank you. I'd read that the hospitality in this place was out of this world, but you've really gone above and beyond. Those granola bars you provide in the room saved me in the middle of the night."

"I'm so glad." Tess watched as the tired young mother headed into the café, ordered her young son to stop standing on the chair, and sat down across from him.

Tess and her friends Janice and LuAnn had opened this inn with the intention of ministering to their guests, and she was happy to hear that Sharon was enjoying her stay. But Tess was still a little unclear as to why, exactly, this family had chosen Wayfarers Inn for their visit. Everyone was welcome here, of course, and they appreciated all the guests who graced their doors, especially as they were still getting the place up and running. But she would have thought a family with young children might be more comfortable at one of the chain hotels in the area that offered suites and indoor pools and arcades. And, she thought as Jack banged his knife against the glass-topped table, their other guests no doubt might be as well.

The café wasn't even officially open yet, but the sweet smell of cinnamon and sugar wafted out of the kitchen. Taylor Smith appeared at Sharon's side and deposited a cup of coffee and a coloring book with crayons, unrequested, and Tess thanked God they'd found him. For a busy college student, the young man had a strong sense of what their guests needed and how best to serve them.

Tess turned back to the iPad in front of her and reviewed the list of upcoming bookings. The reservations slowed down over the next two weeks, but then they picked up again the week of Thanksgiving. There were already six rooms booked for that weekend, and the amount of traffic to the section of their website that showed available rooms indicated that there might be more bookings coming in soon. Praise God. Tess knew that the first year of an inn's life was critical, and so far it looked like they just might make it.

"Excuse me?"

Tess looked up to find Sharon's husband, Moses, standing in front of the check-in desk. He was tall, with thick dark hair. Probably in his midthirties, if she had to guess. His blue eyes were striking against his bronzed skin.

"I'm so sorry. I didn't see you come down."

"That's quite all right. I'm sorry to bother you."

"You're not bothering me. This is my job." She set the iPad down and flashed him a smile. "What can I help you with?"

"I have something of a strange question."

"My favorite kind."

He looked around, and then he pulled something from his pocket. A small piece of paper, folded over.

"This was slipped under the door of our room late last night. I was wondering if you or your business partners saw anyone in the hallways. Or if you have security cameras or anything like that." He was looking around the lobby, scanning for…well, she had no idea for what.

"Goodness." Tess shook her head. "I'm afraid we don't have security cameras here. And I was up in my room by eight, so I didn't see anything. I can ask my partners, though."

"Thank you. That would be great." He put the paper back in his pocket..

"Is everything…is everything okay?" Whatever was on that paper was troubling him, that much was clear.

"Yes. It's…" He looked around again, and then back at Tess. It was almost as if he were trying to read her, the way he studied her face. Then he seemed to come to some sort of decision.

"It's kind of strange, really." He took the paper back out, unfolded it, and held it out so she could see it. It was a note, handwritten, on one of the pads with the Wayfarers Inn logo that they placed in each guest room.

I have the SLC treasure. Leave a cashier's check for $50,000 in an envelope behind the painting in the lobby and wait for further instructions.

"Wow!" Tess read the note again, just to make sure she'd seen it correctly. "What in the world does it mean?"

Moses sighed and shifted his weight from one foot to the other. He looked around again, and then he gave a little half-shrug.

"I got a strange letter in the mail a few weeks ago too," he said. He reached into his pocket again, this time pulling out a business-sized envelope. It was addressed to Moses Willard in Cleveland, and the return address space was blank. He opened the envelope and pulled out a single piece of white paper printed from a computer.

Moses—

Do the letters SLC mean anything to you?

The treasure that was stolen from your family has been recovered. If you want to know more about it, come to the Wayfarers Inn in Marietta, Ohio, on November 5 and wait for further instructions.

"What in the world?" Tess repeated, pulling the note closer and reading it again. But it still didn't make any sense. "What does it mean? What treasure is he talking about? What is SLC?"

She looked up and realized he was studying her again.

"I can promise you, I don't know a thing about this." She pushed the letter back toward him. He couldn't really think… "And neither do my business partners, I assure you."

"No." He leaned back and shook his head. "Judging by your reaction, I don't think you do. I don't think anyone could fake that confusion."

She wasn't sure whether to be relieved or offended, but she was too curious to dwell on it. "Do you have any idea what this is all about?"

Moses didn't say anything for a moment, and then he sighed. "I'll tell you what. Would you mind if I talked about it with all three of you? I need some coffee. I can grab some if you wouldn't mind calling your business partners together. Then I can explain it to all of you at once."

"That sounds like a great idea."

Tess walked over to the service elevator and pressed the button. A moment later she was stepping out onto the fourth floor, where their private rooms were located. She knocked on LuAnn's door first. LuAnn was often up early because she helped in the kitchen, but today there was no sound from inside her apartment. Tess knocked harder, and a moment later, a sleepy-eyed LuAnn pulled open the door, knotting a robe around her waist.

"I'm so sorry. I've woken you," Tess said. She could see the morning light slanting in through LuAnn's windows and realized it was still quite early.

"That's all right. What's going on?"

"One of our guests had a strange note shoved under his door," Tess said. "I think we all need to take a look at it."

LuAnn didn't hesitate. "I'll be right down." She closed the door, and Tess walked over to Janice's room. Janice's door was open and her sitting room empty, but Tess found her in an overstuffed armchair in the corner of the common area, sipping a cup of coffee while she read her Bible.

"Hi there." Janice's blonde curls were pulled back into a ponytail, and she was already dressed for the day in slacks and a light sweater and cozy wool socks.

"I'm sorry to bother you, but I was hoping you could come downstairs for a moment. One of our guests has, well, something of a mystery. Would you come down and hear about it?"

"You had me at mystery." Janice set her coffee on the small walnut side table and closed her Bible, then pushed herself up. "What's going on? Who is it?"

"I'll let him tell us all about it."

A few minutes later, they were all seated around a table in the café, looking down at the note that had come in the mail. Moses cradled a mug of coffee in his hands.

"What is the treasure this letter is talking about?" Janice asked.

"And what is SLC?" LuAnn said. "Salt Lake City?"

Tess smiled, seeing that they had the exact same questions she'd had.

"And why did whoever sent this want you to come to this particular inn?" Tess asked. Though, if her hunch was right, she might already have an inkling about that one.

Moses glanced around again—to make sure no one was listening?—before he spoke. The only other people in the vicinity were his wife and Jack, who were eating bowls of steaming hot oatmeal, and sweet Sadie. Tess was pretty sure the tiny baby wouldn't repeat a word. The oatmeal smelled like cinnamon and brown sugar, and it seemed like the perfect way to start this cool fall day.

"There is a legend in my family," Moses said. "About a treasure that was passed down through the generations. But it was stolen almost a hundred years ago, and no one has seen it since. My grandparents talked about it sometimes, saying how much the family had lost when it was stolen. But, I don't know, I always thought it was nothing more than a legend. Then this showed up, and ..." He let his voice trail off as he shrugged.

"Are you part of the Willard family that lived in Marietta and helped with the Underground Railroad?" LuAnn said, asking what they all wanted to know. When Tess had seen the name Moses Willard pop up in the reservation system, she'd mentioned it to LuAnn and Janice, and they'd all wondered the same thing. They knew the name Moses Willard. Prudence and Jason Willard—a Quaker couple who'd helped shuttle escaped slaves to freedom through the tunnel beneath the building that was now the inn—had named their baby boy Moses.

"That's right." Moses nodded. "Prudence and Jason Willard were my great-great-great-grandparents. I'm Moses Willard the Fifth, named after their son."

"Wow." Tess couldn't believe it. They were talking to a real live descendant of Prudence Willard. After reading Prudence's diary and learning all they could about the selfless acts in which she had risked her life—and the lives of her family members—to carry out, Tess felt like she knew her. And to see one of her descendants in the flesh—one who carried the name she'd given her own son, no less—made her unexpectedly emotional.

"In that case, you are an especially honored guest," Janice said. "Thank you so much for coming."

"This place is beautiful, and it's wonderful to see how you've honored the history here." Moses took a sip of his coffee. "But—excuse me if this sounds flippant—after getting a note like this, I didn't see how I could stay away."

Tess saw his point. "Tell us more about this treasure."

"That's the thing. I don't really know what it was supposed to be. My parents didn't know. The story I heard was that it was a gift given to my great-great-great-grandparents and it was of considerable value. They held on to it and passed it down, but it was stolen from a safe in my great-grandparents' store in 1928, and it's never been seen again."

"Something of considerable value?" Tess puzzled over that. There was something pulling at the edge of her mind. Something she'd read.

"It could be anything," Janice said. "You don't know anything more?"

"The only other thing I know was who supposedly gave the gift to Prudence and Jason. And that's why it's always been more than a little hard to believe."

"Who was it?" Tess asked.

Moses paused for a moment before saying, "Mark Twain."

Tess's first instinct was to laugh. Sure. Mark Twain—one of the most famous American writers of all time—had given Prudence and Jason Willard—soft-spoken Quakers who lived on a farm in rural Ohio—a treasure of great worth? And the Queen of England had given them a jeweled tiara as well.

But then LuAnn whispered, "SLC. Samuel Langhorne Clemens."

Surely not. It was preposterous to even contemplate such a thing. And yet, there was something pulling at the edge of Tess's mind, just out of reach. What was it?

"So you're saying that someone sent you this letter"—LuAnn touched the paper that had been mailed to Moses—"to get you to our inn because of a treasure Mark Twain supposedly gave to your great-great-grandparents."

"You forgot a great in there," Janice said with a smile.

"Great-great-great-grandparents," LuAnn said.

"That's correct," Moses said. He looked a bit sheepish. He glanced over at his wife and kids. Sharon was now holding her phone, taking a picture of Jack eating his oatmeal. "I know. It sounds completely nuts. I get an anonymous note in the mail and pack up and bring my whole family here, on the off chance a family legend is not only true, but that someone who says they have it will show up and give me information about it. I understand how crazy it all sounds."

"But..." Tess could see there was more he wanted to say.

"But, I mean, wouldn't you come?" He shrugged. "If you were in my situation, wouldn't you want to know?"

They all thought about it for a moment, and then they all started nodding.

"I would, especially if that family legend involved Mark Twain." LuAnn, a former English teacher, leaned forward a bit. "He's one of the most fascinating characters in all of American letters."

"And I wouldn't be able to resist the mystery," Janice said. "Even though it's most likely, as you say, nothing more than legend, the idea of solving an old mystery would make me come."

Tess was listening, but on another level, she was elsewhere, paging through faded, cursive handwriting in her mind. She'd read something... And then it clicked.

"But it might not just be legend," she said. She got up and went over to the desk drawer where she kept her set of photocopies of Prudence's diary. As she rejoined the group, Tess flipped to the journal's later pages, looking for the passage she was thinking of. She could have sworn it was toward the back. Aha. There it was.

"Look at this." She set the binder on the table and turned it so Moses could read it. "Look at this journal entry."

"Is this..." Moses squinted. "Whose journal is this?"

"This is a copy of Prudence's journal," Janice said. "We found the original here when we bought the inn."

"The original is at the Marietta Underground Railroad Museum, just a few blocks away," Tess added.

"Wow." He looked down at the image and shook his head. "I'd heard she kept a journal, but I assumed that was just another family legend."

"That legend, at least, is very real," Tess said.

"Which makes you wonder about the other one," LuAnn said, raising her eyebrows.

"But look here. Look what it says." Tess pointed to the passage she'd found.

Moses appeared to struggle to make out Prudence's florid handwritten script, but he carefully read: "'Our acclaimed and esteemed friend's most gracious gift arrived four days ago. What a wonderful treasure! And yet, alas, its possession brings with it an equal measure of danger.'"

"I'd forgotten about that entry," Janice said, shaking her head.

"Do you think she could really be referring to Mark Twain here?" LuAnn asked. "Were Prudence and Jason friends with Mark Twain?"

Moses shrugged. "It seems completely implausible, and my parents didn't put much stock in it, but that's the story."

"But how did they meet him? When did they become friends?" Tess couldn't even begin to wrap her head around this. "What is this gift he gave them?"

"Well, that's why I showed up here," Moses said. "To see if someone out there really does have answers to those questions." He took another sip of his coffee. "I figured, the worst that could happen is we've spent a few days in a great old inn, and I get to introduce my wife and children to the city where my family came from. And if someone out there really does know something about the Twain treasure and what happened to it, then I would be crazy not to come."

Tess agreed with him. She would have done exactly the same thing.

"So where's the note that was slipped under your door last night?" LuAnn asked.

He pulled out last night's note and set it on the table, beside the letter that had come in the mail.

Tess reread the note.

I have the SLC treasure. Leave a cashier's check for $50,000 in an envelope behind the painting in the lobby and wait for further instructions.

Tess looked over to the lobby at the painting that sat on the carved mahogany mantel above the fireplace. They'd picked it up at a flea market over the summer, and it showed a steamboat cruising along the river. People on the banks of the river were dressed in Victorian clothes, and the inn—then the Riverfront House—was one of the buildings that was shown in the background. Janice had set an arrangement of dried gourds and fall leaves on the mantel next to it.

"It's a bit presumptuous, isn't it?" LuAnn asked. "To assume you simply have $50,000 at your disposal?"

Moses shrugged. "I don't have that much cash lying around, that's for sure."

He left it at that, though, which made Tess wonder. It was a princely sum, perfectly and thoroughly out of reach for any of the three of them, who were still stretched to the limit after purchasing the inn. But her husband Jeffrey had managed an exclusive resort on a private golf course, and over the years Tess had had the opportunity to interact with plenty of women who would drop that amount and more in a single trip to Nordstrom. She'd seen men buy a set of golf clubs that cost nearly that much without flinching. Could Moses possibly pay the fee? Would he?

"So what are you going to do?" Janice asked.

"I'm not sure." At the table behind him, Jack was now smearing oatmeal on the table with one hand while grabbing for his mother's phone with the other, and Sharon was doing her best to comfort a whimpering Sadie. Moses pushed himself up, walked over to the table, and held out his hands. Sharon gratefully held out the baby, and he took her, cradled her in his arms, and sat back down. Tess observed his attentiveness to his wife and children with appreciation. "That's why I was hoping one of you either saw something or that you had security cameras."

"I'm afraid not," LuAnn said. "Do you have any idea what time this note was left under your door?"

"We went to bed by nine, but we were up several times in the night with Sadie." He held her up against his shoulder, and the whimpering stopped. "Sharon got up with her around one, and she said there was nothing there then, but I found it when I got up with her just after four."

The dead of night, then. The inn doors were locked at eleven, and the only people who would have been around were the three of them and their guests.

"It has to be from someone staying at the inn, then," Tess said.

"Does anyone else have a key?"

"Winnie has the code to the back door," LuAnn said. "But we had the locks changed when we moved in, and I don't believe anyone else has a key."

"And Winnie wouldn't have had anything to do with this." Janice's voice was confident, and Tess agreed with her. But still, they would probably need to ask her, just to be sure.

"And it wasn't any of the three of us," Tess said. She felt confident of that. None of them would have kept a secret like this, and none of them was a good enough actress to be able to pull off the shocked and confused reactions they'd just displayed. Beyond that, though, none of them would do anything to put the inn and its reputation—not to mention the memory of their beloved Prudence—in jeopardy.

"We have guests in four rooms besides yours," Tess said. "So I guess it has to be one of them."

"It's strange to be suspecting one of our guests of something like this," LuAnn said. Tess agreed, but she didn't see what alternative they had.

Janice was examining the note that had been shoved under the door. "This is clearly written on the notepad from the room. I wonder..."

"I wondered the same thing," Tess said.

Moses looked at Janice, and LuAnn tilted her head.

"We should examine the pads in the rooms to see if there's an indentation left by the pen," Janice said.

"Ah. Good thinking," LuAnn said. "When the guests go out, we can do that."

"And look at this," Tess said, pointing to the postmark on the envelope that had been mailed to Moses. "It was mailed from Columbus. So whoever sent it lives there."

"Or was passing through there on October 25," Janice said, pointing out the date stamped on the letter.

"Or drove there specifically to throw off anyone hoping to figure out where the sender lives," LuAnn added.

Tess nodded, deflated. So maybe it wasn't as great a clue as she had hoped.

"We'll figure this out," she said, hoping she sounded more confident than she felt. "We just need to pay attention to our guests and see what we can learn."

"We'll ask discreet questions," LuAnn said. "To find out what they know. One of them has to know something."

"We can do that," Janice said. "But..." She turned to Moses. "Don't you want to involve the police in this? We could call Chief Mayfield. This is extortion."

"I've thought about that," Moses said. He glanced over at his family again. Sharon had given up the fight over the cell phone and was focused on shoveling in her breakfast as quickly as she could, while Jack took pictures of the room and himself with her phone. "But I don't think I want to alert the police. Not yet, anyway. The last thing I want to do is scare off whoever sent this and lose the treasure." He patted Sadie's back gently. "If it even exists, that is."

"I think that's smart," LuAnn said. "And I also think it makes sense to hold off on handing over the money for now, at least until we've had a chance to do some sleuthing."

"Oh, believe me, I am not in any rush to write a check for that much money," Moses said with a laugh. "Especially without knowing if the treasure is real."

"Well, if it is, we'll do everything we can to help you find it," Tess said.

She didn't know if Moses looked more relieved or frightened by that prospect.

A NOTE FROM THE EDITORS

We hope you enjoy Secrets of Wayfarers Inn, created by the Books and Inspirational Media Division of Guideposts, a nonprofit organization that touches millions of lives every day through products and services that inspire, encourage, help you grow in your faith, and celebrate God's love in every aspect of your daily life.

Thank you for making a difference with your purchase of this book, which helps fund our many outreach programs to military personnel, prisons, hospitals, nursing homes, and educational institutions. To learn more, visit Guideposts Foundation.org.

We also maintain many useful and uplifting online resources. Visit Guideposts.org to read true stories of hope and inspiration, access OurPrayer network, sign up for free newsletters, download free e-books, join our Facebook community, and follow our stimulating blogs.

To learn about other Guideposts publications, including the best-selling devotional *Daily Guideposts*, go to ShopGuideposts .org, call (800) 932-2145, or write to Guideposts, PO Box 5815, Harlan, Iowa 51593.

Sign up for the
Guideposts Fiction Newsletter
and stay up-to-date on the books you love!

You'll get sneak peeks of new releases, recommendations from other Guideposts readers, and special offers just for you . . .
and it's FREE!

Just go to Guideposts.org/Newsletters today to sign up.

Find more inspiring fiction in these best-loved Guideposts series!

Tearoom Mysteries Series

Mix one stately Victorian home, a charming lakeside town in Maine, and two adventurous cousins with a passion for tea and hospitality. Add a large scoop of intriguing mystery and sprinkle generously with faith, family, and friends, and you have the recipe for *Tearoom Mysteries*.

Sugarcreek Amish Mysteries

Be intrigued by the suspense and joyful "aha" moments in these delightful stories. Each book in the series brings together two women of vastly different backgrounds and traditions, who realize there's much more to the "simple life" than meets the eye.

Mysteries of Martha's Vineyard

What does Priscilla Latham Grant, a Kansas farm girl know about hidden treasure and rising tides, maritime history and local isle lore? Not much—but to save her lighthouse and family reputation, she better learn quickly!

Mysteries of Silver Peak

Escape to the historic mining town of Silver Peak, Colorado, and discover how one woman's love of antiques helps her solve mysteries buried deep in the town's checkered past.

To learn more about these books, visit Guideposts.org/Shop